PRA

Suddenly

'While Fleur McDonald has a wonderful way with telling rural stories in a special way, it was the mystery that made this a stellar read in my eyes. I felt that it showed off her skills as a writer even more, luring the reader into a sense of safety and then hitting us with some truths that made events even more shocking! A great summer read that won't disappoint.'

Samstillreading

'*Suddenly One Summer* is a fast-paced, intensely gripping romantic suspense novel by Aussie author Fleur McDonald which I flew through and absolutely loved! The tension in two different states, with two completely different situations was done extremely well. I have to say, I think *Suddenly One Summer* is this author's best work to date! Highly recommended.'

Readingwritingandriesling

'An entertaining and intriguing read with likeable and unlikeable characters plus a well-balanced plot with more twists than a country road.'

Weekly Times

'McDonald has written a suspenseful jigsaw of a story that doesn't fall into place until the final long-held secrets are brought to light . . . *Suddenly One Summer* was a book that kept me guessing with suspenseful storylines, slow burning clue drops and a big finish.'

Beauty and Lace

'Fleur McDonald has once again taken secrets that lie hidden beneath the veneer of many small communities, using them to form the basis of a story which could easily be as true to life as the words she has used to craft this absolutely enjoyable read . . . A great Sunday afternoon in the shade read.'
Blue Wolf Reviews

'[Fleur McDonald's] familiarity with farms and the bush is entrenched in her tenth novel which is set in both Western and South Australia. The effect of isolation on individuals and relationships, the difficulty of coping as people age and the impossibility of solving crimes in the vastness that is regional Australia are all issues that need to be considered as everyone waits for the rains.'
OUTinPerth

'An enthralling read with surprising twists and merging stories.'
Talking Books

Fleur McDonald has lived and worked on farms for much of her life. After growing up in the small town of Orroroo in South Australia, she went jillarooing, eventually co-owning an 8000-acre property in regional Western Australia.

Fleur likes to write about strong women overcoming adversity, drawing inspiration from her own experiences in rural Australia. Fleur currently lives in Esperance with her two children, an energetic kelpie and a Jack Russell terrier.

www.fleurmcdonald.com

OTHER BOOKS

Red Dust

Blue Skies

Purple Roads

Silver Clouds

Crimson Dawn

Emerald Springs

Indigo Storm

Sapphire Falls

Missing Pieces of Us

Fool's Gold

Where the River Runs

FLEUR McDONALD

Suddenly One Summer

ALLEN&UNWIN
SYDNEY • MELBOURNE • AUCKLAND • LONDON

This edition published in 2018
First published in 2017

Allen & Unwin
83 Alexander Street
Crows Nest NSW 2065
Australia
Phone: (61 2) 8425 0100
Email: info@allenandunwin.com
Web: www.allenandunwin.com

A catalogue record for this book is available from the National Library of Australia

ISBN 978 1 76052 884 3

Set in Sabon LT Pro by Bookhouse, Sydney
Printed in Australia by McPherson's Printing Group

10 9 8 7 6 5 4 3 2 1

The paper in this book is FSC® certified. FSC® promotes environmentally responsible, socially beneficial and economically viable management of the world's forests.

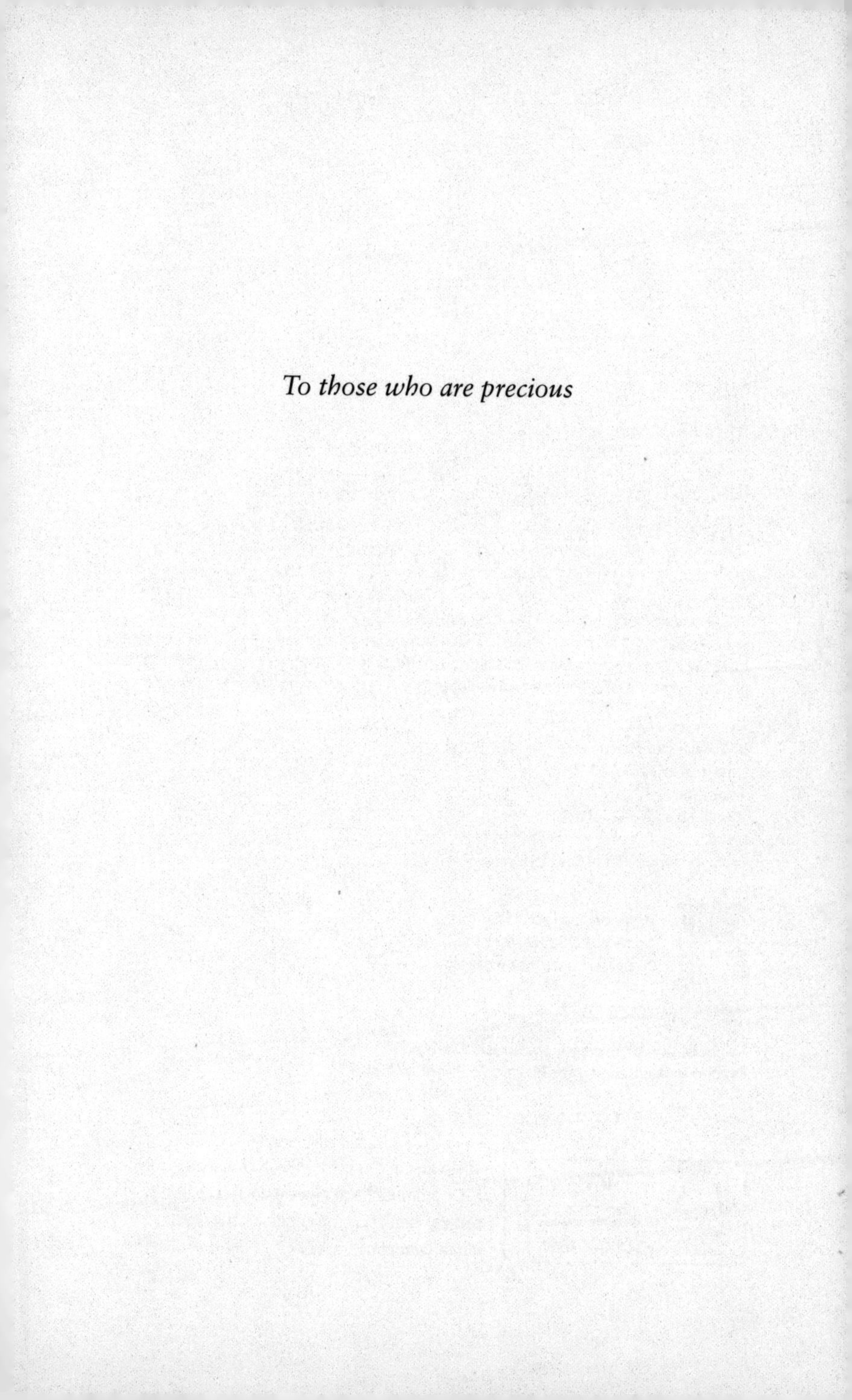

To those who are precious

Prologue

The woman put a shaky hand to her head. She gasped as a searing pain shot through her and she felt something warm and sticky beneath her fingers.

Fear made her whimper.

Where was she? It was pitch black. There wasn't any light filtering in from anywhere and the darkness was suffocating. She couldn't hear a sound. Creeping her fingers along the floor, she felt only dirt and stones.

'Hello?' she whispered. 'Hello?'

Nothing.

Her breath came in short, sharp puffs.

A sudden scrabbling made her jam her hand over her mouth to stop herself from screaming. There was a loud squeaking—angry and sharp—then more scrabbling.

Recognition filtered through. A mouse? A rat? She remembered the sound, but not where she'd heard it.

Panic rushed through her, making her hot and sweaty. Somehow she knew something was very wrong.

How had she got here? Why did her head hurt so much? Her fingers clawed at the dirt, scraping at it, hoping the act of connecting with soil would jolt a memory. Nothing.

'Think,' she said to herself. 'Think.' But as she muttered the words, she realised she didn't even know her own name.

~

She wondered how long she'd been asleep, but when she woke there was enough light for her to see a rat at her sleeve, sniffing her curiously.

Her squeal echoed around the building and the rodent scurried away.

She moved her head—the pain was intense—and tried to take in her surroundings. She was sure she'd never been here before. But there was also a strange sense of recognition. The fear from last night returned. Where *was* she?

'Just get up,' she told herself. If she could get outside, surely she'd work out where she was.

She tried to stand up but the pain was so bad she vomited onto the dirt and slumped back down.

Eventually she dragged herself over to the wall and leaned against it, exhausted from the effort.

Door. She needed to find the door.

There, in the corner.

It took what felt like a superhuman effort to get to it, the pain burning through her whole body but, after what seemed an eternity, she reached the door and pressed down on the handle.

It stayed closed.

'No!'

She leaned her body against it and shoved as hard as she could. The door gave way and she tumbled out onto rich, green grass and looked up at a landscape she didn't recognise.

Chapter 1

Brianna Donahue let out a loud cry as she stepped on a stray piece of Lego. She toppled to one side and grabbed a chair to steady herself. The chair fell and she tumbled on top of it, her phone falling from her hand.

'Bugger!' she swore quietly, hoping the noise wouldn't have woken the boys. 'Far out!' She sat on the floor for a moment, holding her bare foot and massaging the sore area with her thumb. What a way to start her birthday.

Surely Caleb could have checked that the boys had picked up every little piece. He'd been supervising the clean-up last night. For the first time in months.

Squeezing her eyes shut against the frustration, she imagined Caleb driving towards the Merriwell Bay airport in the pre-dawn light. He was returning to work after the Christmas break, having managed to score another two weeks into January as holidays.

Normally she would have got up and made him breakfast. Talked about the next few days, what was ahead for both of them. His court cases, her jobs on the farm. But not this morning. She'd been too tired, and although she wouldn't admit it to anyone else, she was sick of hearing about a career and life she couldn't relate to. It felt like months since she and Caleb had had a conversation that didn't involve the kids, or farming, or the law.

Brianna glanced towards the west and imagined the spotlights of his flash four-wheel drive illuminating the pre-dawn dark. The long streaks of white picking up any stray kangaroos. Caleb had bought the top-of-the-range LandCruiser without telling her, turning up in it one day with a large smile on his face. Brianna could tell he was delighted with it and thought she should be too, but a niggling voice inside her asked why he hadn't talked to her about it first. That was what husbands and wives did, wasn't it? Talked through important decisions, made them together.

Sighing, she dragged her thoughts back to the day at hand.

There was a catastrophic fire danger warning out. The media had been reporting it for the last thirty-six hours, whipping everyone into a frenzy of fear and expectation.

With the pain in her foot subsiding, Brianna got up off the floor, pulling the chair with her. Casting around, she saw her phone, picked it up and switched on the torch. If she turned the lounge-room light on, it would filter into the kids' bedroom and wake them. She needed peace to organise her thoughts for the day ahead.

In the kitchen she flicked on the radio and the morning show crackled to life. The announcer was interviewing a stock agent about a bull sale that had been held the previous day. Still ten minutes before the news and weather. Biting her lip, she tapped at the weather app on her phone, hoping that the forecast had changed. A drop in wind speed or temperature would make her feel a lot more relaxed.

It took an age before the app finally connected and updated. Like everyone out here, she was frustrated by the slow speed of the internet. Scanning the screen she felt a rush of anxiety. The forecast had worsened overnight.

Summer was supposed to be dry. And hot. That was just summer in Australia. But there had been good rainfall during the growing season and, as a result, there was a large volume of dry material still in the paddocks. Which made great fuel for fires. Add to that northerly winds of over fifty kilometres an hour and a temperature of forty-three degrees and everyone started to get jumpy.

There wasn't a shimmer of humidity in the air, so the Fire Danger Index would be in the extreme category. As the day went on, it was almost certain the FDI would reach a reading of catastrophic. Every farmer within the Merriwell Bay shire would be on high alert.

As a precaution, the lawns around the house would need to be dampened. Brianna ran outside and turned on all the taps. She heard the pump kick in, and the sprinklers gurgled and spluttered a couple of times before water burst from them, raining droplets onto the thirsty lawn. A gust of warm wind buffeted her face and for a moment she wished Caleb could be at home today. He was steady and calm, never panicking in a crisis, while she seemed always to be filled with anxiety and adrenalin. Since she'd joined the volunteer fire brigade she'd had to teach herself to remain calm and make decisions under pressure, but for Caleb it seemed to come naturally, perhaps because he always had to think on his feet in the courtroom.

Caleb would know what had to be done on a day like this. He had grown up on a farm, until his parents had gone bankrupt after four bad seasons and a large stock theft that hadn't been covered by insurance. He understood how a farm was run and what life as a farmer entailed, and that was one of the reasons their relationship worked. In the past she hadn't minded him working in Perth and being away a lot. She had plenty of friends and she was happy in her own company, which was probably why farming suited her. The long-term goal was for Caleb to open his own practice in Merriwell Bay and she'd always said that until then they had to do what was necessary to make the situation work. But these days she wasn't quite so sure. It was tough parenting two active boys and running a farm without Caleb by her side.

The high-pitched whistle of the kettle interrupted her thoughts and she made a coffee, taking it outside onto the verandah. A magpie was under the sprinkler, dancing and preening in the droplets, and she made a mental note to tell the boys not to turn off the water today. The birds would need it too.

Feeling unsettled, Brianna gave herself a stern talking-to. *You've always managed. Today won't be any different.* But she recognised she was feeling vulnerable. She *hated* that feeling. And somehow she was blaming Caleb for it. It wasn't his fault that his high pressure job meant he was away a lot. Being a partner in the firm Martin and McIntyre, he needed to be available for important appointments. A fly-in-fly-out lawyer.

Sometimes she thought it would be best if they bought a house in Perth and he stayed up there for the whole week, rather than flying home when he had a spare day. Just come home on the weekends. Thankfully, his employers covered his travel costs and his high salary paid for the toys he accumulated. The Toyota was used all the time, as was the four-wheel motorbike, but the Mustang didn't see the light of day very often. She was glad the farm didn't have to pay for these things; they'd be bankrupt by now if it did.

Brianna pushed thoughts of her husband aside. The first scheduled meeting with all the fire control officers was about twenty minutes away. Peace until then. If the boys stayed asleep.

The smudge of light in the east was now a golden spotlight on the horizon. The sun would slide into view any moment. The smell of eucalyptus came to her on the breeze. The driveway was lined with gum trees planted by her father, Russell, just after he bought Le-Nue thirty-five years ago. It was an add-on block to the original farm he'd grown up on. Russell had always thought of it as his own—a place for him and his family—whereas the home farm was his father's. Brianna could *just* remember walking by his side as he put the seedlings in the ground, covered them with dirt and gave them a long drink from the forty-four-gallon drum he'd rigged up on the back of his ute.

Her dad.

Feelings she couldn't quite name rippled through her. Among them were happiness and love, sadness and pity. She pressed her lips together tightly as she reflected on the changes the last year had brought. Russell was getting older—although his smile was still as bright and sunny as it had been when she was a child, the lines were a bit deeper around his eyes and he seemed to tire more quickly.

Brianna didn't want her dad to grow any older. She couldn't imagine a life without him.

'Mum?'

Brianna turned around and saw her son, Beau, the younger of 'the Terrors', standing in the doorway. The white legs protruding from his boxers looked like matchsticks, as though they might snap at any moment—but looks were deceiving: Beau could run like a cow that had found a gate open into a crop.

'Good morning, sleepyhead,' she said with a smile and put her mug down so she could hug him.

'It's hot already.'

'And it's only going to get hotter, unfortunately. We're in for a rough day. We'll have to shut up the house before the sun gets up completely. Can you pull the curtains in the lounge room for me? I'll make you a Milo.'

Taking a last deep breath of morning air, Brianna went back inside to the kitchen. Two teaspoons of Milo mixed with cold milk and there was the perfect start to a six-year-old's day. Her dad had done this for her every morning until she'd gone to boarding school in Year 8. Brianna had only lasted six months there, being desperately homesick. Russell had brought her home and she'd sworn never to leave Le-Nue again. But, following high school, she had left once more to attend agricultural college and study farm management. That was where she and a handsome young lawyer called Caleb had met, while he'd been giving a guest lecture.

'Here you go, Beau,' she called as she gave the drink one last stir. Just then the windows rattled and a door banged somewhere as a hot breeze swept through the house. Outside, the trees in the driveway were bending towards the ground and there was raised dust in the paddocks.

She thought through the list of things she might need during the day. Most of it was already in the back of her ute. The firefighting unit, petrol, drip torch and pliers. Her uniform was behind the seat and there were eskies full of water for her to drink. It all needed to be there 'just in case'.

She reassured herself that there really shouldn't be any fires today. Her neighbours had finished harvesting and she was expecting a harvest and movement of vehicle ban to be put in place for most of the shire. That meant no one could go out into a paddock unless it was to check water for stock. No one in the paddocks equalled no fires. That was the way it should work, anyway. Still, there could be a thunderstorm, and lightning could strike the tinder-dry bush, or some idiot could drop a lit cigarette.

'Thanks, Mum.'

She turned to her son as he climbed up onto a bar stool at the kitchen bench. 'What do you think you're going to do today?' she asked. 'It's going to be too hot to play outside.' She started to rummage through a bowl sitting on the bench that held all sorts of odds and ends, looking for the Kestrel weather meter, which would help her calculate the FDI. She'd have to take the readings in time for the fire control officers meeting.

Beau shrugged, busy eating the Milo off the top of the milk. 'I don't know. Play with my Lego and build another spaceship.' He frowned. 'It's boring when it gets hot. Can't we go to the beach?'

'We'll see,' Brianna answered, noncommittal. She glanced at the clock again and registered that it was unusual for Trent, the older 'Terror', to be sleeping in this late. She hadn't heard his usual morning noise at all, she realised. Usually he was up before she was, out in the chook pen talking to his girls or playing with the dogs on the front lawn.

'I've got to go and take the readings for the Sked this morning,' she said as her fingers closed around the Kestrel. 'I'll only be a few minutes.' She grabbed her hat and jammed it on her head, stopping only to pull on her boots and take in the worsening weather.

Chapter 2

It must be twenty-five or twenty-six degrees already, Brianna thought. It wasn't even 7 a.m. yet. Wouldn't be long and all the stock would be camped up under the shade of the bush. Her mob of white Suffolk stud ewes, which were in a paddock close to the house, were clustered around the water trough, although a few were breaking away and heading towards the patch of bush on the northern side.

Brianna jumped into her ute, drove quickly to the highest point of the farm and held up the Kestrel. Noting down the readings, she calculated the FDI. Only sixty-two. In the severe category. It would certainly go up. Once it hit forty degrees, twelve percent humidity and forty kilometre an hour winds, which meant an FDI of one hundred, the fire danger would be catastrophic.

Her phone dinged with a message.

Happy birthday, sweetheart. Looking like a bastard of a day. Stay safe. Dad x

So far, he was the only one who had remembered. Caleb had left without mentioning her birthday, but he'd probably had his mind full of work. Apparently, he was preparing a big case, although Brianna didn't know the details. Caleb would no doubt get to Perth and realise he'd forgotten when his phone beeped to remind him. His life ran on beeps. It would be just like him to come home with an extravagant piece of jewellery for her. One she couldn't wear because she spent most of her time outside and wouldn't want to lose a diamond or get the jewellery caught in machinery. One of her friend's mums had had her finger ripped off on a tractor ladder, after her wedding ring caught on it as she was climbing down. Three years ago Caleb had given Brianna a stunning opal necklace, but it had accidentally come loose and fallen off in the muddy yards. By the time she'd realised it was missing, the mud and sheep shit had covered it and no one had ever found it.

She always appreciated the gesture, but these days she'd choose affection and closeness over anything Caleb could ever buy for her. This morning, if he'd put his arms around her waist and pulled her to him and they'd talked quietly for a time, she would have been happy. Or if he'd told her he loved her. Or something even more intimate.

She tried to shake off her melancholy mood. Maybe turning thirty-eight was making her sad. Beau had said a couple of days ago—as only Beau could—'You've lived nearly half your life, Mum.'

Getting into the ute and shoving it into gear, she smiled. Beau could always be relied on to tell things as they were.

The bushfire radio crackled to life—it was 7 a.m.

'Good morning to all across the bushfire network . . .' The professional tones of Nina Jackson filled the ute as if she were sitting in the passenger seat. 'It's twenty-eight degrees . . .'

Brianna could imagine Nina sitting in her Toyota ute, twenty kilometres away, on her farm, the cord of the radio twisted around a finger, the other hand holding the microphone. Her long hair would be piled in a messy bun on her head, and her sunglasses would be perched on the end of her nose while she announced the meter readings from the piece of paper stuck to her steering wheel.

'Before I begin the call-in I'd like to wish Merriwell Bay Five a very happy birthday.'

Brianna's mouth opened as she heard her call sign and registered what Nina had done. 'Bitch,' she whispered with a small smile, half pleased and half horrified that the whole bushfire brigade now knew it was her birthday.

Nina quickly moved on with the Sked, finishing with, 'I have an FDI of seventy-two. Any other check-in stations?'

'Merriwell Bay Nine, check in.' That was Darren Wilson, Brianna's neighbour, three farms away.

'Merriwell Bay Nine, go ahead,' Nina authorised.

'Happy birthday, Bri,' Darren started cheekily, then launched into his readings.

Brianna's phone dinged, dinged again, then once more. Nina's announcement had obviously spurred some of her neighbours to send birthday messages. She flicked through them, grateful for her tightknit community. The last one read: *HB B*. Brianna laughed out loud. Danny Gratton was a man of very few words.

'Merriwell Bay Five, check in,' Brianna called in.

'Go ahead, Merriwell Bay Five.'

She reeled off her figures, then, as a willy-willy of dust rose in front of her, said, 'I'd like a harvest and movement of vehicle ban implemented at 8.30 a.m. This weather is only going to get worse.'

'Agreed,' Nina responded. 'Do any check-in stations have anything else to add?' She waited only a heartbeat before saying, 'A ban will be in place as of 8.30 a.m. Unless there are any other check-in stations, Merriwell Bay Fire Control is signing off.'

The radio went silent.

Brianna leaned her head against the back of the seat and let out a slow breath. She hoped not all her neighbours would use the harvest ban as a forced break and head into town. The fewer people out here, the fewer there would be to call on for help should it be needed.

A mob of sheep that had been watering at the trough to her right started to follow the sheep pad, one by one, and camp underneath the line of scrubby bush against the fence. She watched as the dust rose behind them—they were silent as they walked, their heads down, one foot in front of the other as if already depleted by the heat.

The phone rang.

Nina.

'You are in *so* much trouble,' Brianna said by way of a greeting.

'No, I'm not,' said Nina, laughter bubbling down the phone. 'Did you get breakfast in bed?'

Brianna scoffed. 'Hardly. Caleb was gone before daylight.'

'Oh, crap, is he in Perth today?' said Nina, concern filtering through her voice. 'You going to be okay by yourself?'

'Why wouldn't I be?' Brianna replied, ignoring the anxious feeling that had been swirling around in her stomach all morning. 'There's nothing to worry about. Just a horrible hot day. Not like we haven't had them before.'

'Bloody wind is blowing like a freight train. I was hoping to get the lambs into the feedlot today, but that's not going to happen. Too hot for them to walk that far, anyway. Stock are like kids on windy days—badly behaved. What are you going to do?'

'I want to do a quick check of all the waters, then I'm going to head home,' said Brianna. 'Trent was still in bed when I left. This heat is sapping everyone's energy. I guess I'll have to keep the kids entertained inside. Beau wanted to go to the beach, but I don't like leaving the farm when it's so hot. Hard when it's summer holidays and you've got to keep them in the house.'

'Nah,' Nina said. 'Tell Beau it's too hot for the beach. You couldn't go for a swim if you wanted to—the sun would burn you to a crisp in the blink of an eye and the sand would be scorching.'

'I guess you're right.' Brianna sighed.

'You okay?' her friend asked in a low voice and Brianna got the feeling she knew about her melancholy mood. That was the thing about Nina, she'd always been able to read her. They'd met in high school when Nina's family had moved to Merriwell Bay to manage a ten thousand hectare farm for a large agribusiness company. As it turned out, she didn't leave when her family did. Instead she went to Perth to study agricultural science, then came back to marry John and become a farmer. Not a farmer's wife, as she reminded anyone who cared to listen. 'I'm just as much a farmer and do as much work as John does!' Nina and Brianna had similar interests and an uncanny ability to be able to finish each other's sentences. Brianna knew she'd be lost without Nina's friendship. Yet, right now she wasn't willing to share her thoughts with her friend.

'Yeah, fine.' Brianna turned the key and started the ute. 'Anyway, I'd better get on. I want to get back to the house as soon as I can.'

'Hold on, hold on! What are you doing to celebrate? If lover boy isn't home, you have to do something!'

'I've got a bottle of wine in the fridge. Dad will probably swing by for a quick beer. Maybe Angie too.' She wasn't sure whether or not she wanted to see her father's girlfriend on her birthday. There were days Angie was lots of fun and she could be very amusing. There were also days she wasn't. It was hard to predict her mood.

'I was thinking Lizzie and I could come and help you drink it,' Nina said.

Brianna smiled at the thought of seeing her friends. Even though the three of them lived within a twenty-kilometre radius, they didn't see each other very often. They all led such busy lives.

'Let's see what the day holds, shall we?'

The ute bumped down the gravel track as she drove towards the cement tank centred on the fence line. This was her key tank, which fed water out to other satellite tanks and troughs.

'Typical. Always the cautious one. Righto, well, if we're not fighting fires, I'll be at yours at six. Reckon we'll all be thirsty by then.'

Brianna pulled up at the tank and climbed out, the phone still stuck to her ear. The heat hit her like a furnace. 'Shit, have you been outside since the Sked? It's awful.'

'John's gone to start the pump to make sure the tanks are full, but I'm going to do the troughs, so I'll be out there in a minute. The wind looks like it's got stronger. I can see dust from Jackson Hallow's farm. God, all his topsoil is going to feed the fish by the looks of it. I wish he'd stop overgrazing his place.'

Brianna turned around and stared in the direction of Jackson's farm. It would be hidden behind the hill, but the dust would still filter around. Her farm was south of his and if his topsoil was off to feed the fishes, then she'd be getting it too. Had she taken the clothes off the line last night? She couldn't remember. Dusty clothes always needed rewashing and the rainwater tanks were getting low. 'He's a shocking farmer. Always got skinny sheep. I don't dare drive past when it's like this, it'd make me sick. Did I tell you about last year when I jumped the fence and put down one of his cows?'

'You didn't?' The glee in Nina's voice made Brianna grin.

'I bloody did! Couldn't bear it any longer. She'd been there for about two weeks, obviously had some type of paralysis. So I shot her. It was the kindest thing for her and why he hadn't done it, well . . .' Brianna broke off as she grabbed the ladder lying on the ground and leaned it up against the tank.

'More power to you, Miss Sharp Shooter. Was there any comeback?'

'None. He probably didn't even notice. Besides, unless he'd seen me, there was no way he could've known who it was.'

She scrabbled up the old ladder and looked over the top. The tank was full but there was a dead magpie floating in the middle. Brianna tucked the phone in between her shoulder and ear and reached for the net below her. Leaning over the edge of the tank, she stretched out to try to scoop up the dead bird.

Nina was still talking. 'I'll bring a salad and a couple of bottles of wine, and Lizzie can bring a couple of packets of chops. With any luck there'll be a sea breeze in by then and we can sit on your verandah and look out at the dead paddocks and see if we can conjure up some clouds. Maybe if we get drunk enough we'll do a rain dance!'

'Too early in the season for it to rain,' Brianna said just as the net made contact. 'Gotcha!'

'Never too—' Nina stopped mid-sentence. 'Got what?'

'What? Oh, nothing. Just scraping a bird out of the tank. Anyway, tonight sounds great. Thank you for thinking about me. I'd better get going. I think I said that about five minutes ago!'

'Yep, me too. Oh, whoops, look at the time! John will skin me alive if I don't get over to the other farm and check the troughs. See you tonight!'

The phone went dead and Brianna shoved it into her back pocket before lifting the net out of the water and dumping the bird over the side. It made a thud as it hit the ground, and by the time she'd replaced the net, climbed down and gone to kick the bird into the bush, meat ants were swarming all over it.

Brianna stared at it for a moment. There wouldn't be much more than feathers left by tomorrow, she decided, so it could stay where it was and the ants could continue their meal. After all, the ecosystem had to go on working, didn't it?

~

'Dude, you're slacking.' Jack Higgins, First Class Constable, gave Detective Dave Burrows' feet a slap to remove them from his desk and sat down in his sagging office chair.

'Oi!' replied Dave as he reacted to stop his feet from falling to the ground. 'That's your opinion. I see it as restorative thinking.'

'Keep telling yourself that. You look like you're sleeping to me.' Jack reached over and grabbed a cupcake from the plastic container in the middle of the desk. 'Kim is spoiling us. No wonder my pants aren't fitting properly any more.'

'Self-control,' Dave muttered, closing his eyes again. 'You don't actually have to eat them.' But he felt a surge of pleasure on his wife's behalf. Kim was a great cook, which was why her roadhouse was the most popular on the route to Adelaide from the northern part of the state. It was a known fact that where the truckies stopped to eat always had the best food, and the parking area at Barker Bellissimo was virtually full of trucks.

'What, and let her think I don't appreciate her cooking? Or worse, she might stop bringing us cakes. No, it's my duty to make your wife feel like she's doing a great job.'

Dave scoffed. 'Maybe I should make you do some street patrols. On foot! That'll help with the waistline.'

'Patrol car suits me fine,' Jack said as he licked his fingers and tossed the patty paper in the bin. 'So, what are we doing today? Other than sleeping and eating. We'd better do something or the town will think we're on holidays and go to the dogs.'

'Contrary to your beliefs, I'm always doing something.'

There was a silence and Dave cracked open an eyelid to look at Jack. He was eating another cupcake.

The phone rang and Dave heard Joan answer it at the front desk. He braced himself, as he did every time the phone rang. Although the mid north of South Australia was seductive in its beauty and sleepiness, it was not without its criminal activity. He'd investigated three big cases here in the last two years. It was during the first one that he'd met Kim. Again. They'd fallen in love as teenagers but lived too far apart to stay together, and when Dave had come to Barker to investigate Kim's niece, Millie Bennett, who had been investigated for theft—a charge Dave had cleared her of—he and Kim had reconnected. Dave had not made the decision to move to Barker lightly. He'd been through a messy and painful divorce and had reconciled himself to remaining single for the rest of his life. The rekindling of their relationship had made Dave realise he'd never stopped loving Kim but, for a while, he hadn't seen how he could keep his career on track and be with her. So he'd talked to his boss and snatched at a full-time posting to Barker, with the stipulation he would travel if the department needed him to. His feelings for Kim had been too strong to resist and every day he was grateful for her presence in his life.

Dave could never quite decide which case had been his most satisfying. Perhaps it was the one involving Fiona Forrest, whose husband had been murdered but his death made to look like a suicide. Dave had dug and dug until he'd found the truth and discovered not only two murders but also a sinister predator, Leigh Bounter. Fiona had taken some time to get back on her feet after the investigation, but now, with a small baby in tow, she was living on her farm, Charona, happy and content. The last time Dave had visited with Kim, Rob, the local vet, had been there. Kim had nudged him as they'd left and said, 'I told you so.' He'd given her an exasperated glance. Kim had a knack for seeing things other people missed and she'd predicted that Fiona and Rob would eventually end up together, even though it hadn't looked to him like they were anything more than friends.

Nope, there wasn't anything quiet about this part of South Australia. But Dave loved it here. Funding cuts meant he was the only detective in the area, so he ended up with all the challenging jobs. He liked that.

Clearing his throat, he said to Jack, 'There was a phone call this morning from a farmer on Jacaranda Road—Guy Wood. When you've finished stuffing your face we're going to head out there and have a look around his place. He reckons that he's lost some sheep.'

Jack leaned over and plucked another cupcake out of the container. 'Come on then,' he said, getting up. 'What are we waiting for?'

'Ah, youthful exuberance.' Dave picked up his notebook and put it in his top pocket. Jack had only turned twenty-eight a couple of weeks ago and wasn't yet jaded. He would make a good detective in time.

'Dave?' Joan's voice buzzed through on the intercom.

'Yep?'

'Katrina Jones has just reported a blue ute doing burn-outs on Short Cut Road. Apparently, it just about cleaned her and her kids up as they were coming into town. It was on the top of Chapmans Hill. Thinks it was a Holden but couldn't be sure.'

'Again? How many times has that ute been reported now?' Dave asked, frowning.

'But how can you be sure it's the same one?' Jack asked, his head cocked to one side, a grin on his lips. 'Seem to remember someone telling me, "Don't assume."' He wagged his finger at Dave and shook his head as if he were disappointed in him.

Dave laughed at his own words being thrown back at him. It was the first rule of detective work. Never assume. He'd been drumming it into Jack ever since he'd arrived at Barker.

'Anyway, it'll be gone by the time we get there,' Jack said, tipping Dave's chair back as he walked by.

Dave flung his arms out to stop himself from falling, but Jack gave him a shove forward and the chair rocked back onto its four legs.

'Bastard!' Dave said good-naturedly. 'We'll drive out to Short Cut Road on the way to see Guy,' he told Joan. 'Could you suggest to Mrs Jones that next time she try to get number plate details? That'd make our job a lot easier.'

He leaned over for a cupcake but the container was empty.

Chapter 3

The house was dim when Brianna opened the door into the laundry. The flies were thick under the verandah, trying to escape the heat, and a great wave of them followed her inside.

'Bugger,' she muttered, waving her hands around, trying to stop them from landing on her face. She grabbed a can of fly spray and gave a good squirt, before washing her hands and closing the laundry door behind her.

Shortly there would be dead flies all over the laundry floor, but it was nothing that a vacuum cleaner wouldn't fix. Caleb wasn't here to voice his disapproval at not cleaning them up straightaway—he was a bit of a clean freak. Ridiculous, really, when he lived on a farm with dust in summer and mud in winter. Anyhow, today, she thought happily, she could clean up when it suited her.

The TV was blaring and Beau was parked in front of it, staring mindlessly at the bright cartoon characters dancing across the screen.

'Hi there,' she said, dropping a kiss on his head as she walked past. 'Where's Trent?'

Beau shrugged.

Frowning slightly, Brianna cast a quick look around the kitchen. Nothing had changed since she'd made the Milo for Beau. No toast crumbs or dirty plates to indicate Trent had eaten breakfast. She turned and headed back through the sitting room and down the passage to the bedroom the Terrors shared, expecting to find Trent curled up in his bed, either still asleep or playing a game on his iPad.

'Good morn—' She stopped. 'Oh.'

His bed was empty. She looked around to check whether he was half under it, as he sometimes was when he was playing with his toy cars.

Brianna looked at the crinkled sheets and crumpled doona, then reached out and touched the bed. It was cold. He'd been up for a while.

He must be out making sure the chooks and dogs had water. Still, she hadn't seen him when she'd driven in. But where else would he be on such a stinking hot day? She turned around and headed back to the sitting room.

'Have you seen Trent at all today?' she asked Beau.

Beau looked away from the TV and she smiled when she saw his telltale Milo moustache. 'Nope. He was gone when I got up.'

Brianna bit back her surprise. 'Really?'

'Uh huh.'

Braving the heat and wind again, she went outside and checked the chook pen. Trent had clearly been there that morning because the trough was full and there was a damp patch on the ground under the tree where he'd run the hose. The chooks were scratching into it, burrowing into the damp earth and flicking dirt over their feathers to keep cool. She hoped the heat wouldn't kill any of them. She'd lost three of her hens during the last forty-degree day. Heat and birds weren't a good mix.

Lifting her sunglasses to wipe the sweat from her eyes, she made her way to the kennels. The dogs set off a round of barking as Brianna approached. They stretched to the ends of their chains, straining to get off. She unclipped all three and watched with a smile as Jinx, Rexy and Buddy ran straight to the coolness of the verandah and flopped at the back door, kicking up a black cloud of disgruntled flies.

She shaded her eyes and peered out to see if Trent was in a paddock or down at the shed.

Nothing.

Strange. He usually left a note if he was going out on the bike. Quickly she went to the garage and checked for the other ute. Both the Terrors drove the older, more clapped-out ute.

It was there and the engine was cold.

Jinx, the oldest of the dogs, limped after her as she walked to the fence, and went through the gate and down the well-worn track to the shed.

'Trent?' she yelled, even though she knew it was futile against the wind.

Jinx heard her, though, and barked as he tried to jump up at her.

'Steady there, old fella,' she said, grabbing his paws and lowering him to the ground, before patting his ears. Her dad had given her Jinx when she'd turned twenty-five. He was thirteen now and slowing down. She'd had to retire him the previous year from working the farm, but it was proving difficult as Jinx still stuck to her like glue.

'Trent?' Her voice was snatched from her as the wind raced around the edge of the shed. 'Little bugger,' she muttered to herself and walked inside, keeping a watchful eye out for snakes. It was the perfect day for them.

A piece of tin banged in the wind and, as her eyes adjusted, she realised the four-wheeler was missing.

'Ah, there we go, Jinx. He must be out on the farm somewhere.'

Of course, he wouldn't know about the harvest ban and the fact he shouldn't be out in the paddocks, so she climbed into the tractor and yanked the two-way mic from its holding.

'Trent, you on channel?'

The only answer was hissing silence. She waited a few more moments before repeating the call.

Nothing.

'Little bugger,' she said again, looking down at Jinx. He was now lying at the bottom of the tractor's steps, puffing with the heat.

Pulling out her phone, she texted her dad—*Have you seen Trent?*—before putting another call out over the radio.

Nope. Why? came the reply.

Just haven't seen him today. Probably out checking stock, she texted back quickly. As she hit the send button, a memory flickered. That's right! He'd said he was going to check his mob of ewes. Clearly he'd forgotten to take the handheld two-way, which was annoying because she had a hard and fast rule: if the boys ever went anywhere on the farm, they had to take the two-way.

Those ewes were Trent's pride and joy. The mob, all ten of them, had started when Trent was five and raised a ewe lamb as a pet—its mother had died while giving birth. Wanting to teach the kids responsibility, Brianna had brought it home for them. Beau hadn't been interested, probably because he was too young, but Trent had loved making up the milk every morning, lunch and dinner. Loved the way Lamb Chops—the only name for a pet lamb, Trent had told Brianna—had followed him around. Whenever there was an orphaned ewe lamb now, Brianna brought her home, Trent raised her, and when she was old enough he turned her out into the paddock. Trent had asked to put a ram over them this year so he could sell the offspring to make some money. Russell had joked that Trent would be a millionaire by the time he was twenty if he kept going in this entrepreneurial spirit.

Brianna jumped down from the tractor and brushed away the flies.

'Should I drive around and find him?' she asked Jinx.

Jinx panted up at her.

'If he's not back in half an hour, we'll go for a drive, how does that sound?' She stopped and looked down at the dog. 'On second thoughts, you'd better stay behind. Don't want your feet getting burnt on the tray. I'd race you back to the house but it's too damn hot!'

Back in the house, she checked the table where the two-ways were kept and made a grimace. She was right. He'd forgotten it.

'Mum?' Beau came out of the sitting room looking flushed. 'Where's the fan?'

'In the storage cupboard, mate. How about we put the aircon on?'

'Yes, please,' he said and went back to the TV.

'Great manners, Beau,' she smiled after him. 'I've got some office work I need to do, okay?'

The bank manager, Ashley Spedding, had rung yesterday wanting to make an appointment for a review, but Brianna hadn't started the budget yet. Today would be the perfect day for it, since she wasn't able to get outside.

She opened the accounting package and started to reconcile the last month's bank transactions, before methodically working through filing all of the invoices and grain sales. This side of the business was second nature to her now. It wouldn't be if she hadn't attended agricultural college. The numbers and accounting packages wouldn't have made any sense, nor would the futures markets or GST. Russell was a skilled and experienced farmer, but he couldn't have taught

Brianna everything she needed to know. There had been so many innovations and new practices since he had started.

Initially he'd been dubious about college. 'You don't need all that book learning,' he'd told her. 'You need to understand the weather and soils, not futures markets and quality assurance.' Somehow she'd managed to convince him, and she was glad because she had learned a lot. Besides, she'd made good friends and met Caleb.

As she tapped at the keyboard, she thought about last year's harvest. It had been a positive one, a rare year when good prices and good yields coincided. In fact, Russell had said he didn't remember a year like it. 'A golden year,' he called it.

The profit needed to be managed carefully for the seasons when the prices weren't so high. Farm management deposits were one option, as was putting part of the profit towards new fences and farm structures, which were one hundred percent tax deductible.

She pulled up the farm map and looked at the paddocks, which had been cropped last year, trying to work out what rotations to use. Brianna was careful to manage her farm well, to avoid overworking it and to spell the land when it was needed. She had a different approach to her father, which sometimes caused friction, although they always worked through it. He was very much a stock and pastures man, while Brianna felt that cropping needed to be in the mix to cultivate the soil and clean out the grasses. Russell sometimes thought she put in too much crop. However, they both loved Le-Nue and believed they were custodians of the land, not its owners.

Angie, her father's girlfriend, had different farming methods again, and that had been cause for more than one good-spirited argument over the dinner table. The farm Angie had inherited from her great-uncle was on sand plains and Brianna thought she overstocked it. Money seemed to be Angie's biggest objective, rather than the health of the land—well, that was Brianna's summary, anyway. Russell tended to shy away from disagreements between Angie and Brianna, taking the more neutral path of 'Everyone farms differently'. Brianna had come to realise that. Look at Jackson Hallow, the bloke who continually fed the fishes with his topsoil.

One thing she couldn't understand about Angie was why she had a manager on her place. Angie had strong opinions about how farms should be run, so why wasn't she running hers herself? Bri suspected it was because she didn't like the hard physical work.

Angie was a strange one. She'd once been a local, from what Brianna could glean from her dad, and she knew that her mum and Angie had been friends when they were growing up. She'd left Merriwell Bay, married a grazier in the Riverina and not returned until he'd died and the farm had been sold. Fortuitously, her great-uncle had died just as she'd returned and left her his farm, fifty kilometres east of Le-Nue.

Angie and Russell didn't live together—they both preferred their own space. But Brianna could see how good they were together. Angie could be charming and funny and sociable; her father was steady and kind and a bit of a loner. They seemed to balance each other out.

She glanced down at the bottom of the screen and saw that nearly an hour had passed and Trent still wasn't home.

'Beau, are you sure you haven't heard anything of Trent today?' she called as she got up and went into the kitchen. She checked the clock in there, to make sure she hadn't made a mistake. No, it was nearly 9 a.m.

'Nup.'

Fear began to creep through her. What if he'd fallen off the motorbike? He couldn't call her because he hadn't taken the two-way. Shit, maybe she should have gone looking for him straightaway. But he was a farm kid, and even though he was only eight, he had a good head on his shoulders and knew the land well. But things could always go wrong . . . What if he'd fallen off and broken his neck? She'd *told* Caleb that four-wheel motorbikes were dangerous. God, only last week a boy had been killed when the four-wheeler he had been riding tipped as he rounded a corner too fast.

Her heart started to beat faster and she could feel sweat break out on her already damp brow. Taking deep breaths, she called her dad's number.

'Happy birthday, chickie,' he said as a greeting. She could hear the calves bellowing in the background. He was weaning, which meant the beautiful black Angus calves he bred would be locked in the yards, with hay and water, until they had grown used to being apart from their mothers. It wasn't the best day for them to be in the yards, but there was shade and water and so they should be okay in the heat.

'Have you seen Trent?' She tried to keep the fear out of her voice, but couldn't.

'What's going on?' Her father was instantly on alert.

'I haven't seen him this morning and the motorbike's gone. I thought he'd just gone to check his ewes, but he hasn't come back yet.' As she talked, she grabbed a water bottle and the first aid kit. To Beau, she said, 'Stay here. Ring me immediately if Trent comes back, okay?' Not waiting for an answer, she raced out the door and headed towards her ute.

'Don't panic, love,' Russell said. 'He's probably run out of fuel and is walking back. I'll go for a drive and see what I can see.'

'You know what he's like about checking his ewes, so I'll start there. I'll ring if I find him.'

'I will too. Don't worry. He'll be fine. He's a practical kid and you've raised him well.'

'I hope so,' she muttered, calming a little at her father's reassuring words. He'd always been a steadying presence in her life.

Brianna shoved the ute into gear and revved the engine too hard before racing off down the driveway, leaving a cloud of dust in her wake. She couldn't stop seeing her eldest son's lifeless body lying on the ground with the motorbike on top of him. The hot engine and exhaust burning through his clothes, his skin.

She blinked hard, looking from side to side, squinting against the glare of the sun. In the distance there was a mirage shimmering and for one moment she thought she saw the glint of the motorbike, but when she focused it was gone.

She strained to see Trent's black hair against the washed-out golden pastures, but every paddock she went into, he wasn't there. His ewes were settled in the shade of a tree line so he hadn't been there recently. There were no motorbike tracks, no gates open or shut differently. Nothing. Realistically, if there had been tracks, the wind had probably covered them with dust already.

In frustration she hit the steering wheel. This was so out of character for Trent, who never went out for too long, or at least without leaving a note. He knew it worried both his mother and grandfather, especially given his grandmother had disappeared without a trace.

The glare of the sun through the windscreen made her hot, even with the aircon on.

Her phone rang and she snatched it up.

'Got him?' she asked her father.

'No sign,' he said in a slow and steady voice. The voice he always used when he was trying to keep her calm. 'I've been over the whole of this side of the farm. Can't see any tracks either.'

'Me neither. Where could he have gone?' she asked, her throat so tight she almost couldn't get the words out. 'He knows he's not allowed on the main road with the quad.

Bloody hell, Dad, he'll be lying somewhere and we can't find him. I told Caleb—'

'Now, love, none of that is going to help Trent. What we need to do is find him. I'm going to ring a couple of the neighbours and get them to come over and help.'

Thank God for her dad. She wouldn't have thought of organising a proper search. She would have just kept on looking.

'I'll ring Nina and John and see if they can come too,' Brianna said.

'Let's meet at your house and we'll put a proper search grid into place. If we don't, we'll end up going over ground you and I have already searched. See you in fifteen.'

Chapter 4

'Caleb? It's me,' Brianna said in answer to his voicemail. 'I need you to ring me asap.' She pressed the disconnect button, wishing she could remember his schedule. He'd muttered something about court and meetings but she hadn't paid a lot of attention. It could be hours before he called back.

She dialled another number. 'Nina?' Her voice was shaky.

'What's wrong?' her friend asked immediately.

'We can't find Trent—he's not in the house. The motorbike has gone. I've been everywhere this side of the farm and Dad's been the other. There's no sign of him.'

There was a sharp intake of breath from Nina. It didn't matter how old the child was, there were always dangers on farms: accidents could happen to anyone.

'Okay, we're coming now,' she said and hung up.

Her phone rang immediately. It was Caleb.

'Thank God.'

'Babe, oh bugger, I'm sorry. I forgot your birthday before I left. Happy birthday, beaut—'

Brianna interrupted him. 'Did you see Trent this morning?' She heard him take a breath.

'Caleb?' she said.

'No. No, I didn't. Why? What's going on?'

She explained and then said, 'I'm terrified, Caleb.'

'Shit. Have you tried the cave?' Halfway up the granite hill in the middle of the farm, there was a cave the boys often played in. Pretending they were cowboys or one of the Famous Five, they'd light campfires and roast marshmallows. Later in the evening, Brianna and Caleb, if he were home, would go up and they'd have a barbecue. Sometimes the boys would spend the night up there and be home in time for breakfast. The last time they'd gone to the cave, though, Beau had been stung on the ear by native bees. As far as Brianna knew, they hadn't been back since, and that was over three months ago.

'I don't think he would have gone up there—it's too hot. But Dad is coming over and we're going to set up a proper grid search, so we'll make sure we check it out. Nina and John are due soon.' Just then she saw Nina's blue ute coming up the drive, stirring up the dust.

'SES?' Caleb questioned.

'Not yet.' She heard him say, 'I'll be right there.'

'Look, babe, I've got to go. I'm heading into court, so I'm gonna be off the grid for at least three, maybe four hours. I'm sorry . . . Shit, I need to be there.' There was indecision in his voice.

'It's okay,' Brianna said. 'Don't worry, go and do what you've got to do.'

'Message me the minute you know something. God, how does this even happen?'

'He's a kid, they do this,' she soothed. Then she frowned. Why was she trying to make him feel better? He was the one who was never here. Anger at the injustice flared through her. 'But I told you the four-wheeler was a bad idea.' She knew she sounded accusatory, but she couldn't help it.

'That's not helpful, Bri.' Caleb's tone changed as he adopted the lawyer voice she hated so much. The one that made her feel small and stupid. He lowered his voice. 'Sweetheart, I'm sorry I'm not there. He's my boy too and I'm as frightened as you are. I'll ring you as soon as I'm out. Love you.'

With shaking hands, Brianna threw the phone on the passenger seat and blew out a breath. Nina and John pulled up, and she got out of the ute.

Nina jumped out of the car and pulled Brianna in for a hug. 'We'll find him,' she said in a determined tone. 'Come on,' she guided her friend toward the coolness of the house.

Brianna, having felt the strength of her friend's hug, had to swallow tears.

John patted her on the shoulder as he followed them.

Another ute arrived, then another: Danny Gratton, Jimmy Pearce, Amanda Connors, Jackson Hallow, Lizzie and Phil

Nixon, Craig Lane and Tom McCullum. All farmers, close enough to be considered neighbours. Russell arrived and hugged his daughter close for a moment, before thanking everyone for coming.

Amid the chaos, Bri noticed they all had CamelBaks on their backs, broad-brimmed hats, and two-way radios pinned to their belts. Danny, the man of few words, was carrying a first aid kit.

'Okay, when did you see him last?' Tom asked.

'Last night. I read them both a story, then turned out the lights. I didn't hear him leave this morning and Beau hasn't seen him.'

'Is he driving?' Jackson wanted to know.

'The motorbike is missing.'

'Would he have left the farm? Run away? Did you have a fight?' Jimmy Pearce fired the questions at her like a machine gun.

'Fight?' Brianna felt herself wobble a little. 'No, of course not!' How could Jimmy even ask that? Trent was a good kid; he had a mischievous streak, sure—both kids did—but he was good-natured and usually did as he was told. And she knew he would never do anything to deliberately worry her, she was sure of that.

More questions. More answers.

Kind arms hugged her, while the hum of talking and making plans grew louder.

Finally Russell clapped his hands and everyone quietened.

'Mum? What's going on?'

Brianna felt Beau's small hand slip into hers. 'It's going to be fine, sweetheart,' she said gently. 'We just need a few more people to help find Trent.'

Lizzie appeared at her side and took Beau's other hand. 'Come on,' she whispered to him. 'I've brought a new Wii game for you to beat me at. It's a basketball one.'

'But . . .'

'Come on, Beau, let's leave them all to do their job and find Trent, okay?' Lizzie tugged gently at his hand.

Brianna squatted down and looked him in the eye. 'Can you go with Lizzie, please, darling? We need to find Trent as soon as we can because it's so hot outside. We don't want him getting dehydrated. Lizzie will look after you.' She registered that Beau was looking frightened but her attention was dragged away as her dad took her arm.

'You search with me,' he said.

~

Outside, the fierce sun continued its relentless shining and the wind ripped through the trees. In one way Brianna was grateful for the gale because it dried the sweat almost before it formed on her forehead, but it tore away Trent's name almost before it had left her mouth.

'No point in yelling, love,' Russell said. 'He won't hear. The wind's too strong. Come on, we're going to start in the bush on the boundary, then head up the hill.'

They walked without talking, concentrating on their surrounds, looking for tyre marks or anything unusual. Following winding stock tracks through the bush, seeing only sheep and the occasional kangaroo. The wind tossed around the small scrubby plants, and the leaves of the spindly mallee trees rustled against each other with a scratching sound.

Russell stopped occasionally and lifted the binoculars, searching the landscape. Brianna took from his silence there was nothing to report. They came to the base of the hill and stopped for a few moments. Brianna unscrewed the lid of her water bottle and drank gratefully, then let a small amount of water trickle over her face.

Her dad pointed out four kangaroos lying under a tree, dozing. One used its paw to shoo away the flies. Trent loved watching kangaroos; as a small child he'd spent hours lying in the middle of the paddock, watching them, or tracking echidnas or rabbits, and finding lizards to bring home and raise as pets. What she wouldn't give to see him do that again.

Don't think like that, she told herself. *You can't think like that.*

'Ready?' Russell asked.

Brianna nodded and started along the path. 'There's no motorbike tracks here, Dad.'

'I know, but he could have walked. It's pretty hard to use the bike when you get up higher, anyway.'

'Can't see any footprints either. I don't think he's here.'

'Gotta look, love. Because if you don't, you'll question yourself, even if you're one hundred percent certain he couldn't be.'

Brianna knew he was right. He'd been through this before. When her mum had gone missing.

As they got higher, they could see the others spreading out across the land, in utes and on foot. Russell had handed out maps of Le-Nue before they'd left and he'd sent one team to check all the dams, and one to circumnavigate every paddock boundary, then work across the paddock in a criss-cross pattern. A third group was walking all the little paths in the scrub.

They'd been searching for three hours when Brianna stumbled on a loose rock and went down on her knees. She fought the urge to scream. Choking back a sob, she got to her feet and kept on walking, calling out Trent's name as she went. She didn't care that he probably couldn't hear her. What if he could?

With each passing minute her panic grew. The pictures in her mind became more graphic and desperate. Her brain kept repeating: *This is so unlike him. This is so unlike him.* Isn't that what every parent said when a child disappeared?

The insistent heat and wind had become almost unbearable but she couldn't stop. Even though her head was throbbing and she felt like she needed to curl up and sleep, she had to keep looking. Her baby was out there somewhere, probably frightened and dehydrated.

Instead of sobbing, she yelled his name with every inch of her might.

'Trent!' It turned into a scream. A high-pitched scream that held all the terror and anxiety she was feeling. She took a couple of shaky steps forward, then stopped, tears threatening.

Her dad was next to her in an instant, hand on her shoulders, leaning in close to talk to her.

'Hang in there, love. We'll find him.' His phone dinged with a message. 'Here,' he handed her the nozzle from his CamelBak. 'Have a drink and wipe your face. The cave's not far away now.' He took out his phone and looked at the screen. 'Bugger, only Angie. She's wondering if she needs to come out and help.'

Wearily, Brianna shrugged. 'Whatever. We just need to find him.'

'I think she'd better come.' He used voice recognition to send the message.

'Come on, let's keep going.' Brianna capped the nozzle and handed it back before looking up towards the top of the hill. She guessed there would be about three hundred steps to go. Not many if Trent was at the top.

But she didn't think he was.

A loud buzzing indicated they had arrived at the cave. Standing back, they watched as a swarm of bees hovered at the entrance, while some of the workers buzzed around their ears.

Brianna glanced around. 'Well, he's not here,' she said, her voice catching. 'Should we call the SES and police, Dad?'

Russell was silent. Finally he answered, 'I don't know. I can't understand where he would be. He knows the land, he's good on the bike. But accidents happen. Maybe . . .' His voice trailed off.

Lifting the two-way from his belt, he asked, 'Anyone had any luck?'

'Negative from group one,' answered Tom and Jackson. 'Nothing to indicate he's been around any of the dams.'

Brianna swallowed hard. That was one good thing.

'Negative from group three,' answered Jimmy and Amanda.

'Russell, Craig here. I've just pulled up at a gate on the boundary. I'm on the . . . uh, south side. I'm sure I can make out motorbike tracks leaving the farm. They're very faint, and there are ute tracks across them, so they might be old, but they're heading over the road. John and I are going for a look. I think at this stage we might need to extend the search.'

Brianna's mouth fell open. Over the road?

'Roger that,' Russell replied. He swallowed before saying, 'There's a track which leads down to the waterhole. It's a real deep hole. I think if we haven't found him in another half an hour, we call in the pros.'

~

The dust rose high behind Dave and Jack's vehicle as they travelled down the dirt road towards Guy Wood's farm. Jack had been right. There hadn't been any sign of the burn-out ute, but the evidence it had been there was strong. Deep skid marks in the gravel fishtailed from one side of the road to the other.

The two men had got out and taken a look, standing in the boiling heat, no sound other than a crow cawing, but there was nothing they could do until they had a make or a number plate to go by.

'Maybe we should send a patrol out,' Jack said. 'It's probably only teenagers playing silly buggers, but it wouldn't hurt to give them a touch-up.'

'Good idea,' Dave responded. 'Is that going to be you or me?' There were only two of them at the police station at the moment. Short staffed by two.

He flicked on the blinker and turned into Guy's driveway.

The fences on the way in, he noted, were old and in need of repair. A mob of sheep was camped in the creek line and there was a very old and broken-down Massey tractor on the side of the road.

'Seen better days,' Jack nodded towards the dust-covered, sun-damaged machine.

'So have the sheep. See the way the wool is hanging from their sides? And that one,' Dave pointed to a lone ewe off to the side, 'see how she's biting at herself? She'd got lice for sure. That doesn't usually make for happy neighbours.'

'Why?'

'Decreases the quality of the wool when it's sold.' He pulled up next to the house, then reversed into the shade of the gum tree next to it. 'And it's not nice for the sheep. Imagine being itchy all the time.'

'Looks like there could be some TLC needed here,' Jack observed, getting out.

'Yeah,' responded Dave, then nodded to the elderly man standing on the verandah as if he'd been waiting for them. 'That's probably why.' He raised his voice and hand in greeting. 'G'day, I'm Detective Dave Burrows. Are you Mr Wood?'

'Yeah, yeah, that's me. I've been waiting for you. Come in, come in.' He shook hands with both men before turning on his heel and limping indoors.

'How's the season treating you, mate?' Dave asked as he ducked his head under the low guttering and walked in through the door. Glancing around he saw a dark living room with white sheets over the chairs. It appeared not to be used. The house smelled musty. Dave tried to remember what he knew about Guy Wood. Not much. In fact he wasn't sure he'd heard his name except in passing.

'Hasn't started yet, 'as it?' Guy responded. 'Still only January. Hot as 'ell and no rain in sight for bloody months. C'mon, this way.' He pointed down a narrow passageway and led them past an open door showing an unmade double bed. Even with a quick look Dave could see it was old-fashioned: it had a brown and green bedspread and sheets that were brown and orange. It was clear there wasn't a woman on the scene—they wouldn't be getting scones, jam and cream for morning tea.

'Yeah, I saw on *Landline* last week that the Met is forecasting an El Niño event. Might be a dry year.'

'Could be, mate, but there's no point in worryin' about what's forecast. Just deal with what comes your way. Tea?'

Dave could see Jack glancing around at the dirty kitchen, a look of distaste on his face. He had a silent chuckle to himself. Jack was still young and had been fairly sheltered in his policing. Drunk drivers, speeding and the occasional shoot-out and murder were all he'd come across. He hadn't done a lot of community policing—Dave wasn't sure why, but Jack seemed to shy away from it.

'Nah, we'll be right, thanks. We've got another appointment in an hour or so. I understand you think you're missing some sheep.'

'Yeah. I'm three 'undred short on me shearing count.'

'When did you shear?' Dave asked, taking out his notebook.

'Back in July.'

'And when did you realise they were missing?'

'I 'ad them in the yards the week before Christmas. I remember cos that lady turned up again. She's been turning up now every year for nearly thirty years. Dunno where she comes from or why she's here, but she camps down in me shed—the one you saw when you drove up.'

Dave's forehead creased as Guy continued to speak. The old man was unshaven; his clothes were loose-fitting and dirty, and it looked like there were a couple of days' worth of dishes in the sink. The floor had dirt and dog hair collecting against the walls. Above the open fireplace, paint was peeling and the wall was covered in black soot, as if there had been a fire at some point. Dave gave the man another once-over to make sure he couldn't see any open wounds that needed immediate attention.

Out of the corner of his eye, he could see Jack. His hands were shoved in his pockets as if he were frightened to touch anything.

'Okay,' Dave said, refocusing. 'Can you remember why you had them in the yards?' It was a bit of a trick question. He was testing the old man's memory.

'Oh.' Guy looked up at the ceiling vaguely before looking back at Dave. 'I can't rightly remember. Would 'ave been something to do with lookin' after them properly and the like. You know, drenchin' or needlin' or something. Me memory's not what it was.' He tapped the table with his fingers and looked expectantly at Dave and Jack. 'I reckon me next-door neighbour has come on over 'ere at night and rounded 'em up and taken 'em home with him.' He leaned back in his chair and gave a grin.

'Who is your neighbour?' Jack enquired.

Dave was glad his tone was steady and strong.

'That young upstart Jones,' Guy answered straightaway. 'You know, Alex Jones's son. Never got along with 'im, right from when he was a young fella. Always thought highly of 'imself, so 'e 'as. Doesn't like me much neither, so it's gotta be 'im. Can't remember 'is name . . .' Guy's voice trailed off and he stared dreamily into thin air.

'And who are your other neighbours, Guy?' Dave asked after a few moments of silence.

'Ah, to the west it's Goanna Harris, and Peter O'Neil to the east.'

Dave jotted down the names. 'Right. I just need to be clear. You had the sheep in the week before Christmas and you counted them, found you were down by three hundred; that sound about right?'

'Sure is.' Guy sat back with his arms folded and nodded emphatically.

'And you've waited until the second week in January to report this?'

The old man looked defensive. 'I've been busy. There's always summat to do on a farm.'

Dave made another note in his book. 'How are the fences on your place, Guy?'

'They're all stock proof.'

'Right, and did you see anything at all suspicious that led you to think your sheep were stolen by this—' Dave glanced down at his notes '—"young upstart Jones"?'

Guy leaned forward as if he were about to reveal a secret. 'I 'ear cars at night.'

'Do you? Any particular time of day?'

'It's always late. Dark, like. I don't sleep too good any more—one of them things about getting old, so the night-time radio tells me. When the dog barks, I wake up, see? Then I 'ear 'em and I go out onto the verandah to listen and watch.' He paused. 'I've never seen anything, though. Just hear the engines in the dark. Still, I don't suppose 'e'd use 'is lights if 'e was goin' to nick something, would 'e?' He gave another grin, pleased with his own brilliance. 'Sometimes I think I see a light, but it never turns out to be nothin'.'

'So you can't tell me any details?' Dave hedged. 'What type the car was, what sort of noise it makes?'

'Sometimes it's real quiet like, and others . . . well, there's lots of revving and what 'ave you.'

'Can you remember when you last heard these vehicles?'

'Oh, be last week, maybe. Or was it last night?' He paused, his brow crinkled in thought. 'Nope,' he said finally. 'The actual day escapes me.'

'Hmm, so you heard them *after* you'd realised the sheep were missing? Not before, Guy?' Dave said gently.

The old man looked confused.

'Not before you had your sheep in the yards.'

Guy frowned and stood up. 'I 'ear 'em all the time. Doesn't matter if it was before or after me sheep were nicked, does it? I 'ear 'em! Why are you tryin' to muddle me?'

'Not at all, Guy, I'm trying to establish when you heard the cars. So I can check weather events—see if was a moonlit night or not, see if it was raining. See if what you heard could have had something to do with the sheep going missing.'

Jack nodded in agreement. 'It's all part of the investigation, Mr Wood.'

'I see,' he said. He shrank back in his chair, looking very vulnerable.

'Guy, do you have any family close by?' Dave asked, changing tack.

'Family? Me mum and dad are dead—been dead for years and years. Me younger brother, God rest his soul, was killed in Vietnam. No, it's only me now. Has been for years.'

'What about this lady you mentioned earlier? The one who turns up?'

'She's a strange one, that one. Don't know where she came from, just turned up one day. Stayed for a while, then left in the middle of the night. Didn't say her name or where she was from or nothing like that. Camped down at the shed, like she owned it. Which she doesn't, mind.

'Anyhow, she went away, then came back again. Does it twice every year, without fail. Turns up, cleans my house, cooks a mountain of food and then disappears again.'

'You don't know her at all?'

'Never clapped eyes on 'er until that first day. Strange. Almost got used to 'er now.'

'And she was here the week before Christmas?'

'Sure was.'

'Doesn't stay in the house?' Dave confirmed.

'Nope.'

'Mr Wood, do you visit the doctor often?' Jack asked.

'What would I want with one of them? Fit as a mallee bull, I am.'

'Of course, I can see that,' he answered. 'It's always good to go and get a check-up every now and then, though.'

'Nah,' Guy scoffed. 'Last time I went to see a quack was in 1981, when I 'ad pneumonia. Spent six weeks in the bloody 'ospital. Never again. I got home and all me chooks were dead. No one had been here to look after them, see? That was real bad.' Unexpectedly, his eyes filled with tears. 'Wouldn't want to go through that again, so no chance of me going to a doc, mate.'

There was a silence and Dave looked down at the notes he'd made. His eyes were drawn to two words: *Needs help.*

'I think we've got as much info as necessary,' Dave said, getting up. 'Look, Guy, I'd really like to mention you to the community nurse, Isabelle Davis. Must get pretty lonely out here by yourself. She pops in on landholders who don't get into town often, and checks their blood pressure and things like that. Great service—means people get a visit every day or two. How does that sound?'

'Don't be worrying yourself about me. I'm fine out here just as I am. You get me sheep back and I'll be happy with that.' Guy got up, and led the way back down the passage and opened the front door.

'Can you point out the shed where the lady stays?' Jack asked, stopping to look around.

'That one.' Guy pointed to a rusty corrugated-iron shed in the distance. It was beyond the wool shed, sheep yards and what looked like a rubbish tip where old wire and drums were piled high.

'Can we take a look?' Dave asked.

'Help yourself. But you make sure you find my sheep, mister. That's what I got you out for. Don't be going and interfering in other people's affairs.'

With that, Guy limped down the steps, and walked to a faded mustard-yellow Toyota and stood beside it. 'Bob! Where are ya, ya useless mutt? Bob!'

Dave hadn't noticed the black kelpie snoozing in the shade of the gum tree. It took a couple of goes for Bob to get to his feet, but he did it, and then he staggered over to the ute and looked up at his master.

Guy leaned down, and grabbed Bob by the scruff of the neck and lifted him into the air. Bob didn't like it and let out a loud whine. 'Carn, you old bugger, you could at least 'elp me.' He tried to heave the dog onto the back of the ute again. This time Bob tried to pull away and gave a loud yelp.

Jack leapt off the verandah. 'I'll get him up there for you, Mr Wood. Hang on.'

Putting his arms around Bob's stomach, he gently lifted the dog onto the back of the ute. The dog flopped down again and looked up with watery eyes.

Guy reached out and patted him with gnarled hands. 'There you go, Bob,' he said softly as he kept patting his ears. 'Bit of an effort these days, isn't it? Like that for all of us.'

Dave looked over at Jack and saw he was pressing his lips together hard. 'We'll be in touch, Mr Wood,' he said.

'For sure, lad, for sure.'

~

Brianna licked her dry, cracked lips and pushed her hair back from her sweaty brow. She'd held the two-way tightly in her hand for what seemed like hours and now her muscles were beginning to cramp.

'Come on,' she said, wanting to shake the radio. 'What've you found?'

Russell came to stand alongside her, his shoulder touching hers. She felt him breathing steadily, but one glance at his pale face told her he was as fearful as she was.

Standing silently, they looked in the direction of the swamp and waterhole, waiting.

'I can't bear this any longer,' Brianna whispered. 'I'm going down there.'

'You can't,' her father said.

'I can, he's my son.' Her voice broke on the last word. She turned to head over to her ute.

Russell stepped in front of her and looked at her steadily. 'Bri, you can't go. You've got no idea where—'

'We have Trent. He's alive.' A loud voice laced with adrenalin burst through the speaker.

Brianna froze. She couldn't make her voice work. Or her fingers. She couldn't even raise the two-way to her mouth.

'Can someone call an ambulance? Repeat, we need an ambulance. Copy?'

Russell snatched the two-way from his belt and answered as Brianna pulled out her phone.

'Copy that, you need an ambulance? You've found him, Craig?' he rapped out.

'We're at the swamp . . .'

Brianna didn't hear anything else; she ran for the ute, dialling triple zero as she went.

'We need an ambulance! Hunters Road, about eighty ks west of Merriwell Bay. Eight-year-old boy hurt.' She stayed on the line while the operator asked more questions she could barely comprehend.

In the ute, she grabbed the mic of the two-way.

'What's going on, Craig? I'm coming.'

'It's all okay, Bri,' he answered. 'We've got him.' Even over the muffled radio Brianna could hear the relief and emotion in the burly man's voice. 'We've got him.' There was a silence before he came back on again. 'Trent's a bit banged up and dehydrated, but he'll be fine. An ambulance would be good.'

'I've called one,' she answered. Turning her attention back to the phone, she said, 'Did you get that? He's alive but you need to get here quickly.'

'What is the condition of the patient?' a calm voice asked.

'I don't know. Just follow the directions.'

'Ma'am, can you—'

'I can't tell you any more. Hurry, this is my son! I'll have people waiting on the road to show you in.' She hung up the phone and said to Russell, who was now standing at her window, 'Can you stay at the entrance so the ambulance knows where to turn?'

She didn't wait for an answer, just shoved the ute into gear and roared out of the driveway, across the road and down a narrow track that led to the swamp.

Questions crowded her mind. Would he be all right? What injuries did he have? What was he doing at the waterhole?

As she drove, she said over and over to the vivid blue sky, 'Please let him be okay, please let him be okay.'

Arriving at the waterhole, she couldn't see anyone. 'Trent?' she screamed, tumbling from the ute. 'Trent? Craig, where are you?'

'Bri, follow my voice,' Craig called.

'Where?'

'Keep coming.'

She ran towards his voice, through bushes and pushing branches out of the way. Finally she saw Craig's fluoro yellow shirt reflecting in the sunlight. She focused on the scene and realised the motorbike was on its side. She could smell petrol. But where was Trent? 'Trent? I'm coming, honey.'

'Over here!'

She broke into the clearing. 'Trent?' she gasped and ran to him. Phil was leaning over him, dribbling water into his mouth, and Craig was sitting next to him, bare-chested. It took a couple of seconds to realise that his shirt was hanging from a tree, to shade Trent from the sun.

Brianna felt like her heart was about to burst through her chest.

'He's very dehydrated, Bri,' Craig said softly. 'And that is making him quite confused. Looks like he's taken a tumble from the bike, had a bit of a whack on the head, and of course he's been lying here most of the day. His ankle is really swollen and I suspect there might be a fracture.'

'Can't we get him into the car and take him to hospital? Won't it be quicker?' She stroked her son's arm as his eyes flickered towards her.

'Trent, honey? Mum's here. Hey, what've you done to yourself, you silly sausage?' She kept rubbing his arm so he'd know she was there.

Trent looked at her blankly.

'Trent?'

He turned away and stared up at the shirt that was blocking the sun. It flapped wildly in the wind.

'Here we go, mate, try and get a bit more of this into you,' Phil said as he held the water bottle over the boy's mouth.

Brianna watched as Trent licked greedily at the water. She held out the edge of her shirt for Phil to wet it. Trent's face was covered in dirt and blood and she wiped away what she could.

'Trent? Can you talk to me? It's Mum,' Bri said softly.

She could see his lips were blistered and his face red from sunburn. The trees would have shaded him for a little while, but as the sun had risen, he would have been exposed to the full force of the midday heat.

'Mum?' Trent whispered the word with recognition in his eyes and Brianna burst into tears.

'It's okay, honey. Everything is going to be just fine,' she said with a lot more certainty than she felt.

By the time the ambulance arrived, the water had begun to do its job and Trent seemed a little more alert. 'I just wanted to get you some yabbies as a surprise for your birthday, Mum,' he said as the paramedics loaded him into the back of the ambulance.

Brianna jumped in behind him, not wanting to let him out of her sight even for a moment. Russell's face, pale, dirty and sweaty, appeared just as the door closed. Brianna gave him a brief wave. She hadn't been able to to talk to him yet. She knew he would have found today especially difficult. He'd been through this before when he'd searched for his wife. She hadn't been found.

'What do you mean?' she asked Trent, pushing aside thoughts of her father.

'I figured Dad would forget. Just wanted you to have something nice for breakfast.'

An electric charge of emotions shot through Brianna. How had Trent seen what was happening between his parents? Clearly he was a lot more mature than his years.

Swallowing hard, she patted his hand and avoided the eyes of the paramedic who sat next to Trent. 'Don't worry about any of that now, sweetheart. All we need to do is get you to the hospital and feeling well again.'

At the hospital there were nurses waiting outside to take Trent into Emergency. One of the paramedics held the drip bag and related vital signs while a nurse wrote down all the information.

Brianna stood apart, letting the medical staff do their jobs, then realised she hadn't called Caleb. 'Shit.'

As she got her phone out to call him, it started to ring.

'Bri? Hasn't he been found yet?' Caleb's panicked voice. 'God, it's been almost nine hours!' During the day she'd sent short texts, all saying: *No news.*

'No, it's okay,' she told him and explained where and when Trent had been found. 'Sorry, I meant to call but I've been completely focused on Trent. He's being taken into Emergency now.' She walked a short distance behind the gurney as the nurses wheeled Trent inside.

'It doesn't matter, just so long as he's been found. Thank God!' His breath blew out, hissing down the phone line.

Keeping her distance from the nurses and her voice low, she said, 'Caleb, we've got a lot to talk about. He went to catch yabbies so I'd have something nice to eat on my birthday. That was why this happened. He wanted to do something nice for my birthday because he didn't think anyone else would.'

'What? Why would have he done that? He knows he's not allowed to cross the road. Imagine if it had been harvest. The amount of trucks on that road . . . God!' It took a couple of seconds more for him to add, 'Why would he even *think* that?'

'Don't you see?' she asked. 'He can see what's going on with us.'

'What?' His tone was incredulous. Then came the lawyer's pause, which he always used when he was thinking of what to say next. When he spoke again, his tone was gentle. Placating. As though he were soothing an overwrought child. 'I know you've had a great shock today, darling. We all have and we're probably all a bit emotional. But although it certainly was a nice gesture, Bri, I don't understand why he thought he needed to take it on himself, when there are plenty of others to help. He could have spoken to your dad, or Angie.' There was another pause. 'There will certainly need to be a consequence for this. He's broken our rules.'

A lump rose in Brianna's throat. Everything was so black and white to Caleb. He couldn't see that their son was trying to make her birthday special. Because he could see—at eight!—his father was too busy. Too busy for the important things.

'Caleb.' She stopped. 'Oh, don't worry.' She knew she probably sounded as defeated and sad as she felt. 'We'll talk when you get home. Are you coming on tonight's plane?'

There was a silence. 'No. I was going to if he hadn't been found, but things didn't go our way in court today and I need to be here to prepare for tomorrow. Now I know he's safe in hospital and well looked after, I'll come home at the end of the week as planned.'

Brianna's mouth dropped open. Not coming? Wild horses couldn't have kept her away—she needed to sit next to her son, reach out and touch him, reassure herself he was still there. Clenching her jaw, she tried to find words she wouldn't regret later.

'Fine,' she answered shortly. 'See you in a couple of days then.'

'Bri . . .'

'No, really, Caleb, you stay there and concentrate on work. Trent will be fine. Beau will be too. And so will I—I always am. See you when you get home.' She punched savagely at the red button and blinked back tears as she turned to find Trent looking at her.

'Don't worry, Mum, I'll look after you.'

Brianna sat next to Trent and watched the drip slowly rehydrate her son. His ankle was in a moon boot, X-rays having showed he'd fractured a bone, and a gash to his head had been cleaned and bandaged. Given the amount of painkillers he'd been given, he couldn't have been feeling a thing.

He slept soundly, his face still pale, and he looked much younger than his eight years. She remembered his birth and the feelings of love and protectiveness that had flooded through her when the nurse had placed him on her stomach. She'd known then she would do anything, *anything*, for him. It was the same with Beau. Every mum she'd ever talked to said the same thing. It was as though there were an invisible cord wrapped around her heart, linking her to her children.

Why didn't fathers feel like that? she wondered. She caught herself. Actually, that was an assumption—one that was wrong, because she knew her dad felt like that about her and her kids. Perhaps the better question was, why didn't Caleb feel like that? Or if he did, why did he focus on work and money at the expense of his family? When had Caleb started bringing home presents rather than attention, focus and love?

There was a clattering of heels in the corridor and Angie swept into the room. Brianna was hit by a wave of her heavy perfume before she was swept up in a large hug.

'Oh, *darling*!' she said in a loud whisper. 'What an *ordeal*!' Angie always sounded as though she were speaking in italics.

Brianna let herself feel a moment of relief that someone was here for her, before she pulled back.

'How *is* he? How are *you*?' Angie peered closely at Brianna's face. 'You need sleep.'

Trent stirred and Brianna quickly hushed Angie and pulled her out of the ward.

'Yeah, I'm buggered,' Brianna said when they were standing in the hallway. 'It's been a bastard of a day.' She rubbed tiredly at her forehead, but smiled at her father's girlfriend. 'Thank goodness he's fine. A few bumps and bruises, plus a break, but he'll be okay.'

'It was lucky there were so many people around who could help look for him. Your father said Craig and Phil found him in the swamp.'

'Sounds crazy, doesn't it? He'd gone to catch yabbies.'

Angie tightened her lips. 'Why on earth wouldn't he tell you? He must know how dangerous it can be out there on your own.

'Now, is there anything I can do for you?' She looked around. 'Has the doctor been in? And which doctor? I hope you don't have Don O'Dwyer. The things I've heard about him.' She tutted. 'If Trent is under his care, you simply *must* change doctors.'

Brianna shook her head empathically. Dr O'Dwyer had a reputation as a rough and uncaring medico and there was no way she would entrust Trent to him.

'No, no, it's okay. Our doctor is Sam Chapman. He left only about half an hour ago. He said Trent's dehydrated, obviously. Then there's the break in the ankle and the blow to his head. I'm hoping that his memory will be clearer when he's fully rehydrated; right now, it's a bit patchy. He remembers some things but not others.'

'Oh, memory loss? That doesn't sound good. Is that the result of hitting his head?' Angie asked, smoothing her hair at the sides.

'It could be but it's probably more to do with dehydration—it can make people confused. Trent remembers leaving the house and checking his ewes—he told me in great detail about how Lamb Chops heard the motorbike and came running over to see him. I know he carries lupins in his pocket whenever he goes out there, so she always comes up to get a feed.'

'So cute,' Angie nodded.

'Then he headed up to Dad's to grab the yabby nets out of his shed. He said that he waited a bit to cross the road because there were two trucks coming—he even told me they were stock trucks—and after that, not much. He doesn't remember falling off, or if he hit something to tip the bike.' Brianna touched her throat, distressed, as she spoke. The accident still seemed so unreal. 'He must have lain there for hours. From what I can gather, he left the house before Caleb did, and Caleb was gone by five. He just wanted to surprise me at breakfast with some yabbies.'

'Why yabbies, *darling*? Such a strange idea.'

'I don't know,' she answered, not ready to share the truth with anyone yet. A memory forced its way into her mind. A barbecue on the edge of the dam. Caleb had Beau on his shoulders; they were laughing. She and Trent were at the water's edge, fishing for yabbies with a piece of string. Trent caught one and she said, 'Ah! My favourite fisherman catching my favourite food.'

The lump in her throat that had been threatening to appear all day rose and almost closed over her airway, and she had to swallow hard. There was no way she wanted to cry in front of Angie.

Angie reached out and rubbed her upper arm, making cooing noises. 'What a shock. Horrible.' She dropped her hand and moved away to pace the hallway. Her court shoes clicked on the lino and her white linen pants rustled as she walked.

Brianna realised she looked like the perfect blue-blood grazier's wife, right down to the pearl necklace—neat, tidy, fashionably dressed.

Self-consciously Brianna tried to rub some of the dirt from her shorts. She must look a sight. Putting a hand to her hair, she found it was knotted and tangled.

'I don't suppose you have a hairband, do you, Angie?' she asked, pulling her hair back off her face and twisting it into a knot on the top of her head.

Then she got a whiff of her underarms and she let everything drop.

Angie stopped and opened her handbag, looking through it but coming up empty. 'Don't worry, I'll find something. A shower would be good too.

'Now, I want you to *know*—' Angie's tone changed and became very soft—'*anything* I can do to help, make sure you *call* me. Do you *hear* me? Anything. I'll be in Merriwell Bay again tomorrow.

'I'd *love* to stay and see your father, but I do really need to get home. I've got to *prepare* for this meeting with the shire council. *Why* they can't grade my road, I don't know. Anyway,' she waved her hand dismissively, 'you've got too much on your plate to hear about a pothole-riddled road!'

'Thanks, Angie, I appreciate your support. I'll be here for a few nights, I'm sure.'

Angie started to leave but stopped after she'd taken a few steps. 'Who has Beau?' she asked as if he were an afterthought.

'Dad's bringing him in. I guess he'll take him home and have him stay over until I'm back.'

Angie looked steadily at Brianna. '*Ah*. Caleb not coming home then?'

She shrugged.

'He's in the middle of a very big court case, I believe,' said Angie. 'If you watch tonight's news, you might even see him interviewed.'

What? Brianna thought. Interviewed? Why didn't she know about that? Why indeed? She'd been busy looking for her lost son and not thought about anything else. She frowned.

Angie gave an uncertain smile. 'Well, I guess he'll be *home* as soon as he can. Give my love to Trent when he wakes up. See you tomorrow.'

Brianna watched her go, wondering why, after all this time, her dad had chosen to start a relationship now. There had been a couple of women over the years but they had come and gone very quickly. Thirty years alone was a long time, she supposed, and no one wanted to grow old by themselves. But Russell and Angie were set in their ways and Brianna couldn't imagine them changing enough to live together. Nina said it was about companionship and convenience—someone to talk to and go out with. 'They don't have to live together—they're both really independent people.'

They seemed happy visiting each other's farms and spending time together without having to change too much of their lives. Angie seemed to fit in with them all, and she undoubtedly cared about Russell, as well as Trent and Beau, which was all that mattered to Brianna.

She sat back down next to Trent, who didn't seem to have moved while she was gone.

'How are you holding up, Bri?' Melinda, the nurse looking after Trent, had walked in and started taking his obs.

'Okay, thanks. Do you . . . um, could I . . .?' Bri broke off, looking embarrassed.

'What do you need?' Melinda asked without looking up from the machine, as if she knew that Bri didn't want to draw attention to herself.

'Do you think I could have a shower?' she asked quickly.

'Of course you can. I'll bring you a towel when I've finished here. What about a change of clothes?'

'That's okay, I can put these back on, but . . .'

'I'll see what I can find in the donations box. You don't want to be wearing dirty clothes when you're feeling nice and clean. Leave it with me.' She smiled. 'He's doing so well. Be back on his feet before you know it. Well, on crutches at least!'

Brianna's phone buzzed. She looked down at the screen and felt another flood of anger. 'Hello,' she answered flatly, waving as Melinda left the room.

'How's everything going?' Caleb asked.

'Fine. The doctor's seen him.' She told him everything that had been said, finishing with 'He'll have about six weeks on crutches.'

A cool breeze blew through the room as the door opened and Russell and Beau came in, carrying a bag each.

'I've got to go. Dad has just got here.'

'Oh.' There was a silence, as if he were processing what she'd just said. 'Look I'm sorry—'

'No, Caleb, I don't want to hear it. I have to go. Talk to you later, okay?' She hung up, wondering why he couldn't understand why she was mad with him. Unclenching her jaw, she smiled at her son before saying quietly, 'Hey, Beau! Come here and give me a hug.' She held out her arms and hugged him tightly, looking up and nodding at her dad. Russell seemed to relax as she indicated all was okay. 'Well, this is a bit exciting, isn't it? I don't think you've been to a hospital before, other than when you were born.'

'Is Trent all right?' Beau asked as he looked at his brother sleeping in the bed.

'Yup, he's going to be fine. His ankle's broken and he'll have to use crutches to help him walk around for a few weeks, but he won't be getting out of sport at school for too long.' She gave Beau an extra squeeze and turned to her dad. 'You're looking better than the last time I saw you.'

He held up a bag. 'I've managed to have a shower,' he answered tiredly. 'Pretty sure you need one too. We brought you some clothes.'

'I can't tell you how much I need them!'

Melinda came back in with a towel. 'I heard you've been brought a change of clothes, so you won't want ours. Much nicer to be in your own. Jump in the shower whenever you want.'

'Thank you,' Brianna answered gratefully. She reached out to hug Beau again, then her dad. 'I'm sorry. I stink! Thank you for today.'

'You're welcome,' he answered in a gruff tone. He moved to the bed and looked down at his grandson. 'We'll sit with him. Have a shower and then we can talk. He won't be alone.'

Chapter 5

Dave breathed deeply as he sat staring through the car window. His mind was racing. Guy Wood was a prime target—elderly, a little confused, and unable to defend himself even if he did catch someone coming onto his farm and stealing from him.

Jack got in beside him and looked over. 'I don't ever want to get old,' he said.

'Yeah,' Dave agreed. He turned on the ignition and picked his way over the stony two-wheel track towards the shed.

'What are you going to look for?' Jack wanted to know. 'You won't see anything. He's delusional. There isn't any woman living in his shed. A wild cat maybe, but not a real-life woman.'

'It's worth a look,' answered Dave. 'Never know what you might find.' He tapped his fingers on the steering wheel.

'And I don't think he's delusional. Maybe he's got the start of dementia. But he needs a bit of help looking after himself, that's for sure.'

'Will you give Isabelle a ring?'

'Yeah, as soon as we get back into town. What do you know about him?'

'Nothing. I've only been here twelve months longer than you, remember? I'd never heard of him before today.'

'I wonder—'

Jack looked over at him, incredulous. 'Are you losing your memory too?' he interrupted.

Dave frowned as he pulled up at the shed. Heat blasted him as he opened the door and he leant into the back seat to grab a torch. 'Not that I'm aware of.' He slammed the door shut and walked towards the opening.

'Kim, obviously. If you want to know more about Guy Wood, she's the one to talk to. She's been here since she was a little girl. She knows everyone and how they're related. She could recite a family history in the blink of an eye.'

'You didn't get it right this time,' Dave said, pointing at Jack with a grin. This was their standard joke. Jack seemed to be able to pre-empt what Dave was about to say. Kim said their conversations used predictive text. 'Can I finish my question? I wonder how he came to be here. Whether this is his family's farm. Whether he ever married.'

Jack stayed silent as he followed Dave into the shed. They stood for a moment, letting their eyes adjust to the dimness.

'I reckon he would have lived here all of his life,' Jack said. 'In fact, I'd bet next week's pay on it. It'll be his family's farm and, no, I don't think he would have married.'

'You're probably right.' Dave flicked on the torch and flashed it around. 'But why wouldn't he have married, I wonder?' The shed was empty, with a dirt floor and cobwebs covering the walls. Exposed wooden beams were strung across the roof and there were small shafts of sunlight coming through the rusted-out parts of the tin.

'Told you—nothing to see,' Jack said. 'And perhaps he never met anyone he liked enough. There're slim pickings out here. I'm speaking from experience.'

'Hmm.' Dave walked to the edge of the shed, flashing his torch from side to side. He couldn't see anything that piqued his interest. No areas where the dirt had been disturbed, no recent footprints.

He went back outside and walked the circumference, hoping to see the ashes of a small campfire or something that would indicate a woman had been here.

There was nothing.

'Come on,' he finally called to Jack, who was poking around in a pile of old drench guns and tools at the other end of the shed. 'We'll go and see what Alex Jones's upstart of a son has got to say.'

~

'You've come from Guy Wood? What's he on about this time?' Toby Jones, who Dave guessed to be about twenty-eight or thirty, stood in the airconditioned kitchen with his arms folded across his chest. 'He's always complaining about something.'

Dave had introduced himself after Toby had answered the door—he'd been surprised to find the farmer at home. Even with the heat, farmers were usually out doing something. Water or stock checks at the very least.

'Is he? Well, we're just wanting to ask what the neighbourly relationship is like,' Dave explained. 'Nothing out of the ordinary.'

'But why? It's a little strange for you to turn up on my doorstep unannounced and ask to talk about Guy.'

'Honey?'

A slight blonde woman appeared in the doorway and Dave figured she must be Toby's wife.

'It's fine,' he dismissed her with a brush of his hand. 'They're here to ask about Guy.'

The woman came into the room. 'Oh, I'm very concerned—'

'Meg!' Toby threw her an annoyed glare but Dave ignored him and stepped towards her.

'You're concerned?' he prompted. 'About Guy?'

Meg looked over at Toby, who threw his hands in the air in resignation.

'Say what you want,' he told her. 'But I keep telling you, it's none of our business.'

'And we're his neighbours,' Meg answered as she turned towards Dave. 'Yes, about Guy. I think he's losing his memory,' she said. 'I went over there last week to drop off a couple of frozen meals, but he didn't know who I was and wouldn't let me in the house. I've known him since

I married Toby—that's five years now. I've always taken meals over to him. I know he's all alone and he doesn't cope with the housework very well.'

'That's interesting. He spoke about a woman who came and brought him meals and cleaned his house, but apparently she stays down in the shed. And he doesn't know her name.'

Meg looked puzzled. 'I've never seen any sign of anyone else there.'

'Ha, that'd be right. Concocting some sort of story. That's what he's good at. Likes to make things up or blame others for his shoddy work.'

'Toby!' Meg admonished her husband.

'You know he does, Meg.'

'I don't think he does it on purpose. He's a confused old man.' Meg's brow crinkled with concern.

'What about you, Toby? Sounds as if there's some ill will between the two of you?' Dave turned to see Toby Jones was frowning, his arms still crossed.

'He and my dad were good mates, but I find him cantankerous and arrogant. I've always found him to be very difficult. When I first left school, I had a V8 ute and I used to work it a bit. He rang the police and told them I was cutting up his driveway and I'd knocked over ten white posts at the front of his place.'

'Had you?' Jack asked.

'No, I hadn't. I knew who did—it was one of my mates. It wasn't me.' He nodded his head as if to make the point.

'Later, after Meg and I got married, he rang my father to say I'd let my sheep over the fence and onto his farm to feed.'

Dave opened his mouth to ask another question, but Toby answered it.

'Again, no I didn't. His sheep didn't have any feed in the paddock they were in, so they busted the gate down and got into a paddock that had a heap of feed in it. By the time he got there, they were back camped on the dam in their rightful paddock and the one with the feed in it was almost as bare as the first one. I could reel off a dozen times he's done this. Like I said, he makes up stories, then rings my dad.'

'And what did your father do? Or, rather, what *does* he do? Sounds like it happens a bit.'

Toby narrowed his eyes and looked at Dave. 'I usually get a fair dressing-down for upsetting the old bloke.'

Meg took a couple of steps forward and put her arm around Toby. 'It's really all a bit of a misunderstanding between Guy and Toby,' she said. 'I suspect Guy thinks Toby was born with a silver spoon in his mouth.'

'As in he feels that you act entitled?' Jack turned to Toby.

Toby shrugged and reddened slightly. 'Something like that. I was . . . ah, a bit of a prick when I was in high school. Liked to tell people we were the biggest farmers in the district. You know, teenage bullshit. Arrogance. Of course, he's been farming here forever, done the hard times, through slumps, low wool prices. I was a young bloke running around telling everyone how good our farm was and how important my family was in the district. Anyway, I've never lived it down with old Guy.' He cleared his throat. 'And I'm the first one to admit I wasn't a particularly nice person. Because of all of that, when something goes wrong at his place, I'm the first person he blames. Doesn't matter that I've grown a brain and matured, he still thinks I've caused the problem.'

'I've tried to fix the relationship,' Meg said earnestly. 'I thought by cooking him meals and helping out, he'd see that Toby had changed. Hasn't worked that way.' She looked down and kicked at an imaginary piece of gravel on the lino.

'What kinds of things have happened recently? When I say recently, maybe in the last few years?'

'When doesn't it!' Toby scoffed. 'He never wants to listen to anything I've got to say. I guess the most consistent problem I've had since I started running the farm is his bloody sheep getting through the boundary fence. Dad's retired to Clare, so I had to go and see Guy about putting up a new fence. I wasn't going to put up with his lice-ridden, flyblown mongrel sheep continuing to come onto my place. But do you think I could get the old fella to put up half the cost? Not a freaking chance.' Toby sighed and shook his head. 'It frustrated me like nothing else. That's not the way it's supposed to work. When boundaries need re-fencing, neighbours are supposed to share the cost. Go halves.'

'What happens when one neighbour can't afford it? Like in this instance?'

'Of course he can afford it! He's a miserable old coot who's still got the first dollar he ever made. Only reason he made it difficult was because he doesn't like me! He said it didn't need doing, which was a load of bullshit.

'Anyway, I ended up paying for the whole damn lot. I wasn't going to have my flock infested with lice from his sheep. You got any idea how much that downgrades the quality and price of the wool?'

'Yeah, I do,' Dave said, interrupting the angry tirade.

Toby stopped and looked at him.

'Third son of a farmer from WA,' said Dave. 'They couldn't find any room for me at home, so I chose to be involved in agriculture by working my way up to lead detective in the stock squad.'

'Right. Well then, you'd understand my dilemma. Of course he couldn't even help pull the old fence down.'

'Toby, he's seventy if he's a day,' Meg put in. 'You can't—'

'Yeah, I know.' Toby sighed. 'It annoys me. In the end it was easier to take on the whole job myself. I made sure the fence line was cleared and I got a fencing contractor in to put up the new fence. It was worth the investment, even if he didn't put one cent towards it.'

'Did you re-fence the whole of the boundary or just part of it?'

'The whole lot. I can show you if you want.'

'That won't be necessary right now, but it may be later.'

'Just ask.'

'And your father, they got along okay together?'

'Like I said, they were good mates. It was Dad who told me to pull my head in and just get the fence up. "He's not going to be there forever, son," he said. "Put it up, it'll benefit you in the long run because you'll want to buy the land when he passes away."'

'You want to buy his farm?'

'When it comes up, yep, that would be my plan. This place will be too small if we have sons who want to come home.'

'There isn't any family for Guy to leave it to then?'

'None that I know about. He's lived there by himself for as long as I can remember. Dad told me his brother was killed in the war. I'm sure he's alone in the world.'

'Right, well, thanks for your time. Appreciate your help.'

'No problems. If you need anything else, just ask.'

'Oh, don't worry,' Jack said. 'We will.'

Dave was about to leave the kitchen when he turned to Meg. 'I'll be seeing the community nurse, Isabelle Davis, when I get back to town. Hopefully we can get the old man the help he needs.'

'That's a good idea. I don't know why I didn't think of that. She'll be great with him; have him round her little finger while she's on the first visit.'

'And you'll let me know if you see anyone hanging around over there—especially this lady who stays in his shed.' It was a command not a request.

'Of course. He's a sweet man.' She gave a sad smile. 'Getting old can be such a lonely business out here. Especially when there isn't any family.'

~

Dave stretched his calf muscles, then dropped forward and let himself hang and stretch. He could feel the blood running to his face.

'That was such a good walk,' Kim said, doing the same thing.

'Great way to clear your head at the end of the day.'

'And stay away from the beer fridge.' Kim gave him a shove with her hip as she stood up, and he tumbled over.

'Oi! That's not nice.'

'Sorry,' she answered cheekily, then flopped down on the grass next to him, before leaning over and giving him a kiss.

'Well, if that's the way you're going to apologise, you can do it anytime you want!'

Kim laughed and put her head on his stomach, staring up at the sky.

The first star was just appearing and the corellas were screeching as they found their perches for the night.

'Good day?' she asked quietly.

Dave gave a sigh. 'Confronting day, actually.'

Kim rolled onto her side and looked up at him. 'How so?'

'Have you heard of an old bloke called Guy Wood?'

'Guy Wood? Are you talking about the old farmer? I don't think he's still alive, is he?'

Dave flicked her a quizzical look. 'Three questions in one breath. That's a record even for you!'

Kim gave him a soft whack.

'Yes, but the Guy Wood I met today was alive.'

Kim smiled at him, then frowned, tipping her head to the side. He ducked his head so she didn't see his grin. She always did that when she was thinking hard. 'He's the one who lives on Jacaranda Road, yeah?'

'Uh huh.'

Kim sounded incredulous. 'I could have sworn he was dead. Okay, from memory, and this will be Mum's memory more than mine, cos I would have been really small and, seriously, this is a long time ago . . . His brother was killed in Vietnam and Mr Wood—that's what I always called him—took over the farm after that. Well, probably not took it over, because his dad was still around, but they farmed together. His mum died years and years ago and I can't remember when his dad died—in fact I don't remember them, I only know the stories about them. Strange family. Kept to themselves, dressed in a very old-fashioned way. People used to say they were like the Amish. I remember my mum saying they used to go to church, then they just stopped going—which was weird back then because everyone went. Next thing there were rumours they had started a church out on the farm so they didn't have to come to town and mix with the townies. And . . . this is foggy, but I seem to remember something about there being another child, but no one was ever sure.'

Dave looked over at her, interested. 'What do you mean, never sure?'

'Geez, Dave, this is so long ago, I'm not sure I've got the story right.'

'Just tell me how you remember it. I can do some research if I need to.'

'But that's just it, I can't remember it well enough, but there was always a rumour about another baby after the two boys. Whether someone saw the mum with a baby at some point, I've got no idea. But if there was a child, it certainly didn't grow up. Whether it died, was adopted or was sacrificed . . .' She waved her hands wildly in the air. 'Or perhaps the little bub never even existed. Who knows!'

'Sacrificed? Are you kidding?'

'This is Barker, Dave. The wilder the story, the better gossip it makes.' She rolled her eyes and Dave smirked at her, remembering the gossip that had gone around town like wildfire when they became an item. It felt like an age ago and, at the same time, just yesterday. Their first public kiss had been in the motel's restaurant, and the waitress had just about fallen over herself in her hurry to get back to the kitchen and tell the staff.

'Mr Wood,' Kim said, breaking into his thoughts, 'never married as far as I know and . . . Well, I really thought he was dead!' She gave a small laugh. 'He must be pretty old by now. But as for the baby, that's all I can tell you.'

'The man I met today is having trouble coping by himself. I think his mind is wandering. His house is very dirty, so are his clothes. I'd say he forgets to eat. Meg Jones told me she takes meals over to him, but last time she went over there he didn't know who she was.'

'Now, Meg's a lovely girl. Volunteers for Meals on Wheels. I wonder why she hasn't said anything to them.' Kim stood up. 'Why were you out there?' Putting her hand out to Dave, she continued, 'Come on, I've got to get tea on.'

'Guy rang the station and reported some stolen sheep.' Dave took her hand and hauled himself up, groaning as he went. 'Sometimes I think I'm too old for this shit.'

'This shit will keep you younger longer,' she retorted, then she softened her voice. 'That's pretty sad he's not coping. You know, I've always been worried about dying alone.'

'That's something you'll never have to worry about. You've got more friends than I can count, and you've got me.'

'You might die before me!'

He patted her bum. 'Not if I have anything to do with it. Come on, I'll make the salad and you can cook the steak.'

'Seriously, Dave,' said Kim as they walked slowly back to their house, 'can you imagine? Being so isolated that no one knows when you've died. No one misses you. It would be awful.' She shuddered.

He took her hand and raised it to his mouth, kissing it gently.

'It would be awful,' he agreed.

Chapter 6

The dusty road seemed to go on forever. With each unsteady step she took, the mirage in the distance shimmered. Her mouth was dry, and even though she'd stopped at a water-hole a while ago, she was again craving a drink.

She'd stumbled upon the waterhole, grateful to have found it. She'd washed herself gingerly, finding more bruises and cuts. The gash to her head felt like it was deep and wide, and when she'd tried to clean it, blood had started to seep out again. She'd had to rip off a sleeve of her already bloodied shirt and try to stem the flow.

Somehow she knew that head wounds tended to bleed a lot, but she didn't know how she knew that. Was she a nurse? A doctor? She had no idea.

The heat was oppressive, the sun almost white in its glare. She didn't recognise the dry, dusty landscape. Oh, she knew what the objects in the landscape were—the road, the fence, the dam—they were familiar things. But this road wasn't. This scenery—low scrubby bushes, stones and clumps of grass; tones of red mixed with blues and purples—was unfamiliar. Did that go with not knowing who she was? Was this area in fact her home but she didn't know it?

The terror of feeling so out of control, of not knowing anything about her own self, made her want to lie down on the ground and scream in panic. Did she even have a name? Was anyone missing her? Would anyone come looking for her?

She had no idea but she couldn't let her emotions overcome her. She had to keep walking. Keep on until she found someone to help her. A hospital—ah, there was another word she knew—or a town.

But if she understood she needed a hospital, why didn't she know her own name?

Come on, she coached herself. *One foot in front of the other. And again, again, again.*

She picked up a stone and put it in her mouth, knowing it would help stimulate saliva. Make her feel less thirsty. How did she know that?

The further she walked, the closer the sun dipped towards the horizon. Just as the sun was about to set, she stumbled onto a dry creek lined with tall, imposing gum trees. She found one that had a hollow carved out of it and curled up at the base, still sucking on the stone. The ground was prickly and hard.

Then the sun was gone and the darkness threatened to swallow her. She felt small and insignificant under a very large sky and she had the feeling no one was going to be coming for her.

Her eyes closed, shutting out the vast, frightening world, and she slept.

~

A scream woke her and she sat up quickly, her heart beating so fast she didn't think she could take a breath. Her cheeks were wet.

She heard the scream again and realised it was coming from her. Her arms instinctively flew over her head, as if she were warding off a blow.

Pain shot through her skull and down her spine. If she'd been able to see, her vision would have been blurry, but it was dark and cold and there was nothing to see but blackness.

She groaned, slumping back down on the ground, and curled into a ball.

At that moment everything hurt so badly, she didn't care whether she lived or died.

Chapter 7

Brianna tucked Trent in tightly and sat on the edge of his bed, smiling down at him.

'How are you feeling? Pleased to be home?'

He nodded. 'Sorry I worried you all,' he said for about the hundredth time.

Doctor Chapman had said Trent could leave hospital after two days. He'd been fully rehydrated and the head wound had been cleaned, stitched and bandaged. His memory of the accident hadn't fully returned, but the doctor thought it would probably come back with time.

He'd explained that a blow to the head could result in short-term memory loss, although it was possible he would never remember the accident itself. 'If you're missing those few hours for the rest of your life, I don't think you'll be missing too much,' he'd said, tussling Trent's hair as they waited to leave.

'Honey,' said Brianna now, 'I'm just happy you're fine. I won't say you didn't scare me, because you did, but this is a lesson learned and I'm thankful you've learned it and you are still okay.'

'I mucked up your birthday. I wanted it to be special.' Tears filled his large brown eyes.

'It's one I certainly won't forget,' Brianna smiled.

'It was scary out there, Mum. I didn't think the bush could be scary.'

Brianna waited for him to say more, but nothing more came, so she asked, 'What do you mean, scary? Because it was hot?'

'I don't know,' he shrugged. 'I know I was scared when I woke up but I don't remember falling off the bike. It was like I was the only person in the world and I was really little and the world was really big.' He rubbed the doona between his fingers and looked down as he spoke. 'There wasn't any noise to begin with and it was so hot. Then the wind came and I tried yelling but no one could hear me.'

Feeling her stomach constrict, Brianna tried to keep her face neutral. She didn't want Trent to know how much hearing about his ordeal distressed her.

'I knew you'd be angry with me cos I'd forgotten to take the two-way. I didn't mean to, Mum,' he said, looking up at her. 'I just wanted to get out there and check the nets and I forgot.'

'Bet you don't do that ever again. Forget, I mean,' she said with a wan smile. 'What do you mean, check the nets? Did you already have them in?'

He nodded. 'I put them in the night before.'

Brianna filed that piece of information for later. It meant Trent had broken their rules twice.

'I couldn't move cos my ankle was too sore and my head hurt. I couldn't work out where I was at first, but then I realised. And that made me remember it was your birthday.' A frown appeared on his forehead. 'I got cross then—and yelled and yelled and yelled.

'My voice didn't work after that cos my throat was so dry. Well, not much anyway. It worked enough to scare the eagle away.'

Brianna froze. Eagle? She hadn't even thought about birds of prey. There was a pair who lived on the hill. Often she'd see them soaring so high they were only specks in the deep blue, but she knew their eyesight was impressive and she'd seen them dive fast towards the earth from great heights and pick off a small lizard or rabbit.

'It was circling over my head. I didn't see it at first cos I had my eyes shut. Everything was sore and I thought if I shut my eyes maybe everything bad would go away. But it didn't.'

'What did it do?' Brianna held her breath.

'It swooped a couple of times. Reckon it was checking me out cos it didn't land, then it perched in a tree and watched me. When it came closer I yelled at it and waved my arms lots. Musta decided it wasn't any good cos then it flew off again. It scared me, Mum.'

'Of course it would have, honey. That's a horrible thing to have to go through. But you're safe now.'

The dogs set off a round of barking, making them both look towards the window.

'Who'd be coming to visit us at this time of night?' Brianna wondered out loud.

'Maybe it's Granda,' Trent said, throwing back his doona cover.

'You stay in bed, young man. You've got some rest to catch up on.'

'It's not late, Mum. The sun hasn't even gone down properly. And Beau isn't in bed yet.'

'He didn't fall off a motorbike, bang his head and break his ankle, did he?' She fixed him with a stern look. 'You've had a big ordeal and you need to rest.'

Trent let out an annoyed sigh and flopped back into his pillow.

'Be back in a sec,' she said, pulling the doona up and giving his forehead a kiss.

~

Standing on the front verandah, she realised with a shock it was Caleb's car coming up the drive. Standing with her arms folded, she watched it drive in, not quite sure how she was going to respond to him.

He parked the car carefully in the garage and got out, pulling his briefcase with him. Even after years of marriage, she still found her eyes were drawn to him. He was tall and handsome in a well-cut suit. She'd joked when they'd first met that a suit didn't show off his butt as well as a pair of R.M. Williams jeans would. His hair was salt and pepper grey at the sides and she thought it made him look distinguished. He was seven years older than her and had been married before, although when he and Brianna had met he'd been divorced for twelve months. He was trim, working out at the gym every day he was in Perth. Brianna used to love running her hands over his muscular upper arms. And his hands were strong and smooth-skinned.

Suddenly self-conscious about her own weathered hands, she quickly gathered her dark hair into a ponytail and secured it with a band she'd had on her wrist. She wondered what he saw when he walked towards her. At thirty-eight, she was trim—her work kept her that way—but she still had to lose belly fat from when she'd had the boys. Nina told her it wasn't belly fat at all: 'It's a mummy tummy and it shows you have lots of love in your life.'

Brianna also knew her face was sun-damaged—little red splotches on her cheeks tended to glow redder when she was hot, and a couple of weeks ago she'd noticed two dark sunspots on her left cheek. She was no longer the glowing, youthful girl Caleb had met when he'd delivered a guest lecture on farm security at ag college.

When she'd mentioned this to Nina, her friend had scoffed, 'Don't be ridiculous. You're totally gorgeous. Your eyes show how beautiful you are inside and out. We've all got to age—it's a privilege denied to many. Embrace the way you look now. Wrinkles show you've laughed and the sun has kissed you while you've been working.' Nina had put her hand up to Brianna's face and run her fingers over her cheeks. 'You really are beautiful, Bri. I wish you could see that.'

Now, as Caleb walked towards her, his face grim, she tried to remember the last time she'd felt his arms or even given him a compliment about how he looked. It must have been a long time ago.

Like sex. She couldn't remember the last time they'd had sex either.

Had they started taking each other for granted? Got bored with each other because they'd stopped talking?

'Hi,' said Caleb.

'Hi,' she answered, stopping herself from falling into his arms. God, what she wouldn't do for a comforting hug.

'How is he?'

'Fine.'

Caleb breathed a sigh of relief. 'I'll go in and see him then.'

She stepped out of his way and went to sit down so she could look out across the paddock as the daylight faded. Caleb reached out to touch her shoulder, but she'd already moved out of reach.

His shoes clipped across the wooden floorboards and she heard Beau yell, 'Dad!' as he went inside.

'Hey there, Terror Two,' came Caleb's voice. 'How you doing? I've missed you!'

She could imagine him putting his briefcase down and holding out his arms so Beau could jump into them.

'Have you been in front of the judge again?' Beau asked excitedly.

'Yep.'

'Did he wear his wig?'

'Sure did. A big curly white one. What have you been doing?'

'Riding the motorbike, and yesterday I went out into the bush to look for rabbits. I wanted to try and catch one.'

'And did you?'

'Nah, but I saw a roo and a tiger snake.'

'A tiger snake?'

First I've heard about it! Bri said in her head.

'Uh huh.'

'Tell me you didn't poke it with a stick?'

'I'm not stupid, Dad! I stood still and watched it slide away.'

'Good lad.'

'But I pretended I was Steve Irwin and tracked it for a couple of ks.'

'Steve Irwin, hey? You've been watching those old videos of your mum's haven't you?' Brianna could imagine Caleb's grin. 'Now, where's your brother?'

'Mum said he had to go to bed early cos he's been through an orrr-deeeal . . .' He sounded the word out, as if he were testing it.

'Very wise of your mum. I'd better go and see him.'

There was a sound of footsteps and the TV being turned back on, then the low murmur of voices.

Brianna turned her head towards the sea breeze, thankful the stinking heat had been replaced with a humid, but cool, change. Clearly she was going to have to keep a closer eye on Beau. A tiger snake? Bloody hell! Just like Beau, though, she supposed. Out in the bush, tracking rabbits or roos, pretending he was a wildlife presenter. Trent loved doing the same. The kids weren't called the Terrors for nothing.

And Caleb? He'd obviously decided to arrive early, since he wasn't due until the end of the week. Maybe her shortness had made him realise he was needed at home. A prickle of annoyance ran through her. He shouldn't need her to get angry with him to work that out. When would he realise that family came before everything?

Lizzie and Nina had joked a couple of times that he would have made a good farmer, because that's what farmers did—they put their stock and farm before everyone and everything else. Lizzie's husband, Phil, had missed a family wedding because the heifers were calving and he didn't trust anyone else to look after them. Nina had complained that John hadn't taken a holiday they'd had booked for months because the season had broken much earlier than usual and he'd had to take advantage of the moisture, spray the weeds out and get the crop in. Both women had carried on by themselves, not angry, just disappointed. It was the way life was when you lived on a farm.

'He doesn't look too much the worse for wear,' Caleb said, sitting down beside her.

Brianna jumped, so lost in thought that she hadn't heard him come out.

He handed her a beer and opened one himself before holding it up for her to 'cheers' with. She waited for a split second before raising her bottle. Was there any point in continuing this stalemate? Not if she wanted their marriage to survive.

'No, he was very lucky,' she said.

'What did Sam say about the head wound?'

'It will heal in time. He may not regain his memory of the accident, but he shouldn't suffer any long-term memory loss.'

Caleb took a long swallow of his beer.

Brianna rubbed the condensation away from the outside of her can with her finger. She tried to think of something to say. '*Thanks for coming home,*' would be a good start, but the words wouldn't come. Why was that? She and Caleb had always found it easy to talk to one another. Although, when she thought about it, the last few months Caleb had been distant and preoccupied. Had she been too, or had she just been reacting to his preoccupation? Probably a bit of both, if she was honest.

'Must have been tough on you,' he finally said, breaking the silence that was heavy around them.

'It was scary, that's for sure. But so much worse for Trent. Did he tell you about the eagle?'

Caleb shook his head.

'It thought he could be a meal. Trent couldn't get away, couldn't move. He had to yell and wave his arms to get it away from him. If he'd still been unconscious, who knows what it would would have done.' She wanted to shock him. Wanted to make him hurt. Make him feel some of what she'd been feeling these last few days. Maybe he'd realise then . . .

In his measured way, Caleb didn't respond immediately. It was one of the things that had attracted her to him in the first place. A lot of blokes were loud and talked without thinking, especially after a few beers. Caleb didn't shoot his mouth off, always considered his words carefully. Like her dad.

'Words can hurt, Bri,' he'd told her. 'Once they've been said, you can never take them back.'

Sometimes what *wasn't* said could hurt too.

'How are you, though?' Caleb asked eventually, turning to look at her.

Continuing to stare across the bare paddocks, she shrugged. 'Okay, I guess.'

'Want to talk about it?'

A harsh laugh escaped her.

Oh, she didn't want to say this but she couldn't hold it in. Bitterness and resentment came pouring out. 'Talk about it? What's there to talk about? If you'd been here, you'd know exactly what happened, exactly how we found him and what the ambos and doctors did for him. Known which neighbours came to help us. But instead you were in Perth, in a courtroom, "off the grid". I had to rely on my neighbours to help me find *our* son.' Her voice lowered. 'While you were in Perth. Not doing anything. You didn't even come home, Caleb.'

She sat there, breathing hard, anger spinning around inside her.

Caleb didn't say anything. He sat there for a moment, then put his beer down, got up and went inside, quietly closing the door behind him.

Chapter 8

It was dark by the time Brianna made her way indoors. The mozzies had kept her company, and when she'd heard Caleb suggest to Beau it was time for bed, she'd decided he could play dad, because sitting on the verandah was good for her soul.

Inside, she saw Caleb sitting at his office desk, illuminated by the light of his computer screen. He appeared to be reading a document, but then Brianna realised he was looking down at his hands.

All the anger left her in one heavy sigh. 'I'm sorry,' she said from the doorway.

'I deserved it,' he answered, not turning around.

'No, you didn't. You have to work and your work is in Perth, I know that. The boys know that. We always knew it was going to be like this.' She walked closer so she could put her hand on his shoulder. 'It's getting harder, though.' She forced herself to say the words.

He covered her hand with his but didn't turn around. 'I felt helpless, Bri,' he said. 'There was absolutely nothing I could have done to get out of that courtroom, short of drop dead. It was the longest day of my life.'

Exhaling heavily, she tightened her grip. 'I'm sorry I spoke to you the way I did. I . . .' She paused. 'I'm pleased you're home now.'

'Me too.'

'Have you eaten?'

'Yeah.'

'Is it time for bed, then?'

He swung his chair around and looked up at her. Putting his hands on her hips, he drew her close to him until she could smell his aftershave.

She bent down to kiss him. His lips felt almost strange, it had been so long. Suddenly it was clear to her how easy it was to grow apart. How easy it was to get busy, to have different interests and not have time for each other.

As Caleb's hands roamed over her body she gave herself up to the pleasure of it, with a solemn promise to make more of an effort.

~

'I'm going to Dad's,' Brianna called out.

The Terrors were listening to a story their father was telling them about a witness who was being told off by a judge. They were falling about laughing as Caleb acted it out with a mop head for a wig.

'Will you be long?' Caleb asked, shushing them.

'Not sure. I need to get the okay on this budget so I can send it through to the bank this afternoon.'

Caleb got up and gave her a kiss. 'See you soon, then.'

She smiled up at him. For five days straight he'd been home, helping around the house, spending time with the kids and making life easier. Their relationship was still a little strained, but making love seemed to have reconnected them. They'd talked, not about important issues but about general things, trying to find their footing again. Last night Caleb had even cooked dinner—something he'd not done since Beau was born. Their time together was nice, but occasionally Brianna felt like she was being on her best behaviour, as though she were living with a stranger, not her best friend.

Brianna wondered how he'd got around all his appointments and court appearances. Maybe he'd taken some leave. She hadn't asked him. It didn't matter, he was here.

As she drove to her father's place, the country looked like it had been drained of colour. The dry pastures were bleached white in the glare of the sun. Trying to remember how many tonnes of barley they still had left over in the silo, she wondered if they'd be able to sow another eighty hectares. The budget had included a couple of 'what if' scenarios—the bank liked to see them, apparently. Options, Ashley, the bank manager, called them.

What if the break is late?

What if the price of lambs doesn't hold up?

What if grain prices rise by twenty percent? Or drop by the same amount?

If grain prices rose by twenty percent, she'd be one happy girl!

Brianna saw Angie's car parked at the front of Russell's house. She hadn't seen Angie since Trent had been allowed home, although they'd kept in touch by text, with daily updates on the patient's recovery. Angie had loved hearing about the beach trip she, Caleb and the boys had taken a few days ago. *Enjoy the healing of the waves*, she'd texted to Bri. *The beach is the best place to mend wounds.* Brianna hadn't been sure whether she'd meant Trent's wounds or her marriage's.

That was the interesting thing about Angie, Brianna thought as she walked up the path. She saw things in people that people often didn't see in themselves.

Brianna tapped on the front door and let herself in, calling out, 'Hello?'

'Ah, Bri, you're here. Russell said you were coming. How lovely.' Angie walked out from the pantry holding a freshly baked cake. 'I was just talking about you to a friend in Perth.'

'That could be dangerous! All good, I hope.' She looked around for her dad.

'Of course! Russell just had to pop out for a moment. Jackson Hallow rang and said he had a couple of your sheep in the yards, so Russell has gone to pick them up.'

She took a knife from the drawer and started to slice the cake. 'Cup of tea?'

'No thanks, I'll just have a water. It's too hot for tea.'

'There really isn't another thirst quencher like tea,' Angie said, picking up the kettle and pouring steaming water into her mug.

'If I drink something hot when the weather is like this, all I end up doing is sweating.'

'Oh?' Angie sounded interested. 'Maybe you're coming into early menopause.'

Brianna didn't know how to respond to that.

Angie put a glass of water in front of Brianna as she hoisted herself up onto a bar stool. 'I had a call from one of my oldest friends this morning—that's why I was talking about you.'

'Oh?'

'Haven't spoken to her in *ages*,' Angie continued. 'I knew her when I lived in the Riverina, so you can't imagine how *surprised* I was to find out she's married to a *lawyer* and now lives in Perth.' Angie took a breath. 'So, of course, I *had* to ask if she knew Caleb. And you'll never guess what?'

'What?' Brianna replied dutifully.

'She does! Isn't it such a small world?'

'Really?' Brianna wasn't too surprised. Perth wasn't a large city and Caleb said most lawyers there knew each other.

'I *know*! Incredible, right?'

'What firm does your friend's husband work for?'

'Well now, I completely forgot to ask. I was just so *flabbergasted* she knew him. I'll ask next time I talk to her.'

'Hang on,' Brianna held up her finger. 'It's your friend who knows Caleb, not her husband? The lawyer doesn't know him?' She crinkled her brow as she made the connection.

Angie seemed thrown by the question. 'Uh, gee, I just *assumed* they both did. She mentioned lawyer functions and dinners they all seem to attend. From the way she spoke, I assumed they saw *a lot* of each other. Geena isn't a lawyer, though.'

'Geena?'

'Geena Adams.'

'Hmm, I'll ask him when I get home.'

Angie held out the cake. 'Are you going to have some? I made it especially.'

'No, thanks, I'm fine. Keeping an eye on the waistline for a change. How are the dams holding up at your place?'

'Pretty good, really. I've asked my manager to shift the sheep off one dam because it's getting a bit boggy around the side. I *really* don't want to be dragging sheep out of the mud if I don't have to.' She put down the cake and took a sip of her tea.

'We're the same. Dad's probably already told you. One dam right up the back has got nothing but mud in it. I pulled four ewes out of there about three weeks ago. But that dam has always leaked, ever since we had it dug. I'm not surprised there's nothing left in it.' She tapped her fingers on the counter. 'I can't wait for the weather to change. Just to cool off a little. I don't remember a summer being quite so hot. Maybe I'm just getting old.' She gave a little laugh.

'That's the perfect opening. I've been wanting to have a little chat with you. I know I'm not your mum and I would never try to be, but I see you making some . . . perhaps mistakes isn't the right word, but certainly some decisions that may not be in your long-term interest.'

Brianna stiffened. Indignation rose in her chest. Angie had never been so forward. Mistakes?

'You're right when you say you're getting older. Life slips by very quickly. You think you have all the time in the world with the person you love, and then the next thing, they're gone.' Angie looked down at the bench, tracing the outline of the ring the mug had left. Brianna knew Angie had lost her husband a few years ago; perhaps she was warning her against leaving it too late with Caleb.

Just then a shadow crossed the window and Brianna looked out, realising storm clouds were building up. Large cumulonimbus clouds were piled high over the hill, their dark, foreboding bellies stark against the white of their tips. Brianna frowned and stood up for a better look. She caught the whiff of moisture on the air and shivered, despite the heat.

Storms had been forecast for later in the afternoon, but by the looks of things they might be early. With storms came lightning, and with lightning came the risk of fires. With any luck, the storm would come with enough rain to put out any fires that might start.

She turned her attention back to Angie, who was looking at her keenly, as if expecting Brianna to agree with her.

When Brianna didn't reply, Angie continued, 'Have you thought about following Caleb to Perth? He's there so much. With you down here, it splits the family up. The boys are missing out, you're missing out, and Caleb is too. I think Trent's accident is a sign he needs his father's influence in his life. Think about the boys, Bri. I wonder if you're not being selfish by staying on the farm.'

Brianna could have coped with what Angie was saying—or at least taken it on board—if she hadn't called her selfish. That was one thing she was not.

'I'm sorry?' Brianna stared at her.

Angie opened her mouth, but at that moment the front door banged and Russell walked in. 'Hello, love. How're you going?' He patted Brianna's shoulder and walked past, stopping at Angie. 'Hello, you.'

Brianna could see he was about to kiss Angie and quickly dropped her gaze.

'Hello, you, back,' Angie said, letting her fingers walk up Russell's arm and over his shoulder, before giving him a squeeze. 'Get the sheep?'

'Nope. Don't know what's going on there.' Russell flicked on the kettle. 'Strange. Nothing in the yards, and Jackson was nowhere to be seen. Did he say he was going anywhere?'

Angie shook her head. 'No, nothing. He rang, said he had two yellow-tagged ewes in the yards and could you come and pick them up. That was the whole message.'

'Ah well, who knows. Maybe they jumped out while I was going over there. He'll get them back in. I can't work out how they would have got there in the first place. We don't boundary his place. They must have got over the fence and walked down the road until they found an open gate.' He shrugged before turning his attention to Brianna. 'Reckon there's a storm coming. Building up over the hill. Was there any rain forecast with the storms? I haven't had a chance to check the weather today.'

'Twenty-five percent chance of one to five millimetres,' Angie answered before Brianna could. 'But you know what thunderstorms are like. It depends on whether you're under one, whether you get the rain. Might end up with an inch or nothing.'

'You're spot on there, love,' Russell said. 'So, how's things at your house, Bri? When does Caleb head off again?'

'I'm not sure. He hasn't said anything yet and it's been great having him home for a while. Everything is so much easier with two pairs of hands!'

'That's certainly the case,' Angie put in.

Brianna could have kicked herself: she'd just played straight into Angie's hands. She frowned again. *Of course* everything was easier with two parents at home. It was the way life was supposed to be. Sometimes, however, life didn't go according to plan.

Russell looked at Brianna; he seemed to be about to say something but stopped himself. Brianna saw him glance across at Angie before asking, 'How's Beau?'

'Beau? Just the same as normal. Out pretending to be Steve Irwin every chance he gets. The last few days have been too hot for them to go outside much, so they've been building cubbies in the lounge.'

'Hmm.' Russell poured hot water into a mug and got milk out from the fridge.

'Why do you ask that?'

'I've been watching him. He seems quieter than usual, and I wondered whether he was a little traumatised or feeling left out.'

'I haven't noticed that,' Bri said slowly.

Angie reached across and patted her arm. 'Sometimes we don't notice things when we're busy,' she said softly.

The silence in the kitchen seemed very loud until Russell said, 'Shall we?' and indicated the office.

'We shall.' Brianna jumped off the bar stool and grabbed her laptop.

As her dad led the way down the passage, he said, 'Don't beat yourself up about Beau, okay? I could see from the look on your face, you wanted to run out and fix everything straightaway. You're a great mum and Beau will be absolutely fine. After all, what kid who wants to be the Crocodile Hunter wouldn't be?' He smiled at her reassuringly, then opened the door and ushered her inside.

'Eight hundred hectares of barley, five hundred of wheat and we'll put canola back in over where we grew wheat last year, so that's . . .' Brianna grabbed the calculator and tapped in some figures. 'Four hundred hectares . . .' She sounded hesitant. 'Hang on, that doesn't sound right.' She added up the paddocks again. 'Yeah, that's better, four hundred and thirty-two hectares.' She stopped and looked out of the window as a distant rumble sounded. 'Here it comes.' Two hours on and the blue of the sky could only be seen in patches. The rest was covered in heavy clouds. They kept moving, swapping positions and changing the look of the sky.

Russell got up and peered out the window, his hands behind his back. Brianna could see him thinking. Another rumble and then another.

'One elephant, two elephant, three elephant,' Russell said softly.

'Four elephant, five elephant, six elephant,' Brianna continued. This was a childhood game they'd always played and she'd taught it to her boys too. 'By the time it takes to say the number and "elephant", that's one kilometre, so you count from the lightning until the sound of thunder and that's how far away the storm is,' she'd explained.

'Fifteen kilometres,' her dad said, still looking out of the window.

Again, Brianna thought that if there was thunder, there'd be lightning somewhere too. While lightning without rain could start fires, rain would degrade all the dry feed in the paddocks and they'd have to start supplementary feeding, which made for more work. It was a double-edged sword.

Brianna would have rather had the rain than fires, though.

'Still a way away yet,' she answered. 'Mightn't even come round this side of the hill, anyway.'

'Exactly.' Russell turned back to look at her. 'I think we should start scanning the ewes as soon as possible. I'd be keen to see us quit all the freeloaders as soon as we can. I've been watching the long-range forecast. An El Niño is looking more and more likely. I know we're not near the break of the season yet, but this year has a feeling of dryness about it.' He tapped his pen on the pad in front of him, looking at his scribbled notes.

'I can tee up Luke Noble when I go home,' Brianna offered. 'Got a date in mind?'

'He likes to scan from forty days, doesn't he? Forty days from when the rams came out . . .' He flicked back through his diary. 'Make it the last week in January or the first week of Feb. Great! I think we're all done. The bank should be pretty pleased to have the budget in so early.'

'They don't seem to think it's early. I think that's why I got the phone call. Anyway, I feel so much better when it's done.' She paused. 'Dad, you haven't talked about looking for Trent. That must have been pretty hard on you.'

Russell took off his glasses and rubbed his eyes. 'I'd be lying if I said that damn situation wasn't in the forefront of my mind the whole time we were looking. I was frightened we wouldn't find him—just like your mum.'

Chapter 9

'I'll never forget that day, love,' her dad said. He put his glasses on the desk and blew out a breath.

'I've dreamed about it ever since Trent went missing,' Brianna admitted.

'Do you remember much?'

'Not really. Lots of people talking quietly, there being heaps of people in the house, and the feeling . . . I couldn't have understood what it meant back then, obviously, being only three, but I think it was a mixture of anticipation and worry.'

'No one thought we wouldn't find her. I always thought we'd at least find her body.'

They were silent, reliving painful memories.

In the distance a mobile phone rang and Brianna could hear Angie answer it.

'I still miss her,' her father said quietly, looking down at his weathered hands.

'Do you? Even after so long?'

There was a flash of lightning followed almost immediately by a loud crack of thunder. The smell of moisture reached her and she wanted to close her eyes and breathe it in, but her dad was looking at her. She held his gaze. Her parents had been high-school sweethearts and from all accounts had seemed destined to be together forever.

Her father's parents had owned the farm Russell now lived on, and once her mum and dad had married they'd expanded the farm by buying the neighbouring two farms, one of which Bri lived on.

When she was a kid Brianna used to sit in a quiet spot in the house—usually in a shaft of sunlight near a window—and flick through her parents' wedding album. The photo she loved the most was of them both sitting under a tree looking at each other. They weren't smiling or laughing, as might be expected in a wedding photo; they were just looking at each other. Contentment, respect, friendship and love flowed from the picture. And, as far as Brianna knew, those qualities characterised her parents' marriage.

Russell nodded as he sat back at the desk. 'Josie was my soulmate and she never would have left us without a reason. I never believed any of the theories that she ran away or was having an affair. Or the best one—I murdered her so I could claim her life insurance, because the farm was in trouble.' He gave a harsh laugh. 'It was all such a lot of bullshit. And I still think the group of hippies that

I kicked out of the swamp that night had something to do with Josie's disappearance. It was too coincidental for them not to.' He sighed. 'I'm sure the police never believed my story when it came to them. Anyway, Josie loved you. I'd never seen a mother so smitten with her child—even when you screamed your heart out, which you did a lot!' Russell gave a sad smile. 'She loved me too.

'I wish I knew why she disappeared . . . It's always unfinished business. There's never any closure because I have no idea what happened. And time? Well, it moves on, doesn't it? Doesn't take away the ache of missing her or the need to know what happened, but I guess you learn to live with it.' He swallowed. 'Did I ever tell you about the time we . . .'

Brianna sat back while her father talked. She loved hearing stories about her parents' early life.

'. . . were sitting on the beach in the dark, looking out at the water. It was freezing, but she really wanted to sit there. Watch the waves, she said, but she was shivering so hard! I suggested we get back in the car—we could still see the moon on the water from there and it would have been a damn sight warmer—but she wouldn't leave. Josie wanted to sit there and watch the waves. So we did.

'She'd never let me help her when she was working on the farm. Didn't matter if she was trying to get a sixty-kilo ewe on the back of the ute, she just wouldn't accept help. Damn, that woman could be stubborn!' Russell had a soft smile on his face.

'So I've got a double cross,' Brianna said, leaning over to pat her father's knee.

'Me? Stubborn? Oh, I don't think so!' Russell laughed and got up. 'Right, we done?'

'I think so. I'll email the file to the bank and wait until they tee up an appointment. And I'll let you know when I've organised Luke for preg scanning.' She picked up her computer, ready to leave, and added, 'You're the best dad a girl could hope for, you know. I never once missed Mum. You did a brilliant job as both parents—you know that, don't you?'

'I did my best, love, that's all I ever could have done.' He cocked his head to the side and looked at her. 'You never missed her?'

'I didn't know what to miss, I guess. You can't yearn for what you never had. Didn't mean I didn't miss the *idea* of her, though. When I was in primary school—maybe around Trent's age—I would have daydreams about a mum wearing an apron and making cakes in the kitchen. Ha! Isn't that sexist?'

'And not at all like your mother!'

'I know. There was this one kid and his mother used to send him to school with homemade cakes and biscuits. He'd trade them for my packet biscuits because he never got to have them at home, and I was happy to have his homemade ones because I never got them. I imagined his mum must have been in the kitchen all day baking!'

'I remember you telling me about that. And so I tried to make a chocolate cake and we had to give it to the chooks.'

Brianna laughed. 'That's right! Chooks eat everything, but when I came back later in the day, they still hadn't touched it.'

'Could have sunk a ship with that effort.' Russell was grinning widely at the memory.

'Russ? Russell?' Angie's panicked voice floated down the passageway, followed by running footsteps.

'What's wrong?' Immediately the smile was gone and Brianna could see him tense.

'Looks like there's a fire next door. The lightning . . .'

'What?' Russell shot to his feet and Brianna followed. Without saying anything, they ran outside to see where the smoke was coming from.

Thunder rumbled around them and the still air was hot and steamy.

'Where?' he asked.

'Just there.' Angie pointed in the distance and Brianna squinted. It looked like Jimmy Pearce's place, but smoke always looked closer than it was.

'I'll ring Jimmy.' Russell pulled his phone from his pocket and scrolled through, looking for the number.

Brianna scanned the horizon, searching for any telltale signs, but there were only low clouds. It looked like a black carpet had been rolled out across the sky. Brianna ran to the other side of the house while Angie again tried to point out where she'd seen the smoke.

'I can't see anything,' Brianna yelled, nervous energy shooting through her as she raced for the ute and snatched up the mic. 'Merriwell Bay Five, check in?'

She waited, jiggling up and down on the spot, waiting for someone to answer.

'Merriwell Bay Five, this is Merriwell Bay Fire Control. Go ahead.' Nina's strong, calm voice filtered through to her.

'Merriwell Bay Five wanting to know if there have been any reports of fires within the Zone Four area?'

'Negative, not at this point in time. Any other check-in stations?'

The radio remained silent and Brianna felt a sense of unease seep into her. Had she reacted too quickly? She was only new to the firefighting game, doing her first lot of training two years ago. She'd always known that, being on a farm, you had to attend when there was a fire—it was an unwritten rule of living on the land—and she'd been near many fires, but only as someone who followed along behind the fire truck and extinguished the small fires behind it. Never as a trained firefighter.

'Jimmy can't see anything either, love,' Russell yelled out from the side of the house. 'False alarm, I think.'

Another flash of lightning and then a thunder crack, the noise reverberating around the sky. A heavy, wet drop landed on her head. She looked around and could see a grey curtain of rain moving towards them.

Brianna raised her hand to show she'd heard him, but kept listening to the radio. The silence didn't change.

Finally: 'Negative, Merriwell Bay Five. Thanks for your vigilance. Merriwell Bay Fire Control, out.' Nina's voice died away.

'Merriwell Bay Five, out.' Brianna hung up the microphone feeling embarrassed. Why had she taken Angie at her word? She should have seen the smoke for herself. Sniffing the air, she tried to conjure up the smell of bushfire smoke, but it wasn't there. Only moisture, rain.

She felt another drop on her shoulder—it spread through the cotton shirt she was wearing and was cold against her hot skin. Raising her face to the sky, she felt another and another. Thunder echoed followed by another bolt of lightning and she ran for the verandah.

~

'I'm so sorry, Nina,' Brianna mumbled into the phone as she drove home. 'Angie was sure there was smoke.'

'Don't worry about it, Bri. It's better to be safe than sorry. Especially in these conditions. Thunderstorms can be dangerous. It was good work.'

'I feel like an idiot.'

'I don't see an idiot, but whatever takes your fancy. Now, listen, how about you bring that family of yours over for dinner tonight? The Terrors can have a run around and pretend they're Tarzan on the new rope we've hung from the tree. You can let your hair down. How about it? We never got to celebrate your birthday, so we have to make up for that.'

'Caleb's home.'

'You'd better bring him too, then.' She laughed. 'Don't think you're going to get out of it that easily.'

Brianna giggled, her embarrassment forgotten. 'Sure, what can I bring?'

Chapter 10

With shaking hands, Guy Wood opened the front door and stared at the woman who was standing there.

He tried to remember if he knew her, but he was sure he didn't.

''Ello?' he said, not sure if he should be polite or rude. He hated the way his mind didn't respond as quickly as it used to. These days, faces from the past seemed to merge into the ones he was seeing in the present.

The man who had come a couple of days ago—or was it last week? Guy couldn't remember—he had looked like a church minister he remembered from childhood. Somehow he'd known he wasn't the minister, but that he was a policeman. He was grateful he hadn't called him by the wrong name.

'Hello, Mr Wood, I'm Isabelle Davis, the community nurse. I was passing, and thought I'd call in and introduce myself.'

'I don't need a nurse,' Guy snapped, standing up as tall as he could. It was a bit hard, what with his back being rounded. He was always worried he'd fall over backwards if he straightened too much. 'Why would I need one of them?'

He didn't give her a chance to answer. Closing the door with a bang, he leaned against it in case she decided to force her way in. Why was she here? How had she known about him? He'd kept to himself his whole life. He didn't like people, and his sharp tongue ensured people didn't like him.

'Mr Wood, I'm not here to cause you any harm, but could I talk to you? Would that be possible, please?'

The voice sounded just like his mother's. Soft, with well-rounded vowels. She used to soothe him to sleep when he had nightmares. 'Gently now, Guy,' Mother would say. 'Gently now. Nice and quiet. Shut your eyes.' He felt his eyes beginning to close.

'Mr Wood?'

'Mother?' His eyes snapped open. Had he spoken out loud?

He tried to think; she couldn't be his mother. She was dead. They were all gone. There was only him now.

'What do you want?' he called out.

'I'd really just like to talk to you. Could I come in?' There was a gentle tapping on the door.

'I don't want to buy anything.'

'I'm not here to sell you anything. Just a chat, Mr Wood.'

'What for? I don't know you.'

'Just to see how you're getting along out here. You must get a little lonely by yourself?'

'Like it that way. Got me dog. That's all I need. Lived like this all me life. Don't need anyone else.'

The lady at the door didn't answer. It was quiet. Had she gone?

He opened the door a tiny bit and peered through the crack.

She put her hand on the door and pushed it open, causing him to stumble slightly.

'Thank you so much for letting me in, Mr Wood. Shall I make you a nice hot cup of tea?'

'Ah.' He looked at her, confused. Had he let her in? He didn't think so. 'What's your name again?'

'Isabelle Davis. The community nurse. How about that cup of tea?'

Giving her a hard stare, he shuffled along the passageway to the kitchen.

'Lovely house, Mr Wood. You must have lived here for a long time.'

He knew she was following him because her voice was close. 'Ever since I was born,' he answered. 'Me mother 'ad us kids in the back room. Didn't go to 'ospital in them days.'

'How long ago was that?'

'I was born in 1947.'

'So you're seventy, then. Shall I put the kettle on?'

He indicated where the kettle was and watched as she turned it on. She seemed to know her way around a kitchen. Maybe she'd be useful. Isabelle, was that what she'd said her name was?

Isabelle, he tested the name silently. She looked nice: not too fat, not too skinny, and she wore her hair tucked up in a bun, the way his mother had. She was plain like his mother too.

'How do you take your tea, Mr Wood?'

'Black with one sugar.'

'You live here by yourself?'

'You already know that.' Crossing his arms, he stared at her.

'Do you have any family close by?' Isabelle put the tea leaves in the pot and poured in the boiling water. Guy realised the pot was very dirty—not shiny like it had been when his mother was alive. He wondered when it had become so grubby.

'Nope, they're all gone.' He was hit by that funny flicker of grief he always seemed to feel, even after all this time, when he said that. He reached out to pat Bob, but he couldn't find his head. Bending down, he looked under the table. Bob wasn't there.

Guy frowned. 'Did you see me dog on the way in?'

'No, I don't think I did. Is he missing?' Putting the pot on the table, she pulled two cups from the draining board and gave them a rinse, before pouring the tea into them. 'Where do you keep your sugar?'

'Here, on the table.' He pulled the jar towards him and scooped out one large teaspoonful. 'I 'ope 'e's not missin'. He's me mate. Usually sleeps under the table when I'm inside.' He looked around, hoping he'd see Bob in a different spot.

Isabelle glanced around too. 'Did you want me to go outside and call him? What's his name?'

'Bob. If you want to,' he shrugged, pretending he didn't care one way or the other.

'I'll be right back.'

Guy heard her open the front door and call, 'Bob, where are you, boy? Bob?'

She sounded like she knew how to call a farm dog.

As quickly as his body would allow him, he stood up and took a wooden box, which was sitting on the sideboard, and pushed it up inside the chimney. He hoped it wouldn't fall out while she was here. He'd have to find a better hiding spot later because his mother had made him promise no one would ever be allowed to see inside that box.

He got back to the table and took a sip of his tea just before she walked in.

'Here he is. Lying under the shade of the gum tree outside, weren't you, fella? Trying to keep out of the heat.' Isabelle gave Bob's ears a rub and went to sit down at the table.

Guy felt better now Bob was here. More confident. 'Come 'ere.' He patted his leg and Bob limped over, giving a huge sigh before he slumped next to him. Leaning down, Guy caressed his mate's head roughly, then went back to his tea.

'Glad I could find him.' She sat down at the table and looked across at him. 'Mr Wood, Detective Burrows was concerned about how well you were looking after yourself. Wondered if perhaps you needed some help, which is why he asked me to call on you. People who live by themselves sometimes need a bit of an extra hand; no shame in it, just the way it is.'

'I don't need anyone's help, missy,' said Guy. 'I weren't brought up that way. I can look after meself.'

'And I'm sure you're doing a great job, but wouldn't it make it easier if someone gave you a hand?'

'I'm not leavin' 'ere,' Guy said suddenly. 'I'm not. You'll 'ave to take me out in a coffin.'

'I'm not suggesting that at all. Perhaps I could call in every day, on my rounds, check that you've eaten, had a shower, that type of thing.'

'I do all of that all right.'

'To be very honest, Mr Wood, the kitchen worries me a little bit. There's a lot of dirty dishes here and they could make you sick.'

Guy frowned as he looked at the sink and saw the mess. There were flies buzzing in the window and he guessed there might be maggots in the sink. When had it become like that? He was sure he'd done the dishes last night. Should only be his breakfast dishes there. That was how Mother had taught him: wash up at the end of every day. *'After every meal would be better, but if it's only you,'* she'd said, *'there shouldn't be too many dishes.'*

His stomach rumbled. Had he even had breakfast this morning?

'I'd be more than happy to bring you out meals to put in your freezer. The ladies who cook for Meals on Wheels make lovely food. If you've got some dirty clothes or sheets, I can take them into town and get them washed and bring them back out. What do you say?'

Staring at her, he wondered what the catch was. 'How much does all this cost?' he asked suddenly. 'I'm not made of money, you know.'

'Let's not worry about that. We can get that sorted later. Have you finished your cup of tea? If you have, I'd really like to listen to your heart and take your blood pressure.'

The look she gave him was so hopeful, he didn't think he should disappoint her. 'Ah, get on with whatever you have to do then.'

~

By the time Isabelle had left, Guy'd had a shower and was wearing fresh clothes. His kitchen was clean and the floor swept and she'd left two meals in the fridge, one for lunch and one for tea.

He was a bit confused because there didn't seem to be any clothes left in his bedroom and the bedsheets were ones he hadn't seen before. Maybe she'd changed them while he was in the shower.

In the lounge, he sat in his favourite chair, reading the *Stock Journal.* After all the activity of the day, he was tired. Bob lay beside him, snoring. Occasionally his feet would twitch as if he were chasing something.

'They were the times, old lad,' Guy said to Bob. 'Back in our 'eyday. You could run and I could remember.'

He looked back at the newspaper and started to read the sheep market report. 'Lambs in Dublin made one hundred and fifty dollars, Bob. Never understood why they built those new saleyards. The old yards at Gepps Cross were fine the way they were.'

Bob continued to snore.

'And the wool market looks like it might kick a bit. Might have to sell that wool I've got sitting in the shed. I'll go and see how many bales are there. Reckon there's at least twenty.'

This time when Guy glanced down, it looked like Bob was chasing a rabbit because his nose was trembling, as well as his feet.

He turned the page until he found the 'Flashback' section. It was one of his favourite parts. Black-and-white photos of long-dead farmers, old machinery and times gone by. Often he recognised someone.

'Don't know you. Don't know you.' He tapped a picture of several men standing next to some small square hay bales and a baling machine, squinting to see any familiar faces. 'I remember using a tractor like that, though, Bob. Dad bought one back in 1949 and we used it for years. One of the best pieces of machinery we ever bought. We put 'undreds of acres of crop in with it.' He looked at the next picture. 'Look at all them rabbits 'ung up on the fences. Buggers of things, they were. Dug 'oles like you wouldn't believe. And breed? Never seen anything like it! You woulda 'ad good fun chasin' them, Bob.'

With a sigh, he turned the page and started to read the caption under the photo. '*Mr George Wood with his highest selling wethers, Jamestown market 1957*'.

'Gawd, that's me dad. Look at this, Bob!'

He must have spoken louder than he normally did, because Bob raised his head and looked at him.

'See here!' Guy jabbed at the photo. 'Look at those wethers. Big and wrinkly. They woulda made hard shearing, Bob. And . . .' He drew the paper closer to his eyes to make sure he was seeing properly.

'That's her,' he breathed.

Chapter 11

'I can't believe that John thinks we're going to put in so much canola this year,' Nina said. 'It's such a high-input crop; all the spraying and everything. Takes up a lot of time as well as money.' She put her glass down and looked expectantly at Brianna, as though she thought she'd agree.

The clinking of glasses and laughter had relaxed Brianna and she didn't really feel like talking about farming tonight.

'It's certainly a high-input crop,' she answered. 'But it's also black gold. Very good for the bank account.' She turned to look at Beau, who was playing on the swing set that hung from a backyard gum tree. Trent was leaning against the thick trunk, playing a game on his iPad.

'I think your kids miss mine,' Lizzie observed. 'Normally they'd all be out running around playing spotlight or trying to catch rabbits.'

'How are they going with your mum?' Nina asked. 'Mine are bored witless in Perth.'

'Mum took mine to the water park today, so they've been cruising down slides and eating ice cream.' Lizzie took a sip of wine.

'They would've had a ball,' said Nina. 'I wish my mum would take them places. I mean, she does, but not fun stuff for twelve and fourteen year olds. She doesn't quite get what they like. Anyway, I'm glad to have the break. Their annual two-week Perth holiday is my holiday too.'

Brianna reached for her glass, not saying anything. She wished she had a mum to give her a break. Especially when Caleb was away for weeks on end. She glanced over at the barbecue. The three men looked deep in conversation and she felt a twinge of jealousy at how Caleb was able to slip so easily into her life when she struggled with his. Two years ago she'd gone to a gala dinner with him and felt so uncomfortable she'd sworn she'd never go to one again. And here Caleb was, talking stock prices and feeding regimes as if he farmed every single day of the week. She guessed it was because he came from a farming background, while she didn't know anything about law, other than what he'd told her.

'Earth to Bri,' Nina nudged her with her foot.

'Sorry?'

'What are you daydreaming about? Handsome shirtless men with rippling muscles?' Nina grinned.

'Black gold,' Brianna improvised, unwilling to share what she was really thinking. 'If the crops come home, you'll make a mint.'

'And be shouting us all French champagne,' Lizzie added with a laugh. 'But, according to *Landline*, there's the possibility of an El Niño. We mightn't have a good season.'

'Can't look at it like that,' Nina said firmly. 'Positivity, girls! That's the key to everything.'

There was a blood-curling yell, then a whoosh, as Beau swung on a rope like Tarzan and landed right near Trent's broken ankle.

'Bloody hell,' said Lizzie with her hand flying to her chest. 'Beau, don't do that! You scared the crap out of me!'

'Beau!' Brianna reprimanded. 'If you land on your brother's leg, you'll have me to answer to.'

'I won't! But I'd make a good orang-utan, wouldn't I? Watch this!' Beau yelled as he ran fast around the tree and jumped into the air, hanging onto the swinging rope with one hand.

'Dear God, hold that rope with two hands,' Nina called, her hands covering her eyes.

Brianna turned away so she didn't have to watch. 'They're not called the Terrors for nothing,' she mumbled. 'I think I need more wine!'

Nina grabbed another bottle from the esky, opened it and poured her a full glass.

'How's things at home, Bri?' Lizzie asked with a glance over her shoulder to make sure the men couldn't hear.

She shrugged. 'Fine. It's good to have extra help with the kids and everything else around the house. Especially with Trent and his ankle. He gets bored so easily and Caleb's been great at playing games and doing things with him.'

Nina studied her. 'You sound over the moon.'

'Like I said to Caleb, we knew it was going to be tough when we got married. He works in Perth and I live here. It was always going to be hard. We've got to work through it, not grow apart. Relationships, so I'm told, don't come easy.'

'You're still pissed off with him for not coming home, aren't you?' Nina said, leaning forward and speaking in a low, knowing tone.

Brianna looked down and remembered the hurt and anger she'd felt.

'Course she is,' Lizzie said, reaching out to touch Brianna's hand. 'Anyone would be. But blokes don't have an umbilical cord attached to them, so they don't always get it. Look at Phil. Hell, if he managed to make one of Braydon's assemblies last year, it was a miracle.'

'I *know*!' Nina agreed. 'When I took Louisa to Perth to have her grommets put in, do you reckon John came? Uh uh.' She shook her head. 'Glad Mum and Dad are up there. Until you hear your kid call out 'Mummy, help me', just as they slip under . . .' she gave a shudder. 'I was so glad Mum was there. All I wanted to do was cry.'

'Bit different, don't you think?' Brianna asked. 'For Caleb, I mean. Trent could have been dead.'

'But he wasn't,' Nina reminded her. 'He was in hospital getting the medical treatment he needed.'

'I know,' Brianna said softly. She shot a glance at the men to make sure they were still busy.

'But,' Nina held up her finger as she drew out the word, 'I get where you're coming from, I really do. It's about being a family.'

'That's it,' Lizzie said. 'And you would have felt a lot more supported if he'd come home, and Trent would have too. But, as Phil reminds me every so often, I need to tell him what I want cos he failed mind-reading at school. And you guys have been married for what? Fourteen years? We get complacent with each other.'

'Thirteen,' Brianna said, working the dates out quickly in her head.

'Aha! I know, it's the seven-year itch times two.' Nina grinned and sat back, raising her glass to Brianna.

'I haven't got a seven-year itch,' Bri retorted. 'I'm too busy!'

'Even with thirteen years and two kids behind you, having as much time apart as you guys do would have to put a strain on any marriage,' observed Lizzie.

'Hey, Beau—uh, I mean Orang-utan—I'm watching you! Your mother said don't land on Trent!' Nina told him.

All three women turned to look at Beau, who was holding onto the swinging rope with a look of guilt on his face.

'Yeah, I know what you were going to do,' Nina said. 'See? We're watching!'

'I wasn't going to,' Beau answered, still swinging

'Really? Where were you going to land?' asked Lizzie.

'Here!' He let go of the rope and landed on his feet like a cat on the opposite side of the tree to Trent.

'Yeah, right,' Brianna said, a smile in her voice. 'He turned that around well, didn't he?'

'I'm sure every kid thinks we came down in the last shower and have never been young. Anyway,' Nina turned her attention back to Brianna. 'I think the question is are you happy?'

Brianna took another drink and thought about the question. She was, really. She had the kids, the farm, her dad . . .

'This isn't changing the subject,' she said, 'and it's not that I'm *not* answering your question, but guess what Angie said to me today?'

'I don't think I could,' Lizzie said, picking up a biscuit and plunging it into the dip.

Brianna told them about her strange conversation with Angie and her suggestion that Brianna take the boys and live in Perth with Caleb.

'You're not going to, are you?' Nina asked, horrified.

'Shh,' Bri glanced over at the men. 'I haven't said anything to Caleb about it yet.'

'But you're not.' Lizzie stated the fact. 'It would kill you. You're a country girl through and through. I can't imagine you being happy in the city.'

'No, me neither, but it did get me thinking. Maybe I should do something like that. I made a promise to myself I'd try a bit harder. He's done thirteen years toing and froing from Perth. Maybe it's my turn.' She felt sick even as she said the words; to leave the farm would break her. She couldn't imagine not waking up to sunrises and open spaces. To the smell of grass, moisture and sheep. Her soul lived on Le-Nue; she knew she could only feel at peace when her feet were firmly planted in the soil of her home.

In a practical sense, there was no way her dad would be able to manage without her either as they'd built the business up as a two-person operation; although she had thought about the possibility of hiring a farm worker. Still, that option didn't sit well with her. She didn't like the thought of someone working on the farm who didn't love the place as much as she and her father did.

'That's the stupidest thing I've ever heard you say,' said Nina, her tone huffy. 'Totally ridiculous.' She put her glass down with a bang and frowned at her friend. 'You know that and so do I.'

Lizzie put her hand on Brianna's arm. 'Bri. Don't even consider it.' Her voice was soft but urgent. 'It won't help you. It won't help the boys. They're farm kids too. It would be like stifling them.'

Brianna sighed. 'I know, I know. There's got to be another way to make everything go back to how it was. I just don't know what it is.' She paused, then looked both of her friends in the eye. 'I did wonder whether Angie suggested it to get me off the farm, so she can have Dad to herself.' There, she'd spoken out loud what had been bothering her since the conversation.

Nina and Lizzie glanced at each other.

'I think,' Nina said slowly, 'you've read that wrong. Even if she was suggesting that, and I'm sure she isn't, your dad wouldn't let that happen. Angie was only saying to me a few weeks ago how much she was enjoying having the Terrors in her life. I know she's a bit different, but she's not vindictive, Bri. Anyway, Angie's not the important one here. You and Caleb are.' She paused. 'Okay, I'm going to tell you something really private.' Nina glanced around. A loud burst of laughing came from the barbecue as a flame went up and sizzled.

'Chargrilled steak for tea, by the looks,' Lizzie said.

Both women looked across at Nina expectedly. 'So?' Bri said softly.

'John and I had counselling after Louisa was born.'

Bri grabbed for breath—she'd never known that. How had her friend managed to hide it? She thought they knew everything about each other. She wanted to reach out and hug her, but Nina was sitting upright in her chair and looked as if getting the words out was hard enough. A show of support might bring old emotions tumbling out.

'We'd been having troubles before I got pregnant and we hadn't intended to have a baby so soon. We knew there were issues we had to sort out first, but then Louisa came along and there was no time. I felt so embarrassed because I didn't want people to think we'd failed. John and I were on eggshells around each other all the time—like we were on our best behaviour. Having a brand-new baby on top of the problems made things doubly difficult.' Nina took a breath. 'The counsellor helped us communicate. To talk.' She shook her finger to emphasise her point. 'To listen. Listening is the most important thing. Some people listen but don't hear. Anyway,' she gave a brilliant smile as she looked fondly at John, 'we're great now. The thing was we had the friendship. If you're friends first and foremost, then anything can be fixed.'

'Why didn't you ever say anything?' asked Lizzie. 'We would have supported you.'

'Oh, I know! But there wasn't anything you could do for John and me. And you guys helped in other ways—remember what a crappy sleeper Louisa was? You two took her so I could sleep in the afternoons.'

'I never knew,' Brianna said softly, glancing over at Caleb. Had they been friends first? They'd had a lot of fun together, but perhaps that was because their relationship had been new and exciting.

The women looked up to see the men arriving with a large tray.

'Tea's up,' said John. 'Want to grab the salads, Nina?'

'Absolutely.' She gave him a large smile. Brianna noticed he gave her a discreet pat on the bum as she turned towards the house.

'Do you need a hand?' Lizzie asked.

'Yes, from you. No, from you,' she said, pointing to Brianna. 'You sit there and think about talking and listening.' She swept away to the kitchen, Lizzie in tow.

'Trent, Beau, tea's ready,' Brianna called, glancing at Caleb to see his reaction to Nina's words. He didn't seem to have heard; he was helping Trent get to his feet.

'I'm starving,' she heard Trent say.

'What's for dinner?' asked Beau, appearing at her side.

'Your favourite, by the looks,' she answered. 'Sausages, potato salad and bread. And look, there's Lizzie bringing out the tomato sauce, so I think you're set! Paper plates are at the end of the table.'

'Here, Beau, I'll help you,' Caleb said, coming up and putting his hand on his son's shoulder.

'I want Mum to help me,' he said, turning away.

Brianna looked down at his freckled face and marvelled at how much like Caleb he was. Blond hair and long, dark eyelashes framing deep brown eyes.

She looked over at Caleb, who held her eye and then shrugged.

John was grabbing a beer for Phil, and suddenly she found herself comparing the two men with Caleb. Her friends' husbands had dark, tanned arms and legs, and hands that were scratched and callused from hard work. Caleb, in his beige shorts, looked almost laughable. His legs were white and his fingers were long and delicate; it was clear he worked indoors and pushed nothing more than computer keys.

Was she thinking like that because she was still angry? *Why did you fall in love with him in the first place?* she asked herself. Right then, she couldn't give herself an answer.

'Mum?' Beau pulled at her sleeve.

She refocused. 'How about I hold the plate, Beau, and you can put on it what you want to eat, okay?'

Beau nodded and started to load up with sausages and bread and sauce. Trent did the same and in minutes they were sitting underneath the tree, away from the adults. Brianna smirked as she saw Beau try to pinch a piece of sausage from Trent's plate and get a firm rap over the knuckles.

'Caleb, when do you head back to Perth?' Phil asked as he sat down, his plate full of food.

'In a couple of days. I've taken some leave but I can't stay away for much longer. Even though I'm a partner, I still have to bill the expected number of hours and I have several cases pending.'

'Working on anything exciting?' Lizzie asked, stabbing a piece of steak with her fork.

'Well, the case I was in court for when Trent went missing was about a guy who was lured into a home in the suburbs and killed, then his body was thrown in the sea.'

'Is that how they got rid of him?' Phil asked. 'Not a very good plan—surely the murderer would have known the body would wash back to shore with the tides. Better to drop it over the edge of a cliff in a forty-four-gallon drum filled with cement. Never find the body that way.'

'Got rid of a few, have you?' John asked, looking at his friend with a grin.

Phil laughed. 'Be very afraid, mate!'

'What's it like to look into the eyes of someone who has killed another person? Like a psychopath?' Lizzie asked, taking the frivolity out of the conversation.

Caleb took a swallow of beer and Brianna could see him considering his words. Excitement hit his eyes; the first time she'd seen it in a long while.

She looked down at her hands and started twiddling her thumbs anxiously. She knew Caleb's job was very important to him, and seeing his face light up as he talked about work, she wondered whether there was a future for them.

Surely opening a practice in sleepy Merriwell Bay couldn't match the exhilaration and adrenalin of a city courtroom.

'A psychopath shows no remorse for what they've done. They lack empathy. Yet they can appear completely normal. Sometimes they seem a little cold or emotionally detached, but they can also be extremely charming.

'A client I had about three years ago . . . now, he was an interesting one. Nicest, politest man you could ever meet. But he slit three people's throats and disembowelled them, taking their livers for his cat.'

'Jesus,' said John, putting down his knife and fork and staring at Caleb, while Lizzie and Nina's eyes opened wide with incredulity.

'That's unbelievable,' Phil said, shaking his head.

'Then there's the nurse who was hired to look after an elderly man. She seemed the epitome of a good nurse: medications always administered on time; she bathed him, played cards with him, kept him from being lonely. Then she murdered him. Four men she killed, and each time the family never had one hint she had murderous intentions.'

'How do you do it day after day, dealing with the dark side of human beings?' John said.

'I love it,' Caleb said simply. 'And it's not often I have cases that involve psychopaths. I get paid to read, write, think, talk and argue—what more could anyone want?'

Silence descended over the table until Phil finally said, 'Guess seeing the first lamb of the season isn't as exciting as I thought it was.'

Chapter 12

Dave started his day by turning on the coffee machine and making himself a cup. He freely admitted he was a coffee snob and only the best would do. As far as he was concerned, the greatest addition to the Barker Police Station was the coffee machine he'd bought with his own money and had installed.

Firing up his computer, he thought about what Kim had told him the other night. There was something intriguing about the story of the Wood family out on Jacaranda Road.

It would be interesting to have a quick look through missing persons to see if a baby had ever been reported gone. He could also search through births, deaths and marriages. Had there been a child born to the Woods, then their birth would had to have been recorded. Maybe he could solve a town mystery in a few hours!

'Ah, that's good,' he said, putting his steaming cup on the desk and sitting down with a flourish. 'Right.' Even though he knew it was a long shot, he brought up the missing persons file on the computer and typed in *Wood*, then stopped. There wasn't a first name to go with the surname. He pressed enter and waited to see what would come up.

A long list for the name *Wood* appeared but, as he scrolled through, none of the dates matched. Nothing. Well, that wasn't surprising, as it was too far back for records stored on the computer. He knew he'd end up having to send an email to the Information Release Centre to get them to go searching through the piles of boxes. It might be better to work out if the baby had even been born first.

'Morning.' Joan stuck her head into his office.

'Morning. Got your coffee yet?' He raised his cup to her.

'Just about to. Busy day?'

'Not yet.'

She nodded, and Dave marvelled once again at the way her tight grey curls didn't move an inch. Having manned the front office for ten years, Joan knew the workings of the police station inside out and could handle just about anything. When he'd first met her he'd thought she was a little intimidating. He knew differently now: she was warm and funny, and sometimes had important insights into the cases they worked on.

As Dave turned back to the computer, he had a thought and swung his chair back to face Joan.

'How old are you, Joan?' Seeing the surprised look on her face, he put his hand up in apology. 'Sorry, not asking to be rude. I should rephrase that. Do you remember Guy Wood and his family?'

Joan laughed. 'I was wondering where you were going with that. Yes, I knew the family. Not well—no one in the town ever knew them well. They kept to themselves.'

'So I've heard. Listen, Kim said last night she thought there was another child, but no one could ever confirm it.'

'Hmm, I'd have to think about that. Off the top of my head, I'd have to say I hadn't heard that, but I would have only been a toddler around then. Well, Guy is older than me, how much I couldn't say, but I'm sixty-two. Say Guy is seventy . . .'

'Yeah, Isabelle told me he's seventy.'

Joan nodded. 'That means he was born in 1947. If there was another child, it probably would have been within four or five years. Probably sooner, though, because children were born close together in those days. Not the contraception there is now.'

'There was a younger brother. Guy told me he was killed in Vietnam.'

'Now, those deaths I remember. I was quite young—in my early teens in the latter part of the war—but being a small town, there was this dark cloud that hung over everyone when one of the local boys died. Mum and Dad would come home and we'd sit down for tea and no one would talk. A death always affected the whole town. I think Barker lost about eight men. Their names are on the war memorial in the main street, if you want to check what year Guy's brother died.'

'Great. Thanks, Joan.'

'Why are you asking?'

'More out of my own interest, really.'

'Well, don't bother with the hospital,' Joan said, backing out of the room but still talking. 'So often back then, babies were born at home. If there are any records, they'd be at the church.'

'Church?'

'Yeah, baptisms.'

'Of course,' Dave nodded. The ministers always entered the details of the baptisms into large registers. 'Would they have the records here?'

She came back in holding a steaming mug of coffee. 'I expect so. I can remember the book sitting at the front of the church when we went on Sundays. It held every birth, death and marriage in the area. Alan McSweeny, the minister who was here when I was growing up, would have written down everything that went on in the church.'

'I'll head over there and have a look when I've got time.'

'You know, the other person who might know is Elspeth Williams. She was a nurse who travelled around birthing babies back then. I don't know if she's even still alive.'

Dave made a note and grinned at Joan. 'I reckon I might try and solve me a mystery.'

Joan shook her head at him. 'You must be hard up for something to do.'

'Morning, all.' The front door banged and Jack walked in.

'Morning. I'd best get back to it,' Joan said.

'How was cricket training last night?' Dave asked Jack after he'd made himself a coffee and sat down.

'Hard,' Jack answered. 'Very hard.'

Dave pushed over a plastic container, which held mini quiches Kim had made the night before.

'See, now this is why training is so hard,' Jack said, opening the lid.

'No self-control,' Dave grinned into his coffee and turned back to his computer.

~

'That young upstart Jones has stolen me wool outta me shed!' Guy yelled down the phone.

'Are you sure, Guy?' Dave asked. 'He didn't seem to know anything about the sheep you're missing.'

'What's going on?' Jack whispered.

Dave shrugged.

'Have you found them yet?'

'We're still making enquiries, Guy.'

'You better come out 'ere and 'ave a look at my shearing shed. I know there were at least twenty bales stacked up in the corner. I was saving them until the wool market kicked, and now it has and they're not there.'

'Righto, Guy; Jack and I'll be out later this afternoon. See what we can see, hey?'

'That'd be right good.'

Dave hung up the phone and expelled a breath.

'Bit of investigative work?' Jack asked hopefully.

'Guy Wood again. He seems to think he's had some wool taken out of his shed.'

Jack groaned. 'Do we—?'

'Don't even ask that question. You know we have to. It's community policing. What would have happened to him if he hadn't rung about the sheep and we hadn't got Isabelle out there? He could have died alone.'

'I know, but . . .'

'Come on, Jack! Isabelle's been out there, she's got him cleaned up, and she's calling in every day on her rounds. How she fits everyone in, I've got no idea. Some kind of miracle worker, I reckon.'

Jack looked uncomfortable. 'Actually, I feel awkward about him because he reminds me of my grandfather. Not for any other reason. In this job I've had people spew on me, try and bite me, bleed on me—you know what it's like. But Mr Wood reminds me of my grandfather and it makes me, I dunno . . . sad.' He sat down and looked at the desk, his cheeks red.

Dave tapped his pen on the desk, trying to work out exactly what Jack had just told him.

'Okay. Want to tell me about it?'

He didn't reply, so Dave clicked on his emails and started to scroll through them. The Department of Agriculture had put out a couple of alerts for stolen stock in New South Wales, but not the type of sheep Guy farmed.

'I was supposed to be keeping an eye on him while I was training in Adelaide,' Jack said in a soft voice. 'Mum and Dad were checking on him too, and I only had one day, *one day*, out of the whole week, I had to check in on him. And all I had to was make sure he'd eaten. I didn't even have to do the dishes or anything. No washing, bathing, any of that. Mum did the rest. All she asked of me was to make sure he'd eaten and there weren't any disasters in the house.

'I got busy. Busy partying with my mates from the academy, so I didn't go over the night I was supposed to.' He swallowed hard and Dave could see his jaw working.

'I didn't go that one night and Mum was late to him the next morning. Sometime during the previous day he'd fallen, and of course I hadn't gone to make sure he was okay, so by the time Mum found him he was in a bad way. He'd broken his hip.' He shot Dave a regretful glance. 'You know what that means at that age, don't you? The beginning of the end.' He shrugged. 'That's exactly what it was. He didn't last six months.

'Mum always said it wasn't my fault, but of course it was. If I'd gone there and found him, called an ambulance, it might have made all the difference.'

Dave could hear Jack breathing and Joan's fingers clicking on the keyboard. The tick, tick, tick of the clock was loud.

Finally he cleared his throat. 'It wouldn't have changed the broken hip, Jack.'

Jack nodded slowly. 'I know that, but if I'd got there sooner . . .'

'I think your mother's right, mate. I really do. It's the anaesthetic, the inactivity, the time in hospital—all the stuff that goes with having a broken hip—which wears someone from the older generation down. Not the fact they've laid on the floor for a few hours.

'Sure, if he ended up with pneumonia, that might be a different story, but the hip was broken in the fall. Not because he lay there for a while.' He paused, not wanting to make light of what had happened. 'If anything, it was just a bloody good lesson for you to never shirk your duties. And, can I say, your experience is a reason to make a difference in Guy Wood's life. You can't change what happened to your grandfather, but you can make sure you never do anything like that again.'

'I never ever have,' Jack said with an intensity Dave hadn't heard from him before.

'Well then, lesson learned. Come on, let's go and see Guy.'

Chapter 13

It was on the tip of Brianna's tongue to suggest she and the boys go to Perth with Caleb when he left this time. Only for a little while. A week or two.

She'd noticed the emails dinging constantly on his computer and knew Caleb had a lot of work waiting for him at the office. He couldn't stay at home for much longer.

Lying in bed, staring into the darkness, she mulled over the possibilities. Maybe he could fly and she could drive up with the boys. Or perhaps she could go after the next hot spell, which was forecast to be in two days' time. Unsure what to do, she tossed and turned, unable to sleep, until finally she gave up and got out of bed.

It was warm enough to sit on the verandah and look at the stars, so she poured herself a glass of water and went out. Occasionally there was the murmur of the sheep, the bellow of a cow. Far in the distance a fox barked, but she had to listen hard for that.

'What to do?' she whispered to herself. If she took the boys to the city they could go to the zoo while Caleb was at work, eat tea on the beach at Cottesloe after he'd finished for the day. Go to the movies, even see if there were a show on. The Terrors had never been to the theatre. She'd heard that *Frozen the Musical* was coming, but she wasn't sure they'd enjoy that one!

The more she thought about it, the more she knew she couldn't go. There was no way she could leave Russell to cope on his own. Not that he wasn't capable—he most certainly was—but the size of the farm required two people, not one. Especially in summer, when there was hand-feeding to do and waters to check. And the possibility of fire.

'Can't you sleep?'

Brianna jumped. 'Shit! You scared me,' she said to Caleb. 'I didn't hear you.'

'Sorry. I couldn't sleep either.' He let out a large sigh as he pulled a chair up and sat down next to her. 'So peaceful,' he said. 'And so many stars.'

'Best view in the world,' Brianna answered.

They sat quietly, then Caleb reached out to take her hand, stroking her thumb with his.

She looked across at him and wondered again how they'd got to this point—having this distance between them. Nina had told her to talk and listen and she wondered what she could say to start a conversation about their relationship. Even thinking about a conversation like that made her feel uncomfortable. Maybe she was scared of the outcome. What were the options? They could continue the way they were, they made changes, or they split up. The last one was what she feared most, so surely that meant she loved Caleb and wanted to stay with him? Didn't it?

'I've thought about coming up to Perth with you,' Brianna started to say, but stopped when he shook his head. 'You don't want me to?' She couldn't keep the surprise out of her voice.

He shrugged. 'You're needed here and the Terrors would go crazy without the space. They're always outside, unless it's stinking hot.'

'But there's the zoo and—'

'It's more important you're here. Your dad needs you. I understand all of that.'

Again, silence stretched between them. Was there a reason he didn't want them up there, or did he comprehend that it was hard for her to go?

Glancing at Caleb out of the corner of her eye, she wondered what he was thinking. The way the moon shone on his hair made Brianna remember a night when Caleb first visited Merriwell Bay, about three months after they'd started seeing each other. She'd organised a camping trip to the beach, complete with campfire, swag, red wine and finger food.

They'd sat and talked about their passion for their prospective jobs—he liked making a difference; helping people. 'The law never gets boring,' he'd told her. 'There's always something different happening—it never sleeps.'

She'd understood his reasoning; farming was the same. No day was the same and there was always something to do.

Caleb had described a case where a young man had stolen electrical appliances out of his own parents' home so he could buy drugs. His parents had made the heart-breaking decision to press charges against their son, so he could get the help he needed, which was more than they could give after trying everything within their power.

Caleb, in his pro bono work, had asked that instead of time in jail, he be sent to a rehab clinic. The judge had agreed. Three months later the young man had emerged clean, fit and healthy. The beauty of this story, Caleb had told her, was that he hadn't reoffended yet.

'Five years on and he's still off the drugs and alcohol. I make sure I catch up with him once every month or so and have a coffee. I made a real difference to his life and I want to keep on making differences. It doesn't always happen like that, so I need to celebrate the successes. Pro bono work is where that usually happens, but then there's my other paid work and that's where the hard slog takes place, but it's still never the same thing every day. I never know what's going to walk through my door and I really enjoy that.'

'I know exactly what you mean,' Brianna had said as the waves rolled in and the moonlight shimmered on the water. She'd poured them another glass of red and sat back looking into the fire. 'The days are never the same on the farm—there's always something different happening, whether it be stock checks, all the way through to the frenetic pace of seeding or shearing.

'We make sure the land is looked after and left in better condition than when we came to it. I enjoy talking to people who love agriculture as much as I do.' She shrugged. 'I don't know, it's great just being so involved!'

Caleb had laughed and reached out, taking her hand. 'Yeah, that's it! Being involved. Birds of a feather,' he'd said before he'd kissed her.

Brianna's thoughts were broken by a noise inside the house.

'What's that?' she whispered, then shot up from the chair and raced inside to the boys' bedroom. 'Hey, what's up?' she asked Trent, who was sitting up in bed crying. Looking at him, she wasn't even sure he was awake, but there were tears rolling down his cheeks. She sat on the bed and he tried to scramble back from her.

'Don't!' he gasped, putting his hands over his face. 'Don't come near me.'

'Trent, honey? It's Mum, you're having a bad dream.' She looked up and saw Caleb hovering at the door. 'Can you get a drink of milk?'

He nodded and disappeared.

'Trent!' Her voice was a little firmer this time.

'Just don't!' he whimpered, before sliding down into the bed and curling up. In seconds his chest had stopped heaving and he was breathing evenly again.

Brianna sat with him, stroking his head until she was sure he was in a deep sleep.

'What was that about?' Caleb asked when he came back into the room. He held the cup out to her questioningly. She shook her head and tried very gently to extract herself from Trent's bed without waking him.

'He's asleep again,' she said. 'Must have been a nightmare. Strange, he hasn't had a nightmare since he was in kindy. Do you remember those weeks he kept waking up and climbing into bed with us?'

Caleb shook his head. 'Vaguely,' he said. 'Anyway, that's where I'm heading now. Bed. Are you coming?'

'I might sit outside for a bit longer. I'm not sleepy.'

In the morning Caleb's computer began to ding crazily. It seemed like every second there was an email landing in his inbox. The noise was driving her mad.

The dogs barked, and from where she was folding the washing she could see dust coming up the driveway. Looked like her dad's ute.

Smiling, she went to switch on the kettle.

'Hello, you all home?' called Russell as he opened the door. 'Angie and I are here for a cuppa.'

'Come in!' she said. 'I'll call the boys. They're out the back on the motorbike.'

'I heard them,' Angie said as she walked in. 'I do hope they're being careful.'

'I'm sure they're doing things I don't want to see,' Brianna answered. 'Oh, you've had your hair cut, Angie. It looks nice.'

Angie's hand flew straight to her head and smoothed the short bob. 'Thank you. I thought it was time for a change. I was thinking of having some deep purple streaks put through it, but I might save that for next time.'

'You're very adventurous with your hair, aren't you; always trying something new,' Brianna observed. She knocked on the office door. 'Caleb? Dad and Angie are here.' She heard him grunt distractedly and rolled her eyes, doubting he would take time to come out and see them.

Outside, she watched the boys tear up the driveway. Even though their faces were hidden by their helmets, she knew their grins would be a mile wide, as they revelled in the wind and speed. Trent was driving and Beau was holding onto his waist, his head peering out from behind his brother's shoulder. Trent revved the engine and flung the quad around quickly, spraying gravel behind them. His moon boot hadn't slowed him down at all.

Standing with her hands on her hips, Brianna gave them a hard stare and yelled, 'Stop that! You know you're not supposed to do burn-outs. And if you make too much of a mess of my road, I'll make you grade it by hand.'

They ripped their helmets off and she could hear their groans from where she stood.

'We weren't doing anything bad, Mum,' Beau called.

'Not like we're going to tip it,' Trent added.

'I know you both think you're invincible, but you're not,' she said in a stern tone as the boys approached the house. 'One wrong move . . .'

'Ah, love, let them be,' Russell said from behind her. 'Kids will be kids!'

'Hi, Granda.' Beau ran over to him and threw his arms around his waist. 'What are you doing here?'

'Can't I come and visit my grandsons without a reason? Well, let me think of one.' He put his arms around the boys' shoulders and steered them inside the house. 'Hmm, maybe I needed to see your smiling faces. Now, what's for morning tea? Milo or chocolate milk?'

'Chocolate milk for me,' Beau said.

'Me too,' from Trent.

'Great idea. Afterwards I want you both to come with me while I check the dam out in East Five. It's getting a little low and we might need to pull some sheep out. And if we don't, which,' he looked down at both boys, 'I hope we don't, we're going to shift them to East Three. So, you'll need your quad bike, helmets and a water bottle. Okay?'

'Oh yeah!' said Beau, punching the air. 'Mum said we could go and shift Trent's ewes by ourselves tomorrow.'

'Wash your hands, boys,' Brianna reminded them.

'Hello there, you two,' Angie said, greeting them as they walked in. She was standing at the bench cutting a cake into slices.

Dutifully they answered her and went to wash their hands, before clambering up on the bar stools to drink the chocolate milk Brianna put in front of them.

'How are you, Trent?' Angie asked.

'Good,' he answered, slurping at the milk. Beau started to blow bubbles and before Brianna could reprimand them,

Angie said, 'Manners please. Goodness, have you been brought up in the wild?'

Brianna blinked and pursed her lips.

'My mother always told me you need to have manners that would allow you to dine with the Queen of England or to eat with the shearers.'

'Don't worry, love,' Russell said, nudging Angie. 'They've got them. Sometimes forget to use them, that's all. They're hungry boys.'

'Granda, I've drawn some pictures of a raft I want to build. Can you help me?' Beau asked, a milk moustache on his upper lip.

'I'd love to. Where are they? What do you want to make it out of?'

Beau climbed off the chair and went to get them. 'We need a pallet and two drums,' he called over his shoulder.

Brianna laughed. 'Got your work cut out for you there, Dad.'

'Russell, should you be encouraging him to do that? It means he'll want to take it on the water and you know neither of the boys is very good at swimming,' Angie said in a low voice.

Brianna was about to make a comment when Beau came running back into the room with a piece of paper and gave it to Russell. It had a rough outline of a raft drawn in crayon.

'Wow, mate, that looks pretty cool. What's this bit here?' Russell pointed to the end of the raft where Beau had drawn an arrow and what looked like a blob.

'That's where I want to put my fishing-rod holders.'

'Ah, I see. Many fish in the dam, are there?'

Beau looked at him seriously. 'I don't know, that's why I want to see if I can catch one.'

Brianna saw Angie frowning and wondered what the problem was. Then she saw Beau had picked out all the sultanas and left most of the cake. Oops.

'Finished?' she asked quickly, wanting to get rid of the evidence.

Beau pushed the plate over to his mum and focused on his granda again. 'My friend Jack caught a big fish at his uncle's farm. It was this big.' He opened his arms to full stretch.

'Did he? Do you know what type it was?'

Beau shook his head.

'Are you going to waste the cake I made?' Angie asked.

'I don't like sultanas,' Beau said. 'They're all squishy.'

'Me too,' Trent said, finally breaking his silence. Brianna had almost forgotten he was sitting at the table behind them.

Angie looked up at him, her cheeks going a little red. 'Oh, that hurts my feelings, Beau,' she said. 'I made it specially for you.'

He shrugged. 'Sultanas are gross.'

Russell gave a laugh and patted her leg. 'Chocolate cake all the way for these kids, my love! But, not to worry, I'll have a slice. I *love* sultanas.'

'Yeah,' agreed Beau. 'I *love* chocolate cake.' He imitated his grandfather and Brianna hid a smile. The pout on Angie's face made her look like a petulant teenager. Without the youthfulness.

A door opened and Caleb came out into the kitchen, his glasses perched on the end of his nose. 'Hello, all. Sorry, I got caught up.'

'Caleb, good to see you, mate.' Russell said. 'How's things?'

'Just getting ready to head back to Perth. What have you got on today?'

'It's so *dry*, I can't *wait* for the opening rains,' Angie said, making all eyes turn to her. 'I know it's too soon, but to be able to stop hand-feeding would be great. I always *love* new beginnings and the new season is just that, a new beginning.'

'Yes. Yes, you're right of course,' Caleb answered, sounding distracted. 'A bit too early, though.'

Russell leaned back and stretched. 'I'm letting the last lot of my weaner calves out of the yards today. They've had five days in there, and finally the bellowing has stopped and the mums are more interested in the hay than losing their babies. Think it's safe for them to go back out now. Want to come for a look when I put them out?'

'Ah, I probably can't today,' Caleb answered, reaching over for a piece of cake. 'I'm working on a brief I need to have done by the end of the day.' He took a huge bite. 'Delicious cake,' he said through a mouthful.

'Nice to see someone appreciates it,' Angie said.

Chapter 14

Dave was surprised to see Guy in a fresh set of clothes and looking clean and tidy. Isabelle must work quickly, he thought.

The old man was waiting outside the shearing shed, with Bob at his feet, and if Dave hadn't known he had trouble with his memory, he would have thought the man looked fit and well for a seventy year old. Sure, he walked with a limp and he was a bit stooped, but generally he appeared in good health . . . now he was showered, shaved and dressed in clean clothes.

'G'day, Guy, you're looking well.'

'Course I'm well. Told you last time, I don't need any doctor or nurse.'

'Did Isabelle come by?'

'A nice little lady did, for sure. Got a real nice dinner in me fridge now.'

'That's great, I'm glad she called in.'

'About me wool . . .'

'Yeah, tell me about your wool,' Dave said, walking into the shearing shed to get out of the hot sun. The flies followed him, but it was good to escape the penetrating heat.

'You remember my colleague Jack?' Dave indicated to where Jack was following behind. He was pleased to see Jack seemed a little more comfortable this time, holding out his hand quickly to the old man.

'Jack,' Guy nodded towards him.

'So, you're missing some wool? Where was it stacked?' Dave asked, looking around. It didn't seem like the shed had been used in many months. There was a light covering of dust over the floor and there were no visible footprints or drag marks.

'Over here.' Guy pointed. 'I had them piled on top of one another against the wall. There were twenty bales.'

'From the last time you shore?' Dave asked as he inspected the floor, his heart sinking just a little. There was nothing to indicate the bales had ever been there in the first place. No dusty outline and, again, no drag marks. There was no possible way the bales could have been shifted without marking the dust.

Jack seemed to know what Dave was thinking because he came to stand next to him and inspected the floor too.

'Unless the wind has blown away the marks,' Jack said softly. 'Or it happened a week ago and the evidence has gone.'

Surprised at Jack's observation, Dave nodded his agreement. He always knew Jack would make a good detective, even though he claimed not to have the desire to become one. His intuition was often spot on—a good trait for a detective.

'From shearing a few years ago. Sent the last clip off . . . geez, be three or four months ago, I reckon. But I saved these in case I ever needed some money. Sorta like me nest egg.'

'You need money now?' Dave looked over at him and suddenly Guy seemed to shrink.

'No, no,' Guy said slowly, shaking his head.

His long, stringy grey hair, which had been combed back, came loose and flopped over his eyes. Hopefully, Isabelle would be able to convince him to get a haircut soon.

'Just read in the *Stock Journal* the price 'as kicked, so thought it'd be a good time. Nothin' like needing any money, or that.'

Dave studied the old man. Was there something more going on here?

'Okay; well, I've got an idea. Why don't we go into the house and have a look at some of the paperwork, while Jack has a look around the shed and sees if he can find any evidence of trucks or vehicles that could have taken the bales away? Being twenty, they would have needed at least a small truck. Wouldn't have been able to get that many on the back of the ute, even if he was pulling a trailer.'

'Dead right there, young fella,' Guy nodded. 'Could it have something to do with those vehicles I keep hearing at night?'

'Have you heard them again?' Dave asked instantly. He was beginning to wonder if Guy were as mentally unfit as he'd first thought.

'Last night Bob started to bark. I got up to have a look around but it was a full moon so I couldn't really see any lights. Beautiful night, though. When I was young, I spent a lot of time killing rabbits. The moonlit nights were the good ones cos you could see where you were walking.'

Dave nodded to Jack, who disappeared outside, then turned to Guy. 'Let's go up to the house. I'd be really interested to hear about your younger days.'

Noticing an immediate difference in the house, Dave was pleased he'd gone straight to Isabelle. The kitchen sparkled and the floors were clean, although a coating of dust came off Bob's fur when he flopped down after following them inside.

'Do you have an office?' Dave asked.

'Yeah, down the hall. Put the kettle on.'

Dave could only imagine the state of Guy's office. 'Can I have a look at your wool sales, bank statements and maybe even your freight bills? Should tell me on the invoice how many they carted for you.'

Guy nodded and limped off down the hall. Dave could hear the shifting of papers and the old man muttering to himself. Taking the opportunity to look around, he saw photos on the dresser he hadn't noticed last time he was here. He picked one up, trying to work out which of the group in it was Guy. The man was tall with a moustache and straight back, while the woman was wearing large skirts and an apron. Her hair was pulled back into a bun and she wasn't smiling. There were two little boys in shorts and suspenders. Old-fashioned clothing aside, Dave was sure one of the boys was Guy.

The muttering from the office stopped, then there was shuffling and a plonk as a heavy file was dropped on the kitchen table, along with crumpled loose-leaf sheets. Dave caught a glimpse of the logo of the local Landmark store . . . and coffee stains on the top sheet. He stifled a sigh. Trying to reconcile what bales of wool had been sold and stored might take a lot of time.

Dave held out the photo. 'These your parents?' he asked.

'Yeah. And me brother.'

'Fine-looking bunch, aren't they?'

Guy humphed and looked away. 'They're all right, I suppose.'

'When was it taken?'

'Wouldn't 'ave a clue.' He glanced down at the photo. 'Maybe I was six or seven.'

'Must've been an idyllic childhood. A lot of freedom. Where's the tea leaves?' Dave asked as he put the photo back down and went over to the bench.

'There was a lot of freedom, for sure,' Guy answered, pulling out a chair and sitting down without answering Dave's question. 'And a lot of work.'

Dave hunted for the tea and was rewarded by the second jar he opened.

'We spent hours mucking around creek beds and trapping rabbits. I liked to track animals—I learned to track me dad, following his footprints. I could track roos and sheep . . . humans . . .' His voice trailed off.

'It was only the four of you?' Dave poured water into the newly gleaming pot and set it on the table, along with the mugs. 'Quite a small family for back then.'

Guy smacked his lips together and squinted. 'Only the four of us,' he said after a pause. 'Better pour the tea there, lad.' He opened the file and flipped through some pages until he found what he wanted and unclicked the leaver. Flicking the pages across the table to Dave, he said, 'There's me wool sales documents for last year. I sold a 'undred and twenty-one bales.'

Dave gave a low whistle. 'Nice amount.'

'And the year before was 'undred and forty-three. Season was as good as we'd had an' me girls cut good kilos. Could buy in some more ewes since things were lookin' as good as they were.'

'And have you got your wool books around? I'd like to see the shearing count, wool book and day tallies if I can.'

'I'll 'ave me cup o' tea first.' Guy held out his hand for the mug.

'Here you go. Do you need milk?' Dave went to open the fridge.

'I 'ave me tea the way the stockmen do. Black 'n' sweet. Learned that when I was out in the stock camps. No milk out there, unless they took a cow with 'em.'

'You worked in stock camps? Where, up the Territory?'

'Did a couple of years up there when I was eighteen. Dad didn't have enough work here and there wasn't the money to keep me. Most young fellas stayed and tried to find extra work around 'ere cos they didn't want to leave. I wanted to see different things, how other places worked.'

'Where'd you work?'

'Out of Alice, towards the Simpson Desert. Place called Narrabine. Owned by the Palmers. Got sold a few years back. Some multinational company bought it, more's the shame.'

There was a tapping on the door and then Jack's voice filtered through. 'Can I come in?'

'In the kitchen,' Guy answered before Dave had a chance.

Dave grinned to himself. The old man still liked to be in control. He could understand that. When his father was dying, he'd had so much taken away, he wanted to maintain whatever control was left to him. It had taken Dave and his family a long time to understand that, in the end, it didn't matter if he went out and pruned his roses, or took himself for a drive around the cattle. If something happened to him while he was out there, he would have died doing what he loved.

Dave poured Jack a cuppa and sat down. 'When you grab the wool books, if I could get you to get the wool sales from the year you didn't sell all your wool, that would be great too. How did your parents come to be here in Barker?'

'Me dad bought the land in 1938 and built it up, sheep by sheep. They didn't have much when they first arrived. Mum lived in a humpy, but by the time us kids were born, she had this house. They never 'ad much but we were always 'appy.

'Didn't mix a lot with the townspeople. Dad never had time for that. 'E was always trying to make a quid.

'Dad loved his sheep, so that was what we farmed. Then grain for a while, but the seasons never seemed to suit us. Not enough rain. Too far north of Goyder's Line. But all of us round here 'ad a go at growing crop at some time. Wheat, mostly.

'When we gave it away, we just went back to sheep.'

'How many do you run here now, Mr Wood?' Jack asked.

'Oh, I guess it'd be about two and half thousand.' He stirred his tea and took a sip. 'Less the ones I'm missing,' he reminded Dave.

Dave hid a grin. In some ways, Guy was on to everything. 'While we're here I'd like to have a look at the paddock you think the sheep went missing from. Check out the fences, that sort of thing.'

'Bob and I'll take you. No worries.'

Chapter 15

'Are you all right?'

The woman's eyes twitched open and she stared blearily up into the brightly lit sky. At first she couldn't focus, but she could make out a head and a hat. She licked her lips and tried to move—her back was sore and stiff from a night on the ground and there was a pain in her head making her squint.

'Here, have a drink.' Rough hands held her head as something was put against her lips. She wanted to struggle; it felt like he had her in a vice-like grip. Was he going to hurt her? Then the cool wetness of water touched her lips and she opened her mouth, trying to take in as much as she could.

'Steady, you'll choke.'

The water was taken away and she finished swallowing. 'More,' she croaked. 'Please.'

Again, the water was held to her lips and she drank deeply.

'What are you doing out here?' he asked. She felt him sit down beside her and she turned her head, trying to bring him into focus.

Her mouth moved but nothing came out.

'You look in pretty bad shape,' the voice continued. 'Where've you come from?'

'Where?' There! Finally! A word.

'What's that?'

A movement beside her, and then the stench of body odour and bad breath. Was it her or him?

Trying again, she formed the word carefully. 'Where?'

'Where are you? In the middle of nowhere. About eighty miles from Port Augusta.'

Port Augusta—her mind tried to find the word in her vocabulary but it didn't seem to be there. Port Augusta . . .

'That's a nasty bang you've got on the head there. You should get that seen to. And you're pretty burnt. I reckon getting you out of the sun would be a good idea.'

Her eyes had begun to focus now and she could see the man sitting next to her. He was well dressed, clean shaven and wore a broad-brimmed hat. As muddled as her brain was, she recognised the hat as an Akubra—a type favoured by stockmen.

'Who?'

Silence. The man frowned.

'Who. Am. I?' The question seemed to sap her energy and she felt her eyes closing under the heat of the sun. It would be easier to go to sleep and not wake up again.

'Hey! Don't you fade on me,' the man said. 'I need to get you to a hospital.'

'Leave.' She worked her tongue from the roof of her mouth where it was stuck again.

'Here, more water for you.'

The water was sweet and wet and lovely. Wanting the taste to last forever, she closed her eyes and concentrated on the feeling.

'I'm not leaving you here,' he said once he'd taken the water away. 'You're going to have to stand and walk to my motor car.' He put his hands under her arms and said, 'On the count of three. One, two, three . . .'

The world swam in front of her eyes and she gasped in pain.

'That's the way. Stand there for a moment and get your balance. Don't worry about falling. I've got you.' The man seemed to need to make conversation. 'I'd love to know how you got all the way out here in your condition. Did you fall out of a moving vehicle or something?

'Gee, look at those crows over there. Flock of them getting a drink from the waterhole. Did you know a flock of crows is called a murder? Murder of crows. Has a real menacing type of ring to it, doesn't it?'

Murder. The word echoed around her mind. Murder. Memories flickered. The immediate pain in her head, then darkness. Waking up in the shed. She remembered that, all right. The terror as she realised she didn't know where she was or who she was. Pure white-hot terror.

Had someone tried to murder her?

'What's your name?' the man finally asked. The long, painful trip to the car was over and she was sitting in the front seat.

She didn't want to answer his questions, wishing for the oblivion of sleep. Not thinking was what she'd rather do right now, but he seemed insistent because he asked again.

'I don't know.'

Feeling him looking at her, she turned away and let her eyes flutter shut.

'What do you mean, you don't know?'

She shrugged. 'I don't know my name.' It was the longest sentence she'd spoken for days. 'I don't know who I am.'

Chapter 16

Dave ran his fingers through his hair. It shouldn't be hard, working out if the wool had been stolen, because it was simply a matter of matching the number of bales from the wool book and the sales to the bank statements. If there were twenty bales that hadn't been paid for, then Guy would be missing the wool.

But no, it wasn't turning out to be that easy. The paperwork Guy had handed over was a mess. Some of it was filed correctly, in chronological order. But there were tax invoices on the sale of wool and several bank statements missing too. Taken over several years, that was a lot of paperwork.

The earlier years were more organised and most of the necessary paperwork was in the files Guy had supplied. Dave could see the decline in the book-keeping in the past three years. Guy had made an effort—obviously it was engrained in him, like a routine job that needed to be done—but there were mistakes and gaps in the paperwork. He pushed the folder away from him and sighed deeply.

'I'm heading out,' he said to Jack, who was sitting opposite him, poring over another lot of bank statements. 'Need some air.' The constant hum of the airconditioning wasn't helping him focus.

'Uh huh.'

By the way Jack answered, Dave knew he was concentrating, so he quietly pushed back his chair and left the room.

Outside, he stretched, doing a couple of lunges and squats to get his blood flowing again, and looked around. The air reminded him of laundry that had been dried on the line: crisp, clean and smelling of dried gum leaves.

He started to walk down the wide street. It used to be that coffee kept him alert during investigations. Now it was exercise. Both he and Kim had made a concerted effort to get healthier after Kim had been misdiagnosed with breast cancer. The coffee still featured in his diet, but he'd added water and exercise and decreased fatty foods and he felt a hundred times better. In fact, he'd lost six kilos and Kim had lost eight.

The gum trees lining the street gave off a eucalyptus scent and the agapanthus, which were planted in between the gums, were flowering. He stopped to look at one, pinching it between his fingers and inspecting the flower closely. Tiny black ants were running in and out of the flowers, gathering the pollen, and overhead, in the clear blue sky, there was a flurry of feathers and an elegant parrot glided down, landing in the birdbath on the lawn of the church. The bird flapped its wings in the water to cool itself down, and Dave watched for a moment before he wandered into the small graveyard.

None of the names meant anything to him. The graves were enclosed by iron fences, aged by time, and he was intrigued to see how neat and tidy they were. There must be a gardener employed. The first date he found was 1902—a Mr Albert Dutton. He'd lived to a ripe old age of ninety-three, but the next one hadn't been so lucky. *Jacqueline Smythe, Born 3rd March 1910, Died 7th April 1920.* It didn't say why the child had died, but there could have been any number of reasons back then: measles, scarlet fever, snakebite, dehydration.

'Can I help you, Detective?'

Dave turned and saw the elderly minister, Chris Connelly, looking at him curiously.

'Good afternoon, Chris. You're looking mighty fit today,' said Dave, smiling.

'Any day above ground is a good one, sir. But the ones after will be better. Was there something I could help you with, or were you just passing?'

'I could certainly do with your help. Would we be able to go inside? It's hot today.'

'It feels like it's never going to end, this heat.' Chris took a key from his pocket and indicated for Dave to follow him. 'But I believe I feel the heat more as I grow older. Are you busy at the station?' he asked as he shuffled along the path and up the stairs.

'It's quiet, thank goodness. Just the normal things of making sure no one is speeding or drink-driving. There's a hoon I haven't been able to catch, but I'm working on it.'

'You must enjoy it when most people are behaving themselves.' The minister leaned on the doors and they opened smoothly.

'It can get a little monotonous sometimes,' Dave admitted. 'Not that I'm an adrenalin junkie or anything like that, but it's good to keep the mind active.'

'Is that why you're here? To keep your mind active?'

The church was dark and cool, and echoed as they talked.

'Well, it's more that I'm curious.'

'Ah, a mystery of sorts then.' Chris gave a smile. 'Come and sit. I'll help you with what I can.'

For an instant Dave was reminded of the Frontier Services minister he'd met in Blinman during an investigation. Dessie had had a similar gentle manner to Chris—a certain peacefulness. He felt a stab of sadness. Dessie had passed away less than six months ago. He and Kim had gone to the funeral, which had been held in his beloved town of Blinman, and watched as his coffin had been lowered into the hard red earth he loved so much.

He cleared his throat. 'I appreciate that. Tell me, do you know Guy Wood?'

Chris sat down on the front pew. His eyes rested briefly on the cross that hung from the wall and then he closed his eyes.

Dave sat and waited. He could see a large book on a stand right next to the pulpit. Whether it was a Bible or the record books, he wasn't sure.

'I do know Guy, yes. I believe he's still on the farm on Jacaranda Road, is that right?'

'Yep, he's getting on a bit now. When my partner and I went to see him last week, I thought it might be a good idea to bring the community nurse in, which seems to have made a lot of difference to him.'

'Ah, great program, the community nursing. Isabelle is to be commended for the job she does.'

'She's an excellent nurse. So, you knew Guy—did you know his family?'

Chris shook his head. 'No, my predecessor, Alan McSweeny, would have. I didn't come here until 1980. Both parents and the brother, I believe, were gone by then. I have some recollection the mother died in an accident—she fell from a horse, I think. But like I said, this was well before my time. I just remember people speaking of it and how tragic it was for the children to be left alone when they were so young.'

He wasn't sure why he lowered his voice, but Dave found himself speaking quietly. It must have been the atmosphere in the church. He guessed it would be the coolest place in Barker right now. 'Would you have a record of their deaths?'

'If they were buried by the minister in this church, yes, there would be a record. Alan was a compulsive record-keeper. But even if it wasn't here, the council office would have a record of who is buried where. I imagine if the funerals weren't in this church, then they would have been in the Catholic church and, again, there should be records there.' There was a pause before Chris turned to Dave and said, 'Can I know why you're asking?'

Dave stretched his arm along the back of the pew and twisted around to face Chris. 'I was having an interesting conversation with my wife, Kim, and she mentioned that Guy may have had another sibling, although no one was really sure. It interested me and I thought I'd do a bit of research. See what I could find.'

Chris folded his hands over his stomach before answering. 'You know it may be difficult to find that information. Often children who died shortly after birth were buried in lonely graves somewhere on farms or along roadsides as the family travelled. Life was very different back then. In fact, unless the child was christened, we may not have a record of the birth at all.' He drew in a breath. 'But you're more than welcome to look.'

Dave felt his heart give a little leap of excitement. 'Thank you,' he said. 'It may not mean anything, whether there was another child or not, but I'd like to try and find out.'

'What do you know about the family already?'

'Absolutely nothing. Brother was killed in Nam.' He shrugged. 'That's all.'

'Everything you tell me here is in confidence.' Chris stopped.

Dave had noticed he did that a lot—gave a funny little pause before he asked a big question or made a statement.

'Can you tell me why you went out there in the first place?'

'Well, he reported some sheep stolen, then he reported that some bales of wool had been taken out of his shed. The sheep—' Dave waggled his hand from side to side in a 'maybe, maybe not' motion—'I'm fairly certain they haven't been stolen. The bales of wool, well, I need to look into them a bit more.

'It's hard because sometimes it's clear his mind is wandering, but other times he makes perfect sense and has total recall. Makes it very difficult to know whether what he's telling me is true or a figment of his imagination.'

'About thirty-odd years ago, there was quite a lot of crime in this area,' Chris said. 'Not here in Barker itself, but in the mid-north area. Have you heard about it?'

'Can't say I have.'

'Hmm, it was an interesting time, with sheep being slaughtered during the night and only the skin and insides left behind. Quite a few stockhorses were stolen and never recovered. Cattle disappeared overnight and farmers started carrying their guns with them. The worst of the crimes was when a little boy was taken from his bed. He was found wandering down the main street in nothing but a pair of shorts on a winter's morning. Thankfully, he didn't appear hurt in any way.

'I can remember the fear it created throughout the town. It seemed nobody trusted anyone. Even their neighbour.'

Frowning, Dave started to speak, but Chris interrupted him. 'It just stopped over time. No one was ever caught, or charged. There was a common belief it was an outsider, in the area for temporary employment, but no one was certain.'

'I can't believe I've never heard about this.'

'I don't think the townspeople like to talk about it. I rarely hear it mentioned either, but I'm telling you, Dave, this town isn't a stranger to crime.'

'Interesting. Were the police involved at all?'

'They were when little Jerry Mayther went missing. Detectives from Adelaide came up here, but there was nothing to see, no evidence to find. His family packed up and moved away very soon afterwards.

'Like I said, no one really likes to talk about it.'

'Are you telling me this for a reason, Chris?' Dave asked, narrowing his eyes. 'Is there something I should know?'

Chris gave a little laugh. 'Like I said, everything I'm told is confidential, but I have been here a long time, and I know many things.'

'Confessions?' Dave asked.

Again, the laugh. 'This is not the Catholic church, Dave. I don't hear confessions.'

Dave was beginning to get confused. Chris was talking in riddles and he felt sure he was telling him something. 'Going back to the Wood family,' he said.

'Yes, the Wood family,' Chris nodded. 'At the risk of stating the obvious, have you thought to ask Guy whether he had another sibling?'

'Yeah, I've thought about asking, but I was a bit worried, given his confusion, it might upset him or throw him off kilter.'

'That's very kind of you,' Chris answered, the surprise clear in his tone.

'What? You think I'm a blundering philistine or something?' Dave asked in a wry tone.

Laughing, Chris got up. 'Well, Detective, perhaps I did. I admit I am surprised at your sensitivity. Come on, this way.'

Chapter 17

In the inner sanctum of the minister's office, Dave ran his fingers along the spines of the books that lined the walls. The books were large and thick, with old, cracked spines of faded red.

'Do you know what year you need?' Chris asked.

'Starting from 1947, I think. The year Guy was born. Children were born almost year after year in those days.'

Chris reached up to a high shelf and took down a book, opening the front cover. 'Nineteen sixty-five. Nope, need to go back further.' He walked along counting the spines until he came to 1947. 'If Guy's birth isn't recorded here, then it would be safe to say the other siblings won't be either.'

'Well, he was definitely born in the area. He told me his mum had him in the back room of their house.'

'I'll leave you to your searching, then. If you need anything more, just call.' Chris nodded his head and left the room.

Dave tilted his head to take in all the books, then looked around the room. The walls were uneven and painted white, and hung with framed pictures of Christ and quotes from the Bible. Carefully he took the book Chris had given him and placed it on the desk. Opening the first page, he felt how thick and creamy the paper was. The writing was beautiful old-style cursive, loopy, neat and easy to read.

1 January 1947: The start of the new year. A fresh year, just like the Lord gives us every day. I pray that for every one of my parishioners and people in the mid north, it's a good, healthy, God-fearing year. Today, being a Wednesday, the church is quiet, except for Mrs Martin who came to say her daily prayers.

2 January 1947: Again, Mrs Martin was the church's only user.

5 January 1947: Sad news reached us today of the 1 January hailstorm in Sydney. It has caused a million pounds' worth of damage, but the human cost was more, with over one thousand people injured. A public holiday and many people were on the beach, making the toll more than it might have been.

Dave flicked through the pages, stopping only to read the births, deaths and marriages.

8 March 1947: The nuptials of grazier George Rankin and nurse Annie Davis were held today, attended by local and surrounding station owners. Early rains made the gardens surrounding our church look lovely and fresh. May the Lord bless their union.

He stopped at 1 April.

Tis a sad day for humankind, especially for us here in the mid north, with the government confirming that Woomera will be the rocket range site for Australia and Britain.

This fella would have made a great historian, Dave thought. He had everything in there.

His phone beeped with a text message. Jack.

Where are you?

At church, he texted back.

Praying for your soul?

Funny man.

I found something with the wool. When are you coming back?

Give me an hour.

More entries, but Dave didn't see any mention of Guy or the Wood family. He sighed and ran his fingers through his hair, admitting this was much more fun than matching figures with wool sales in bank accounts. This Alan McSweeny had a sense of humour.

11 May 1947: The church was almost full today. My sermon was based on the verse Be still and know I am God *and I spoke of needing to be quiet to hear the word of the Lord. At the end I reminded everyone about this quiet time, then I asked all the children, who were in the front row, why it was good to be quiet in church. They had been listening, because they said, 'To hear God's voice.' I shook my head and said: 'No! It's because people are sleeping.' And with that, Jack Hooper, who had been asleep since the first hymn, gave a loud snore and the congregation erupted.*

Dave laughed, imagining the scene.

28 September 1947: My sermon today was on being content with what we have. There was a general rustling of discomfort, as most are not—they always want more. Adam Parker, who is all of eight, was asked to read the Bible verse. Standing at the front, with his own Bible, he opened it to the page and started to read. As he did, something floated to the ground. From where I was, I could see it looked like a pressed leaf. He stopped reading and looked down in amazement. I asked if he needed any help to continue. He shook his head, then picked up the leaf and said, 'I hope you were all listening, because this is a sign from God.'

'Really?' I asked. 'What type of sign?'

'I think he's sent us Adam's underwear!'

Well, it was a little hard to get everyone under control after that.

Dave laughed out loud. Quick kid, that one. Fancy thinking it was a fig leaf!'

14 December 1947: There were two baptisms within the service today. George and Annie Rankin's little baby girl, Caroline Grace, and Warren and Joy Wood's firstborn son, Guy Archibald. I had heard general mutterings of a 'honeymoon baby' for the Rankins. She was a delight, not crying once when I crossed her with water. Guy has a good set of lungs on him, but it didn't matter. I was pleased to have the Woods in church as they don't often make the services. I pray God blesses their lives.

'Gotcha,' Dave said aloud. Okay, he could work from here. It would be at least nine months before there was another baby on the scene. He needed to start looking from August 1948 for the next baby. He glanced at his watch and saw it was past the time he'd told Jack he'd be back at the station.

He put the book away and went to find Chris, who was sitting in the garden reading a book, a cup of tea and a scone at his side. 'Did you find what you were looking for?' he asked, peering over his glasses at Dave.

'I found part of what I was looking for. Could I come back tomorrow and look through the 1948 record?'

'Of course, I'll make sure I've got it out for you.'

'Great, thanks. Alan McSweeny, didn't he have a sense of humour?'

Chris gave a laugh. 'He most certainly did. He could have been a novelist—he had a keen eye for human behaviour.'

'Guess you blokes need to have that when you're dealing with people all the time.'

'As I'm sure you do, Detective.'

~

'What did you find?' Dave asked Jack when he arrived back.

'I think he's had the wool stolen,' Jack said.

'What makes you say that? I was missing some of the wool sales I needed to check.'

'I rang Landmark and got them to send through the missing information.' Jack pushed over the paperwork. 'Okay, look at the 2015 wool clip. One hundred and forty-three bales were marked in the wool book, stencilled and written up in the specifications for sale. That's not something that can be forged, yeah?'

Dave nodded. 'Nope, the wool classer has to write the species up, and with the bales numbered, there isn't any way extras can be added in.'

'Right, so the wool was sold, through Landmark, in the September of 2015. If you refer to the paperwork, you'll see only a hundred and twenty-three were sold—a deficit of twenty. Exactly the number Guy said he was missing.'

Dave looked at the wool sale in front of him, taking note of the gross figure Guy had been paid. He looked across at the bank statements, where Jack had highlighted the payment from Landmark, and saw they were the same.

'And you haven't found a payment for another twenty since 2015?'

'Exactly. I can match every other credit from Landmark and marry them up with the recipient tax invoice. But there are still twenty bales that haven't been sold and he hasn't been paid for.'

The office was silent while Dave cross-matched the highlighted figures, dates and payments. Jack was right. Guy was missing twenty bales of wool.

Dave pushed back his chair and rubbed at his chin. 'Now, that's interesting,' he said. 'Maybe we should have another look at the sheep situation.'

Jack shook his head. 'Nah, I don't reckon. The wool theft is different. The sheep theft report is a result of his muddled brain. We've driven over the farm and seen the fence. It's new. It's tight. Nothing was going to get through that sucker. And Toby Jones didn't want Guy's sheep anyway, remember? Lice and so on. That was why he put the fence up in the first place. I know anyone could have come onto his place and taken the sheep—mustered them and loaded them out of a paddock. Anyone with a good dog could do that, but I'm really not thinking anyone would want his sheep because of the lack of husbandry skills here.'

'Sure, but lice is easily treated. How's this for a scenario? Toby is pissed off with Guy because he didn't put up the money for his half of the fence, so he decides to get it back another way. He waits for a moonlit night, drops the fence, musters what he wants, takes them back to his yards, keeps them there until he's treated them, then lets them out.' He dusted off his hands and smiled. 'Just got his money back for the fence.'

'I think you're grasping at straws,' Jack said. 'What about his wife? She would've known he was up to something.'

'Maybe, maybe not. Come on, Jack, you know how easy it is to do something out there and not get caught. Wait until she wasn't home for a night, tell her he's going fox shooting—the excuses are endless. Maybe he said he was off for a night with the boys and went rustling sheep instead.'

Jack still looked unconvinced.

'He's been hearing cars at night,' Dave reminded him.

'He's confused. None of this would stand up in court and you know it, Dave.'

'Ah, Jack.' Dave got up from his chair and clapped him on the shoulder. 'Always raining on my parade. My point is, if the wool has been stolen, the sheep might have been stolen too. Maybe we have something interesting on our hands here. Come on, let's go and have a chat to Mr Jones again. Oh.' He grabbed his keys from his desk and pointed a finger at Jack. 'Good work.'

Chapter 18

'You need to learn how to tie knots that won't come undone,' Russell said to Beau. 'You don't want to get out into the middle of the dam and find your knots coming undone and the drums floating away from you.'

'No, I don't,' Beau said, his brown eyes turned up towards his grandfather. 'I don't want to worry Mum the way Trent did.'

Brianna felt her heart constrict as she heard her son's sad tone. Beau hadn't said anything to her about Trent's accident. She'd thought the severity hadn't really registered with him because he was that little bit younger. Making a mental note to speak with him about it later, she walked down towards the shed.

It had taken her father a week to gather all the materials needed for the raft and today was the first day they had found the time to work on it. Caleb was back in Perth and

Trent had gone with Angie to her farm. She wasn't sure why Trent had decided to do that; perhaps it had been the lure of the new Poll Dorsett rams she'd bought. She hoped it wasn't. Poll Dorsett rams weren't as prevalent as they once were. There were other breeds butchers preferred.

Trent's small flock of ewes didn't have a sire to go over them yet and Brianna was beginning to think he was going to ask Angie to borrow hers. In which case, she was going to have to do some fast talking, because she didn't want animals that hadn't been tested for brucellosis on her farm. Like any sexually transmitted disease it could be passed on to her flock and Brianna wasn't having that. Angie didn't seem to care about things like biosecurity, which was a puzzle to Brianna. Brucellosis was a fertility disease, rendering rams infertile. She'd care when she was expecting one hundred percent lambing and only got seventy.

Perhaps it was because Angie was old-school. Nina had told her that John's father had always advised them to stay away from quality assurance programs and the like for as long as they could. The paperwork was a load of rot and they wouldn't get any better prices, just more work. Brianna disagreed. There were diseases that could be financially crippling, passed on through straying stock or vehicles going from one farm to the other. Nope, Angie really should up her game when it came to biosecurity. She was being very short-sighted by not doing so.

Brianna grabbed a broom and started sweeping the floor. The last few days had been windy and there was a thick coating of sand through the whole shed. It didn't matter on the cement area, but the shearing board couldn't be sandy and she'd organised shearing for two weeks' time.

Her phone dinged with a message and, seeing it was from Caleb, she put down the broom and read it.

Business function I have to attend in ten days. Can you come?

Ten days? How could she answer that? There could be a harvest ban on, and she'd be getting the sheep ready for shearing. She looked at the calendar on her phone. Preg scanning was booked for the day before.

No, sorry, preg scanning/shearing afterwards. Is it really important?

It's okay. Don't worry, was the answer.

Clicking on the music app, Brianna set it to the McClymonts and picked up the broom again. Humming along to 'Like We Used To' she put all her energy into finishing the sweeping, then checked the wool packs and the stock of bale fasteners.

Going over everything she'd need in the next two weeks, she made a list. Rattle for marking the dry ewes on the back, bale ink for the wool, drench. Russell had suggested they vaccinate the pregnant ewes after they'd finished scanning. Then the dry girls could go straight into the shed, be shorn, then sold to the local meat buyer. It would be good not to have to carry any extra mouths when feed was getting to be at a premium, thanks to summer.

Once she had her list, she hooked the feed-out cart onto her ute, drove under the auger and started it, watching as the lupins filled the cart.

Jinx had been lying in the shade, under the silo, but when he realised she was going feeding, he came out and looked wistfully up at the back of the ute.

'You wanna come for a ride, hey, old fella?' she asked. 'How's your balance? You're not going to fall off, are you?' She lifted him up onto the tray, then, deciding on caution, clipped him onto the chain that was already there.

In the paddock the dry grass was really beginning to power up and there would be very little nutritional value in it. She might need to up the supplementary feeding she was already doing. She looked around at the tall waving ryegrass bleached by the long, hot summer days. Gaps in the pastures were opening up as the feed started to deteriorate. Peeling open one of the heads of a ryegrass plant, she checked to see if there were any little withered black seeds in there. Ergot was a poison that could kill a mob of cattle or sheep easily. A horrid little fungus that infected the plant's seed head. Thankfully, she didn't see any.

Brushing the flies away, she tried to see where the sheep were. Under the shade of the bush shelter belt or near the dam, she surmised. The sky shimmered and as she looked towards the south she could see the sea breeze sitting out there, just waiting to sweep across the land and cool everything down. It was one of the things she loved about living on the coast. Rarely were there two hot days in a row and rarely did she have to sleep without a doona on.

Leaning against the tray, she patted Jinx absentmindedly, all the while looking across her country. The glare of the sun hurt her eyes, while the grey leaves of the bush didn't move in the stifling heat. She still couldn't see the sheep, but because they were almost the same colour as the land right now, it was hardly surprising.

'Let's feed these girls, Jinx,' she said with one last pat. 'Did I tell you? These are the ones I bought from Wagin—they've got great wool. Can't wait to shear them and see how many kilos they cut.'

The ewes were, as predicted, asleep on top of the dam. One raised her head as she heard the noise of the ute and feed cart, let out a baa and, as one, the whole mob rose and ran towards Brianna, all baaing in greeting. As they ran, the small cloud of dust they created with their hooves rose into the sky.

Brianna got out and grabbed the rope attached to the trapdoor of the feed-out cart, then looped it back into the driver's window so she could trail-feed the lupins. She could smell sheep manure and dust and it made her smile. This was her life, and as dirty and hard as it could be, she loved every minute of it.

The ewes fell into line after the ute, nibbling at the small, round lupin seeds. They were in good condition, with about three inches of wool on them and clean arses. She noticed there were a few grass seeds around their faces but that would get tidied up when she crutched the pregnant ones after scanning.

She nodded her approval and drove back towards the shed, slightly high on life.

❧

Angie dropped Trent back a few hours later, just as the sea breeze was whipping the loose dirt into the air.

'Ugh,' Angie said as she followed Trent inside and gave Brianna a dry kiss on the cheek. 'This time of year always seems to feel *gritty*. Everywhere, not just outside. All the dust comes in underneath the doors, all over the floor. I come out of the sheep yards feeling like I could wash away a tonne of dirt off me, let *alone* what gets into my nose and ears! And every time I bite down on my teeth I can feel the sand there *too*!'

Brianna smiled. 'I know. You should have seen the colour of the water when I washed my hair last night. I could feel the dirt scratching my scalp when I rubbed in the shampoo.'

'Summer in Western Australia!' Angie plopped herself down in a chair. 'Now, I'd *love* a glass of wine,' she said pointedly.

Brianna blinked and shot a glance at the clock. Four in the afternoon wasn't too early, she supposed.

'You've got your nails done and your hair re-coloured,' Brianna said, taking in the long, bright red fingernails tapping on the arm of the chair.

'I had an hour spare yesterday, so I thought I'd pop in to the hairdresser. Not joining me?' Angie asked as Brianna placed the glass of wine in front of her.

'No thanks, I've still got a few jobs to do.' She wondered how Angie managed to do her farm work with nails like that. Her manager did most of the work, she realised, but Angie often talked about getting into the sheep yards, drenching or being around the lamb-marking cradle. And she'd certainly done it when she'd helped Russell. Brianna had been surprised at how skilled Angie was when mustering sheep or drafting.

Angie took out her phone and opened the Facebook app. 'I tagged you in a photo this morning, did you see it?'

Brianna shook her head. 'I haven't been on Facebook for a few days,' she answered, getting out a jug of lemon cordial and pouring herself a glass.

'Do you remember how I told you about my friend Geena Adams? She knew Caleb?'

'Hmm,' Brianna answered, taking a drink.

'She put up this *stunning* photo of Caleb and his friend Heidi. Thought you'd like to see it.' She turned the phone around and showed Brianna.

Brianna felt like her heart had stopped. Taking the phone out of Angie's hand, she looked at the picture closely. This was the woman he'd told her about. The one who worked at his firm and sometimes went with him to business functions. Oh, she knew about Heidi, but Brianna had never seen a photo of her and she was stunning. Not at all how Caleb had made her sound. They looked comfortable together, with Heidi's arm through Caleb's, both smiling for the camera.

'*Lovely* photo, isn't it? Caleb is looking very handsome. The grey around his ears suits him, don't you think?'

Swallowing, Brianna handed the phone back to Angie and made herself smile. 'Yeah, it does,' she agreed. 'Caleb told me he was taking her.' Actually, she wasn't quite sure he had, not to this particular function, but she wasn't going to tell Angie that.

Angie enlarged the photo and held it up. 'Such a different world up there, isn't it? All glitz and glamour. *So* different from a dusty farm. I guess they work quite closely together since they're at the same firm.'

Brianna shrugged. 'I don't know. He's never mentioned they've had a case together.' She paused. 'Just need to go to the loo. Excuse me a minute.' Putting her glass down, she made a beeline for the bathroom.

Dragging in breaths, she tried to slow her heart rate. Even though she knew Caleb had been to functions with Heidi, to see them together, standing arm in arm, hurt her.

Why wouldn't Caleb want to have a glamorous, beautiful woman on his arm? She would be able to hold conversations with clients without sounding staged and awkward. Being a lawyer, Heidi was obviously very smart—a quality Caleb liked in people. He would have more in common with Heidi than with Brianna at the moment. Law, a workplace, a social life.

And the photo was on Facebook. Everyone would see it.

She took her phone out of her pocket and opened the Facebook app to look at the post again. Zooming in on Heidi's face, Brianna knew there was no possible way she was as beautiful or poised as the woman in the picture. She stared at Heidi's face; the blue eyes looked back her as if taunting her: *I'm standing next to him and you're not. You're on a farm in the middle of nowhere, dirty, smelly, with callused hands. You are nothing like me.*

She looked up and stared at her own face, the sunspots and wrinkles around her eyes. Heidi's skin looked flawless. Her hair was long, straight and blonde, and perfectly styled—a contrast to Brianna's own mousey brown mop, which refused to stay in a ponytail or any other style she tried to tame it into.

With a firestorm of emotions running though her, Brianna jabbed at the screen to shut the picture down. That photo, that woman, represented every feeling she was having right now: worthlessness, inferiority, shame.

As if on cue, her phone beeped.

Nina.

What's with the photo Angie tagged you in on Facebook?

Chapter 19

'Mum?' Beau called from his bedroom. 'Can you read me a story?'

'Sure can,' she answered. 'I'll finish the washing-up first, won't be long.' She crashed down the plate with unusual force, then swore as a porcelain chip flew onto the floor.

'Mum?' Beau appeared at the door with a worried look on his face. 'What's wrong?'

'Nothing, sweetheart. The plate was still a bit wet and it slipped when I was putting it into the cupboard, that's all.' How could she explain her melting pot of feelings to a six year old?

'Are you worried about something?' he asked, coming into the kitchen and putting his arms around her. 'Because if you are, I promise I won't ever do anything to worry you.'

Brianna returned the hug tightly. 'I'm not worried about anything,' she said, trying to make her tone light. 'And you, mister, don't you be concerned about Trent making me worry. That's all part of you being kids. I'm a mum and it's my job to worry about you both. Trent didn't mean to frighten me, it's just what happened.'

'But I saw the look on your face. It wasn't very nice.'

Pulling him tighter to her, she kissed the top of his head. 'That's very sweet of you. What would I do without you both?' The lump in her throat made it hard to talk.

'I've already promised I'm never doing anything like that again either,' Trent said, coming into the room. 'And I've promised Mum I'll always look after her.'

'We'll look after each other,' she promised them both.

Later that night Brianna was sitting in the office paying bills, trying to distract herself.

In her heart, she knew Caleb would never have an affair. It just wasn't him. He would end their relationship before he started another one, she was convinced of that. So why did the idea keep coming back to her?

The landline rang and she frowned, looking at the clock. It was late for anyone to be calling.

'It's me,' Nina said.

'Oh.' The lump in her throat suddenly reappeared.

'What's going on?'

'Nothing.' Brianna tried to make her tone convincing.

'Really? Doesn't look that way.'

'Why does everyone suddenly assume there's something going on? Have you thought they might have posed for the photo?' Lashing out felt good.

The silence coming from the other end of the phone didn't feel so good.

'Sorry,' she muttered.

'That's okay. I guess it did sound like I was assuming there was something untoward about it.'

Brianna's toned softened. 'I don't know, I guess Angie was just showing me the photo because it was of Caleb. My reaction is my own problem, but it made me feel like she was hinting at something else, you know?'

'We've already had this conversation. I don't think Angie is vindictive. Do you?'

'Not that I've ever noticed. Occasionally she has a bit of a go at the kids for their manners or something minor, but that's the worst I've ever seen. She's usually really nice.'

'And do you think Caleb would . . .' She paused. 'Do something?'

'No! He's already told me about this woman,' Brianna said. 'She escorts him to these big functions where he's supposed to have a woman on his arm.'

'She's a *prostitute*?' Nina's voice rose an octave in disbelief.

Unable to help herself, Brianna laughed. 'No, she's a lawyer too,' and she went on to tell her friend what she knew of Heidi.

On the other end of the line Nina blew out a breath. 'Isn't it awful when I can understand why he's got to do this?' she said in a low voice.

'I know.'

They were quiet.

'How do you feel?' Nina asked.

Brianna found it hard to find the right words. 'I guess I know he's not having an affair. He's not that type of bloke. Even with all the distance between us right now . . .' Her voice trailed off.

'Exactly,' Nina agreed quickly. 'He'd end the marriage before he started a relationship with someone else. This is part of his job and that's all there is to it. So, what are you doing tomorrow?'

Glad for the change of subject, Brianna turned back to the computer and looked at the freight bill she needed to pay. 'Feeding again. Cows are going to need a bit more hay and I'm going to try feeding hay to the ewes, plus the lupins. Hey, how much do you pay per kilometre for your grain freight? I'm sure this codger I've been using is overcharging me. I've just been looking at his invoice.'

'Who do you use?'

Brianna could hear the rustle of papers in the background as Nina searched for a bill.

'MacDune Freight Lines. My last bill was about four grand more than I thought it should be.'

Nina let out a low whistle. 'Okay, per kilometre it's . . .' She quoted the price and Brianna gave a snort.

'Thought so. Mine's four dollars more than yours. I'll have to talk to him in the morning.' Her voice was louder than she intended. Suddenly she felt overwhelmed by the prospect of having to deal with this problem on top of everything else. Tears blurred her vision.

Nina must have sensed she was upset because she asked quietly, 'Do you want me to come over?'

'No, I'm fine,' she answered after a momentary pause. 'I'll talk to you tomorrow.'

'I'm not doing anything if you want me to come there for a coffee. Or I can sit in the tractor with you or do whatever.'

'Honest, Nina, I'll be . . .' She was interrupted by a yell coming from the Terrors' end of the house. 'Shit! Gotta go.'

Running down to Trent's room, she saw him sitting up, staring blindly into the dim light, just as he'd been last time he'd had a nightmare. 'No!' He put his hands out as if to ward something off.

'Hey, hey, hey.' Brianna was beside him in an instant, holding his arms. He turned, pushing her away.

'No! Don't!'

Brianna overbalanced with the shove he gave her and stumbled to the floor. 'Trent!' she said loudly.

He stopped immediately and recognition came back into his eyes. 'What?'

'You're okay,' she said, getting to her feet. 'It's fine. You were having a nightmare.'

His breath was coming in short, sharp gasps, and as she gathered him to her she could feel his heart beating fast. Then the hot tears started.

'Oh, Trent, honey, what's going on? What were you dreaming about?'

He shook his head against her shoulder, trying to say something, but she couldn't understand what it was. Instead of asking again, she held him until the sobbing stopped.

A little while later she brought him a cup of hot milk and sat on the bed, the night light a soft glow in the corner.

'Want to tell me what the dream was about?' she asked.

'I don't know.' He looked down and fidgeted.

Brianna frowned. Trent always fidgeted when he told a lie. If he'd been standing, he would have hopped from one foot to the other.

'Oh. Well, sometimes that happens with dreams. You forget them as soon as you wake up.'

Trent didn't say anything, just kept looking down.

'Shove over,' she said, nudging him. He moved over in the bed and she got in beside him and put her arm around his shoulders. 'Did I ever tell you about the bad dreams I used to have? I wasn't much younger than you, I think.'

'No.' His voice was low.

'I'll tell you about them now, if you like.'

'Okay.' He put the cup on the bedside table, pulled the doona up to his chin and looked up at her if she were about to tell him a bedtime story.

'You know how when I was three my mum went missing?'

He nodded.

'It was like she just disappeared into thin air. These dreams—they were the same every time. One was I'd find her but she'd be . . .' She paused, not sure how to tell him about the dream without frightening him. After all, dreaming about finding her mother's body half mauled by foxes and crawling with bull ants probably wasn't the way to fix his nightmares. 'She'd be alive, living in a cave, but not sure where she was,' she improvised. 'The other was finding Granda crying. I dreamed about that all the time. And it would make me wake up feeling like crying too.'

She hugged him and kissed his head. 'It's a horrible feeling, but I promise you your dreams will go away in time.'

Hers hadn't. They'd just become less frequent.

Trent's eyes were shut now but he murmured, 'I always dream about the accident. Like I know something else happened but I can't remember what it is. I get really scared.'

'You know what, sweetie? It's just a dream. It's not a memory or an actual happening. It's just a horrible nightmare. So you don't have to be frightened of it.' She spoke slowly, in a soothing, singsong tone, trying to lull him back to sleep. If she had to sit here all night and hold him, she would. Whatever he was dreaming about, she would chase it away. Because that's what mothers did.

By the time Brianna fell into bed at two in the morning, she was so tired she thought she'd fall asleep instantly. Instead, she tossed and turned, keeping one ear open for Trent.

During the time in between wakefulness and sleep, Heidi and Caleb found her. They were laughing at her, telling her she wouldn't fit in with their circle of friends. She was a hillbilly, a country bumpkin.

'Honey,' Heidi said in a syrupy tone, 'I'm much more suited to Caleb than you are, why not just give him up? You know I want him.'

Frantically Brianna turned to Caleb. 'That's not true, is it?'

Caleb only smiled. He merged into her mother. She beckoned Brianna closer and closer, until Brianna could feel her breath on her face. 'I didn't want you,' she whispered. 'That's why I ran away.'

Her lips tried to form the words 'That's not true. Dad told me how much you loved me . . .' but in the heaviness of sleep they wouldn't work.

Brianna awoke with a start, feeling the despair of the dream seeping through her.

She needed to take note of her own words to Trent: 'It's just a horrible nightmare. So you don't have to be frightened of it.'

Even so, she wished it were her mother saying those words to her.

Chapter 20

Sitting under the stark white light of the examination room, she tried and tried to remember her name.

Gentle hands cleaned the wound on her head.

'Okay, there's going to be a prick now . . .'

Trying not to flinch as the needle went in, she concentrated on the lines in the floor. Counting twenty one way and twenty the other. The pressure on her head was from the doctor closing the wound with stitches.

Her hands and feet stung from the disinfectant the nurse had cleaned them with. At least it was good pain, she told herself. A healing pain, not the sort that made her want to die.

The good Samaritan had dropped her at the hospital door and walked inside. For some reason he thought she might try to run away. He was wrong: she knew she needed a doctor.

'There we are, good as new,' the doctor said to her. 'Now, this memory problem you're having . . .' he spoke in a slow voice so she couldn't misunderstand him.

'I've lost my memory, doctor, I'm not stupid.' She blinked. Where on earth had that come from? Being too frightened, she hadn't said more than a few words since a kind nurse had admitted her. It had been the good Samaritan who had told the hospital she'd lost her memory.

'Ah, yes,' the doctor spluttered. 'Of course. It's called retrograde amnesia. Often caused by a traumatic event, or a head injury such as the one you're sporting. Sometimes memories come back and other times they don't. You'll need to have some treatment—perhaps work with a psychologist. Also, the police will have to be informed, and I certainly want to keep you in hospital for the time being. We can't let you leave without any money or identity. You don't have any, do you?'

She shook her head. As far as she knew, her pockets had been empty when she'd left the shed and there had been nothing on the ground next to her that could help identify her. Maybe it was supposed to be like that, she thought. Maybe someone had tried to kill her.

A spark . . .

Yes, she'd already had that thought, hadn't she? While she'd been in the car with the good Samaritan. She glanced around, suddenly fearful. Who could it be? How would she know who to stay away from if she didn't know who had tried to kill her? What if it were someone in this room?

A monitor beeped beside her and the nurse said, 'Your heart rate has suddenly gone up a little.' The nurse jotted down a note on the record sheet and then reached out to hold her hand. 'It's okay,' she said softly. 'You're safe here. I'll be with you; you can trust me, I promise.'

The doctor cleared his throat. 'Maybe a sedative would be in order.'

A sedative? To make her go to sleep? So she could be made pliable?

'No!' The word held every ounce of dread she was feeling.

The doctor seemed unsure of what to do. She realised he was young—so young he couldn't possibly be a medical practitioner. No, she was sure this was all some kind of trick.

Trying to get down from the table, she said, 'I need to go.'

'How about we get you into a little ward all by yourself and you can have a shower and a good rest?' the nurse said soothingly.

Wobbling a little bit, she reached out to grab a support and connected with the nurse standing alongside her. With warm hands, the nurse helped her into a wheelchair and took her away from the bright lights and the pretend doctor.

'Now, I think the first thing we need to do is give you a name. I can't talk to you if you don't have a name, now can I? It will only be until we find out who you are.'

'I don't know.'

'What about Dolly? As in Dolly Parton; she's my favourite country singer of all time.'

'I haven't heard of her.'

'I don't suppose you would have. Okay, so not Dolly.' She turned the wheelchair down a brightly lit corridor and then in through the first door they came to.

'What's yours?' she asked.

'My name? Here, on my badge. Sister Williams. Elspeth Williams. What about Sally?'

'No, I don't think so. Something pretty.'

'Something pretty? Good idea. Crystal?'

'That sounds like something shiny.'

'Shiny can be pretty.'

'Yes.' She sounded unconvinced.

'Audrey, Kathleen, Sarah . . . Hmm, what else? Anna?'

'Anna,' she said. 'Yes. Anna. I like that.'

'Well, Anna, I'm Elspeth. It's really nice to meet you.'

Chapter 21

Toby had a mob of sheep in the yards when Dave and Jack arrived, and as they got closer, Dave could see they were lambs.

At the front of the race was a set of scales, and at the back there was a black and tan kelpie, energetically barking and herding the lambs into the raceway. Toby was at the front, reading the weights, and Meg was halfway down, making sure the lambs couldn't turn around.

'G'day, what are you fellas doing back here?' Toby asked as he pushed another lamb into the crate, recorded the weight, then ran a blue rattle mark down its back. Instead of letting it straight through with the rest of the mob, he opened a side gate and let it through to where about fifty lambs, all with blue stripes, were milling around.

'The blue line of death, huh?' Dave said. 'The agricultural answer to the IT blue screen of death! How are you, Meg?'

She waved but didn't say anything. She had a handkerchief tied around her nose and mouth to protect them from the dust.

'Getting rid of what's ready to go to market,' Toby said. 'No point in them staying here eating when someone could be eating them.'

'Look in great nick for this time of the year.'

'I run a feedlot, so there's always some ready. Background them on stubbles, after harvest, then put them straight onto grain. They go like the clappers once they're used to the diet.' He ran a red mark down the next one and put it in a different pen.

'What's the difference?' Dave asked, indicating the three different mobs. There was a large mob Toby had put straight out the front of the race that didn't have any marks on them at all.

'Blue is ready for market, red is the right weight to go into the feedlot, and the others, they'll be put back on stubbles; hoping to get a few more kilos on them before they go into the feedlot. I don't like feeding until they're a certain weight. Costs too much to get the extra kilos on them.'

Dave watched as Toby methodically checked the weight and decided which pen the lamb was going to be put in. 'Looks like you've got more to go back on stubbles than anything.' He kicked at the ground and noted the grain coming through in the shit. Classic sign the lambs were on a grain diet.

'I've already got four thousand in the feedlot. This is the next background mob to go in, so it's unusual to have a lot going back into the paddock.'

The kelpie barked and pushed a bit too hard, and a few lambs doubled back on him and smashed their heads into the fence, before jumping up again and running back to the raceway.

'Jip!' Toby roared. 'Siddown, you bloody mongrel!'

The dog, with his tongue hanging out and puffing heavily, gave Toby a reproachful look as if to say, *C'mon, boss, it was only a bit of fun.*

'Yeah, all fun and games until one breaks its neck,' Toby grumbled. 'Good lamb worth one hundred and fifty bucks and he rams its head into the yards and kills it. Can't afford to have those types of things happen. Got to have much better control over the dog. I'm going to do a low-stress stock-handling course, see if I can get a better handle on Jip. He's young, has got too much energy and hasn't grown a brain yet.'

'That's kelpies for you, isn't it?' Jack said. 'They'd work in the sheep yards all day and still run home at night.'

Toby nodded in agreement, his eyes on the readout and hands on the levers that worked the crate.

'I've heard about those low-stress courses. Supposed to be very good.' Dave leaned against the yards and adjusted his hat. 'I know a couple from up north who've done them. They run a team of dogs now; in high demand for mustering, apparently.'

'I'd just like control over one, don't need a whole team!' Toby said with a wry smile. The last lamb entered the crate with Jip at its heels. He dropped and never took his eyes off it, while Toby finished and set it off into the feedlot mob.

'Go back,' Toby said and Jip effortlessly soared over the railings and loped around the edge of the compound, gathering all the lambs together and pushing them towards the gate.

Meg had run over to open the gate, which led out into what looked to Dave like barley stubble. The sheep streamed through, their heads down. They ran until they went over the dam bank, presumably straight to the water's edge for a drink.

'So how can I help you fellas?' Toby asked again. He took out a notebook and wrote down some figures, snapped it shut and turned to look at them.

'We'd like to talk to you about the sheep Guy Wood has reported stolen,' Jack said.

A deep frown appeared on Toby's face. He looked down, hoisted up his jeans and adjusted his ten-gallon hat before squinting up at Dave.

'Why do you want to talk to me? He's confused. Never makes any sense. He won't be missing any sheep.'

'Actually, we have had more information come to light that indicates he's had some wool stolen. We thought we'd look into the sheep side of things a bit more and make sure you weren't missing anything yourself.'

'Wool stolen? Really? Well, you'd better come up to the house for a cold drink and tell me all about it.'

In the house, Meg put a cold jug of water and a bottle of cordial in front of Dave and Jack, before hurrying off to the bathroom after Toby to wash her face.

Toby came out drying his hands and face, threw the towel over the back of the chair and stood in front of the airconditioner, letting it blow on his hair.

'It doesn't seem to be getting any cooler,' he sighed. 'Sometimes I'd give anything for a slight breeze to get rid of the flies and dry the sweat, but then a bloody great gale starts and we get a dust storm! So maybe it's better when it's hot.'

'So many people are commenting on the heat this year,' Dave agreed. 'It's summer in the mid north, though. I'm think we should expect it to be warm.'

'True.'

'Maybe a break at the beach would be a good idea?'

'That's the trouble with having stock. They need work all year round. January used to be the month for holidays, but not any more. If I'm not making mixes, I'm feeding the lambs, or checking waters, or weighing lambs for market.'

Dave poured himself a glass of water and then offered the jug to everyone else. 'Where will the blue stripes go? Over the hooks or into the saleyards?'

'Over the hooks. Most people around here sell through the yards—lots of buyers around who can push the price up at the yards. But I've got a deal with one of the abattoirs who sell to the chain supermarkets. They look after me. I've got a consistent product and they like that.'

Dave nodded his understanding.

'So old man Wood has had some wool stolen?' Toby asked.

'What?' The surprise in Meg's voice was clear as she stood at the sink, filling the kettle from the tap. 'What's happened?'

'We're still investigating,' Dave said, 'but we do believe there have been twenty bales stolen from his shearing shed. Have you noticed anything strange, or are you missing anything?' he asked Toby.

'I don't think so, but I haven't had my ewes in the yards for a while. We shore back in October and there hasn't been any reason to get them back in. I put the rams over them, but I took the rams to them rather than bringing them in.'

'We know exactly how many feedlot lambs we have, though, and all the lambs in the paddocks. We're not missing any of them because we deal with them all the time. I don't think I've seen anything odd,' Meg put in. 'Oh, except the ute we keep hearing. Remember, Toby?'

'Oh yeah, I still haven't worked out who owns it. Must be a young bloke who's just got his licence or a new car. I'm finding skids all over the road. You would have seen them coming out.'

'Hmm, I did see some,' Jack nodded. 'Have you seen the ute?'

'Nope, I've only heard it. You know how noise travels so far when it's quiet and still. You can hear the engine from miles away, how he runs through the gears. I've never bothered to go and have a look to see if I can see it. He'll get sick of it soon enough. Happens this time every year. Young blokes leaving school, bit of independence, new car. You know how it is.'

Dave jotted down a note. 'Not missing any tools, or diesel?'

'Not that I'm aware of, but I'd have to say we haven't really been checking. We'll keep an eye out and if we notice anything we'll give you a call.'

'That would be great.' Jack handed over his card.

'So how did these bales go missing? And when? Sounds far-fetched to me.'

'I can guarantee you that nothing is too implausible out here. You'd not believe some of the cases I've worked,' Dave said with a grin.

'I'm not clear what you're expecting from me. Do you think I stole them? I don't think I have any bushrangers in my family.' Toby crossed his arms and looked at Dave, a glimmer of humour in his eyes.

'Oh, Toby, don't be silly, of course he doesn't!' Meg said.

'No, Meg's right. Not at all,' Dave responded carefully. 'I'm trying to establish facts. And, really, all I'm wanting from you now is, firstly, to know whether you've seen anything odd. You've told us about the ute, but has anyone driven onto your farm recently, saying they were lost or looking for people who don't live here? Have the dogs barked at odd times . . . You know, that type of thing. And, secondly, if you think you've had anything taken? Which you don't.'

'I can get the sheep in and count them if you need me to,' Toby offered.

'That's completely up to you. Often farmers don't realise they're missing stock until they muster, so it's months before we get to be involved in an investigation—that's if anyone reports it.'

Toby shifted uncomfortably. 'Feels a bit strange to think someone might have been on the farm without me knowing,'

'It can feel like a violation, that's for sure,' Dave agreed.

Meg pushed her hair back from her face and put her arms around herself. 'Do you think whoever did it is dangerous?' she asked with a concerned frown.

'Anyone who is interrupted doing something illegal is potentially dangerous,' Dave answered. 'Stay away from them and call the police. Don't ever try and stop them yourself.'

Toby moved over to her and put his arm around her shoulders. 'Don't stress about it. No one's gonna come here. The dogs wouldn't let them on the place.'

Time to change the subject, Dave thought, and opened his mouth, but Jack beat him to it.

'Did it annoy you having to pay for the boundary fence all by yourself?'

Toby refocused on Jack. 'Yeah, it did.' He took his arm away from Meg, put his hands on the table and leaned towards the policeman. 'It stuck in my throat. Tight old bugger over there, probably got more money than a bull could shit and he wouldn't put anything towards it. Yeah, it annoyed me, all right.'

'But like you said, we'll buy the place in the end, so it was going to be an investment, really,' Meg soothed.

'And you didn't think of trying to recoup the costs anyway? Law court, that type of thing?' Dave asked.

'I did, actually,' Toby admitted. 'But when I talked it through with Dad, like I told you before, he said not to worry about it. In the end, that was good advice because it's certainly made running my stock easier. I'm not forever having to jet for lice. Put it this way, in the long run I've saved more money than it cost me to put the fence up in the first place.'

Dave nodded. 'Well, if you do notice something, make sure to let us know.' He took a card out of his pocket and placed it next to Jack's. 'We'll be more than happy to come out and take a look.'

They stood and Jack picked up the glasses to take them to the sink.

'Oh, by the way,' Dave said, 'is it quite usual to store wool for long periods of time?'

'Sure. If the price isn't great because of an oversupply, or you've got a tax problem. It's one of the few commodities in farming you can store and sell when you want to. Grain you can too, but that can be risky. If you're storing on-farm—you know, if weevils get into it, or something happens, then you wouldn't be able to deliver it. You've got to weigh up the options of keeping it in your shed or silo, or in a store where it's safe and covered by insurance. It would only take a fire or natural disaster to come through and you could lose thousands of dollars' worth of income. Most companies charge some type of storage fee, whereas you don't have that on a farm.' He paused. 'But Guy is old-school and I imagine that would mean he wouldn't think about storing it anywhere other than his place.'

Dave held out his hand. 'Thanks for your time. We'll be touching base with other farmers around the district to see if there's been any thefts that haven't been reported; maybe you could mention this to your friends too. Get them to give us a call if there's any concerns.'

Chapter 22

'G'day, Alice, it's Dave Burrows from Barker Police Station here. How are you?'

'Dave! Great to hear from you. To what do I owe the pleasure?'

He could hear the urgency in her tone and assumed she was on a deadline. Radio announcers always ran against the clock.

'Could I get a segment on your show today? I want to put some feelers out to the public about a case.'

'Can't do today,' she said. 'Maybe tomorrow, 4.45 p.m. That okay?'

'Perfect.'

'I'll call in the morning and get a grip on what you want to talk about, okay? Same number?'

'As always. Talk to you then.' He hung up the phone and wrote a note in his diary to make sure he remembered.

After he and Jack had visited Toby and Meg, they'd called in on three other farmers on the way back into town. They all told the same story: hadn't noticed anything odd, hadn't noticed anything stolen. Didn't mean it hadn't been, just they hadn't noticed it yet. At each farm the vehicle doing burn-outs was mentioned, but Dave had pretty much concluded it wasn't anything to be concerned about. Criminals usually preferred silence to drawing attention to themselves.

When they had arrived back at the police station, there had been a message waiting for them from Goanna Harris, Guy's neighbour. He'd had a tank of diesel drained or stolen, and his neighbour on the other side, Peter O'Neil, was missing some tools. Dave had noted it all down and issued an incident report so they could make an insurance claim but, realistically, unless they caught someone in the act of taking those smaller items, there wasn't much they could do.

'I'm heading back to the church,' he told Jack now. 'Why don't you head out on a patrol?'

'Sure, might even call into some more farmers in Guy's area, since his neighbours seemed to have been touched up. Have a chat there.'

'No worries. Take it gently, though, won't you? Don't put anyone offside by making them think you're accusing them.'

'No worries, boss, I think I can manage that.' He shook his head in annoyance and grabbed his hat off the back of the chair.

'Right, catch you back here a bit later.'

Jack didn't wave.

'What's up with him?' he asked Joan.

'Don't know. Came in this morning in a foul mood. Maybe he's got girl troubles.'

'He hasn't got a girl.'

'Maybe that's the problem.'

Dave sighed. 'If anyone wants me, I'm at the church.'

Joan let out a peal of laughter. 'Praying for Jack? You'd better say two then.'

~

The room was exactly the way it had been yesterday, but there were four record books sitting on the desk and a note from Chris: *Help yourself to what you need.*

It took a good half-hour to find the birth of Guy's brother, Brett Wood.

> *5 October 1948: Today I brought into the house of the Lord, Brett Joseph Wood, second son of Warren and Joy Wood. Brother to Guy. I pray the Lord blesses their lives.*

'Got him!' Dave muttered. 'I want 1949 now . . .' He flicked through the next book but realised it was 1950. They must be out of order. Turning to the front of another book he glanced at the date: 1962.

Strange. He flicked through, letting the pages of beautiful handwriting move in front of his eyes. A name jumped out at him and he stopped, flicking back, trying to find it again.

> *6 June 1962: Today we buried the earthly body of Joy Anne Wood, wife of Warren and mother to Guy and Brett. Plot*

78 in the cemetery. Born on 12 April 1922, leaving this world on the 4 June 1962. A horseriding accident.

'Shit, the boys weren't that old,' Dave muttered, quickly calculating the dates. Guy was fourteen and his brother thirteen. Then Brett went to Nam and was killed six years later.

He took down more books from the shelves, trying to find the years from the Vietnam War to see if Brett's body had been returned and buried here. Apparently not, because the only reference he found was to a memorial service for three of the lads killed on the same day—10 July 1968.

'Tragic,' Dave said to himself. He left the record books open at the pages he needed, then turned his attention back to 1949.

An hour later he got up and stretched, his neck and shoulders sore from sitting in the same position for so long.

'How's it going, Dave?' Chris asked from the doorway. 'I'm sorry I wasn't here to meet you. I was called out.'

'Good, thanks, Chris. I've found some of what I was looking for. Just not another child. I'm halfway through 1952. But if she's not in here, that's four years after the last baby was born, so there may not have been any more.'

'Quite possible. If there were stillborns and they were given a Christian burial, they'd be recorded here too, but not if there were any miscarriages or if they were buried on a farm somewhere,' Chris noted.

'Maybe she had three or four miscarriages before she managed to have another baby. Anyway, I'll keep looking. I don't give up easily.' He flashed a smile at Chris. 'Oh, by the way, there were a couple of the books out of date order.' He indicated the ones stacked on the edge of the desk. 'The year 1962 was here—although I'm pleased it was, because I found that Guy's mother died that year.'

Chris moved into the room and looked down at the book. 'That should narrow your search down.' He read the entry. 'So young,' he said with a sad shake of his head.

Dave stretched out his neck muscles and sat down again. 'Everyone seemed to die young back then,' he observed. 'Tough times in tough country.'

'Very true. Not having easy access to medical treatment certainly made for more deaths than there should have been.'

'Before I forget,' Dave said, holding up his hand. 'Is Alan McSweeny still alive?'

'He is. He's in Parish Care in Adelaide. It's a nursing home for ministers and priests.'

'Is he . . . ?' Dave searched for the right words.

'With it?' Chris asked with a smile. 'He's pretty good for ninety. I saw him last time I went down to Adelaide and he asked about many of the parishioners by name. Some of them have passed, and of course that made him sad, but he could still remember them and some of the jokes they shared. Humour, as you picked up yesterday, is very important to Alan.'

Dave flicked a page and ran his eyes down the entries, looking for familiar names. 'I better keep looking; otherwise, I'll be late and Kim will wonder where I am.' He glanced at his watch. 'Bugger, only another half an hour.'

'Get to it, Dave,' Chris said. 'I'll be out here if you need me.'

Dave ran his finger down the column of names, saying them aloud: 'Osborne, Forrest, Richard, Fullwood . . .' He'd perfected his method by now and it only took a minute to read both pages of the large book, then flick over to the next page. 'Miller, Pearce, Needer, Smith, Wood, Hunter.' He shook himself and looked two lines up. 'Wood.' He looked up, then down again. 'Wood! You little beauty!'

3 August 1952: Warren and Joy Wood welcomed a little girl, Rachael Carol, into the house of the Lord. The baptism was straightforward.

Dave reread the entry. There was something wrong with it. Alan McSweeny always made some comment about praying for their lives to be blessed. The entry felt too short and emotionless, unlike Alan's other posts.

He picked up the book and photocopied the page, then repeated the action for Joy's death and Brett's christening. He'd do some more research, but he could now say he'd solved one mystery. The Woods had had a daughter.

But now there was another one. What had happened to her?

~

'In three, two, one. Good afternoon, I'm Alice Burton on ABC radio and you're listening to the Drive program. It's 4.45 p.m. and the temperature is thirty-nine degrees here in Port Pirie. I hope today is treating you well and you're able to stay cool somewhere.

'My next guest is a regular on the show. Detective Dave Burrows from Barker Police Station joins us for another update on police matters in the mid north. How are you today, Detective?'

'Hi, Alice, great to be here. Thanks for your time today.'

'I understand you have some information you'd like to make the public aware of?'

'Yes, Alice. There have been reports of farm theft in the Barker area recently, and I'd like to ask everyone to keep an eye out for any strange behaviours, cars you haven't seen before, or the same car in the same place over a period of time. Perhaps someone arriving at a homestead needing directions, or looking for a person who doesn't live there. Criminals have ingenious ways of casing people's places.'

'Can you tell us what's been taken?'

'At this stage, tools and diesel; however, we are looking into some missing bales of wool.'

'Wool?' Alice sounded surprised. 'That would have taken some doing. The bales aren't light.'

'You're right there. A ute or a truck would have been needed.'

'I guess if someone knows something, you'd ask them to give you a call?'

'Yes, Alice.' He recited the station's phone number before continuing. 'We ask farmers and stations owners to be vigilant in their security and to check their sheds and stock to see if anything has been taken.'

'Gee, sounds like you've got your work cut out for you, Detective. Do you have any leads at all?'

'We're still in the early stages of our investigation, Alice. Any information would be gratefully received.'

'Sure, and what would be the best advice you could give to farmers and people living in isolated areas?'

'Often, people living away from towns forget the basics of home security. Even if you're living somewhere quite isolated, it's still imperative you remember to lock up and stay aware of your surroundings.'

'Thanks for coming on the show, Detective Burrows. We hope you find the perpetrator. It's five away from five and here's "I Shot the Sheriff" by Bob Marley to lead you into the news.'

Dave waited until he knew she was off air before saying, 'Great choice of song, Alice! That's the way to get people to help me.'

'I thought it was perfect,' she laughed down the phone line.

'Appreciate you getting me on air, thanks for that. We'll have to start up our monthly musings section again. Seem to have let that slide.'

'You know what it's like, Dave, the call on airtime is huge. Give me a yell anytime you need help.'

The clunk of the phone being hung up echoed in his ear. He sighed. Five o'clock. Tonight, he decided, he was having a beer instead of a walk.

~

'So you really found a record of the christening?' Kim asked as she poured herself a glass of wine and put a beer in front of Dave.

He was sitting at the table in the roadhouse Kim ran, a large T-bone steak, covered in mushroom sauce, and chips in front of him. He'd decided that since he was breaking the rules, he might as well break them properly.

'And the funeral of the mother and death of the brother.'

'Why wouldn't have Guy told you about her, do you think?'

'I really don't know. Short of going through all the record books, it's not going to be easy to find her date of death, and I want to know if they reported it.'

Kim grinned wickedly. 'What if she didn't die? What if she ran away or was sold or—'

'This is Australia, not a third world country!' He took a mouthful. 'God, that's good.'

Kim looked down at the butter chicken she'd ordered and poked at it with her fork.

'How's the new girl working out?' Dave asked, nodding towards the kitchen.

'Okay. She knows enough to cover for me when I'm not here. Although this chicken doesn't look like how I'd make it.'

Kim had hired a kitchen hand, to give her some extra time at home to focus on the new business she'd set up last year: running meals to people who had family in hospitals and needed a bit of extra support. Her first client had been Fiona Forrest, a friend she'd met through the roadhouse and whose husband's suicide Dave had been investigating. Since then it had taken off. Elderly men whose wives had been taken to hospital, or dads who had to look after a couple of kids while Mum was in hospital having a baby, were her biggest clients. Kim, with her big heart and large laugh, would drop the meals in, have a chat, then move on to the next house. She didn't just love it, she *revelled* in helping people.

Dave reached over and shovelled some of Kim's dinner onto his fork, then chewed with great concentration.

'Still pretty good,' he said. 'But I don't think she's going to replace you.'

Kim smiled at him and took a sip of wine. 'What are you going to do about this—what was the daughter's name?'

'Rachael Carol Wood. Now I've found she existed, I really need to know what's happened to her. That's the way my mind works. There are a few things troubling me, though.'

She raised her eyebrows at him and waited.

'Okay, one: why didn't Guy tell me when I asked? He would have been five when she was born. Not an age you'd forget there was a newborn baby in the house. Agree?'

'Of course.'

'Right, so, two: why wasn't her death reported?'

'How do you know it wasn't?'

'I don't,' Dave admitted. 'But I did send an enquiry off to the Information Release Centre and I haven't heard anything back. It doesn't usually take too long for them to respond. And I'm going on a hunch, because if the town didn't know the girl existed, then the family couldn't have spent much time with other people, or else they didn't take the child with them if they did. Again, that begs the question why.'

'Yes, I agree with that too.'

'And, three: why didn't the town know she existed?'

Kim shrugged.

'The last one—actually, I think it's two—how did she die and where is she buried?'

Chapter 23

Brianna picked up the phone and dialled Caleb's number. She'd put it off for too long.

It rang twice then switched to message bank.

'Thanks for calling Caleb Donahue of Martin and McIntyre. I'm unavailable right now, but please leave . . .' Brianna listened to the message, all the while trying to work out what to say.

'Hi, Caleb, I'm wondering if you're having affair with the "date" you keep taking to functions?'

Or perhaps: *'I saw the photo of you and Heidi. You look . . . close. Anything going on there?'*

There was also the option of: *'Heidi is pretty. You guys look good together.'*

None of them was appropriate, she knew, but the snarky voice in her head kept suggesting options, until the message was finished.

Eventually she decided on: 'Hi, it's me. Call when you can.'

Stabbing at the disconnect button, she blew out a long breath. Nothing she could do now except wait for his call back. Slapping her hands on her thighs, she got up and went to the shed. She checked the oil and water in the John Deere tractor and refilled the hydraulic oil. Russell had told her about the small leak in the three-point linkage. If it didn't have enough oil, the hay feed-out cart wouldn't work and she wouldn't be able to feed the cows.

Brianna started the tractor and backed into the cart, before loading it with hay and trundling down the laneway to the cows.

She still couldn't work out how she'd got to the point where she needed to ask Caleb about Heidi. The image of the two of them together wouldn't leave her mind. Maybe Heidi was the reason he hadn't wanted her to take the kids to Perth and spend a week up there. Maybe he could, in fact, spend more time at home but chose not because of Heidi. Maybe, maybe, maybe.

'Or maybe,' she muttered to herself as the cattle heard the tractor and started to run towards her, 'I've blown it way out of proportion and there is nothing going on.'

The cattle knew it was feed time by the sound of the tractor engine and they were bellowing as they lined the fence and followed her along to the gate. She smiled; the cattle distracted her from her thoughts for a little while. These were her father's 'babies'. He was the cattle man, she was the sheep woman. Her white Suffolk stud ewes were her pride and joy, and Russell could take or leave sheep, although he grudgingly admitted they were helpful in the cropping program. However, her part of Le-Nue was more suited to cattle, so feeding them was her job.

'Are you lot going to be well mannered today?' she asked, climbing down to open the gate. 'Ha! Get away with you,' she yelled at them, to make them move back from the gate. They were just as likely to wander out and start chewing on the hay before she'd even managed to get through the gate, the way they were behaving. 'It's not like you're starving,' she told them. 'Jenny Craig would be good for you all.'

Finally she managed to shift them, and get the tractor through and to the area where she fed the hay. Her father had always taught her to feed it in one spot, so only one part of the paddock would blow when things got really dry. The constant hooves following the hay powdered the grass up quickly and left the area bare.

Fishing out her pocket knife from the console, she jumped down and cut the netting before making sure it was safe to roll out.

In the tractor again, she turned to watch out the back window as the hay rolled out, roll by roll, with the shiny Angus cattle chasing her, trying to get the first and sweetest mouthful.

When she'd finished, Brianna got out of the tractor again and started to roll up the netting. She'd seen cattle try to eat the wrapping and get it stuck in their mouths or stomach. The ending wasn't pretty.

The cow with tag K65 watched her while she munched on the hay. Knowing she was the quietest of the mob, Brianna walked slowly over to her, watching her large brown eyes. She picked up a bit of hay and held it out to her.

K65 regarded her carefully before taking a step towards her.

'Hi there, gorgeous. You're looking rather beautiful today. So shiny and fat. I'm a bit proud we've got you this far into the summer and you girls haven't lost much condition at all. I reckon it all goes back to the quality of the hay we made last season and not overstocking.'

K65 stretched her neck out to sniff Brianna's hand. It tickled, but she held still, willing the cow to take it. Her tongue twisted out and Brianna felt the roughness of it on her skin, before K65 took the hay into her mouth and stepped back, still watching her carefully.

Taylor Swift music filled the air with a loud, sharp chorus of 'Shake it off'. For a split second the whole mob was still, but then their heads jerked up and they shied away from the noise, cantering in the direction of the dam.

'Shit,' Brianna said, frowning. 'Oh.' It was Caleb.

'Hi,' she said and climbed back into the tractor, lifted up the three-point linkage and headed towards the gate.

'What's up?' He sounded distracted.

'Nothing really. Wanted to say hi.'

'It's court day, Bri. I'm just about to head over there.'

To her it sounded like he was chiding her. 'Sure, no worries. I'll let you go.' She waited for a moment. 'Who are you working the case with?'

'Ah,' he sounded distracted.

Imagining him with the phone tucked in between his ear and shoulder, packing his briefcase, made her smile. He was off to save the world in his own small way. To make a difference.

Then she remembered Heidi.

Finally he named two other lawyers Bri had heard him talk about.

'Not Heidi?'

'Heidi? What, no. She's in finance, not criminal. Why?'

'I was just wondering.'

'I haven't got time for this now, Bri.'

Anger surged through her. 'Time for what? A discussion of whether you're having an affair or not?'

Pause.

'I beg your pardon?'

Now she had his full attention.

'I saw the photo of the two of you.'

'And?' His voice was dangerously low.

'You looked . . .' She suddenly floundered. Fuck, she shouldn't have made this phone call. Wrong time, wrong place, wrong everything. 'Nothing. Look, I'm sorry. Ignore me. Ignore the call. I'm really sorry.'

'No, I think you'd better explain what you mean.'

'I just thought . . . I don't know.'

A tense pause before Caleb said, 'I can't believe you would even think I'd have an affair. That shows just how far apart we've grown.'

She could hear him swallow hard and she cursed herself. She cursed Angie for putting the thought into her head.

But if you didn't have a tiny thought it could be true, you wouldn't have even considered the idea, a little voice inside her heart told her.

'Thanks for the faith, Brianna,' he finished, his tone hard.

Then he was gone.

The tears started even before he'd finished speaking and she let the phone fall from her hands onto the tractor floor. Leaning her head against the window, she cried until she didn't have any tears left.

Chapter 24

'I don't understand your father,' Angie said to Brianna as she took the glass of wine Brianna held out to her.

Brianna didn't say anything, but had a small sip of her drink. Angie was the last person she wanted to see right now. Her phone had remained quiet since she'd spoken to Caleb. She knew she'd made a dreadful mistake to have rung him.

'I was only trying to *protect* Beau. I know how busy you always are and, like I've said time and time again, both boys should be able to swim *much better* than they can. After all, we live right next to one of the best beaches in the world. Being farm kids, they need to be able to get themselves out of trouble if they *accidentally* fall into a dam or something of the like; a *tank* even, God forbid! I just yelled before I could stop myself. I think I even swore. Told him to sit his arse down.'

'I appreciate you were thinking about the boys,' Brianna said. 'But—' It was time to stand up to this woman.

'Russell was so *angry* with me,' Angie interrupted. 'I can't understand why. He completely overreacted.' She gave a little sniff and touched her finger to the corner of her eye. 'I was so *worried* that something might go wrong. Can you *imagine* if he'd fallen in and we hadn't been able to get to him in time? The water is all muddy and you can't see to the bottom. He would have sunk and we wouldn't have been able to see where he was to fish him out.'

Oh God! she thought. Her stomach lurched with horror as she imagined that scenario. *God, Angie was right! Damn it all, she was right.*

'And the water is so *cold* in dams. Everyone knows you shouldn't swim in them, so if Russell had gone out to get Beau and got cramp because it was so cold, then he could have gone under too! Imagine losing them both in one accident!'

Brianna put her hand to her chest. She could see it all happening: the frantic splashing, the cries. Beau's frightened face gasping for air, then slipping under the water. Russell running and jumping in, searching, desperate grasping at air, then a yell of pain, and slowly he disappeared too. She couldn't lose her kids, her dad. She'd already lost Caleb, she was sure, but she could never, ever lose her kids.

'It happens too, doesn't it? I've heard of a lot of adults who drown trying to save their kids.'

Brianna refocused, trying to control her heart, which seemed to have started racing. 'Sorry?'

Angie reached over and grabbed her hand. 'I'm sorry I got a little cross with Beau but, really, I did have his best interest in mind.'

'It's okay, Angie,' Brianna answered. The words wanted to stick in her throat, but she had to admit Angie could have been right. 'Look, it's fine. Thankfully, nothing happened. The boys were upset, but I understand why you reacted so strongly. Don't worry about it.'

'Oh, *thank you* for understanding, Bri. I wouldn't want us to fall out over anything so silly. And all because I got a little cross with Beau.'

A little cross? Beau hadn't told it like that. He'd said, 'She screamed like a witch, Mum, and told Granda off real bad.' Her dad hadn't said anything other than 'Angie got a little uptight at the dam today, but I think we've got it all sorted.'

'Did you want another glass of wine?' Brianna looked at Angie's empty glass, which she was sure she'd only just filled.

'No, thanks. I'd better get going. I've got a meeting tonight. The local progressive women's day is coming up and we're still organising it. You should come along, Bri. Get you off the farm and doing something different. You look a little peaky. You could do with a change of scenery.'

'Oh no, that's not my cup of tea, thanks very much.' She got up and took Angie's glass to the sink. What she really wanted to do was cry and cry and perhaps drink a bottle of wine. She would do neither because her kids needed her.

'Come on, now. You could come with me and I'd *introduce* you around. Make sure you weren't left standing on your own. Nothing *worse*, when you go into those things by yourself and *everyone* turns to look at you.' Angie took a breath. 'Nina sometimes goes,' she added as a sweetener.

Brianna gritted her teeth, all her generous feelings towards Angie gone. 'No. Thanks anyway.'

'The offer is always there. Right, well, I'll be off then. I'll just say goodbye to the Terrors.'

Brianna had to hurry to keep up with her as she strode outside to where the boys were on the motorbike again. Brianna motioned at the boys to stop and come over. They seemed to take a fraction longer than normal to pull up.

'See you later, kidlets,' Angie said when the bike had been switched off. 'I'll bring a chocolate cake next time I come over.' She beamed at them.

'Bye,' they said simultaneously and then shoved their helmets back on, before roaring off in a cloud of dust.

Angie coughed as the dust covered them both.

Wait until I get hold of you two later, Brianna thought. She turned her attention back to Angie.

'See you next time,' she said.

'Of course, *darling*.' Angie leaned in and air-kissed Brianna's cheek. 'Oh, by the way, I've been wanting to say to you since Trent's accident, if you ever want to hear any stories about your mother . . . I know I've offered before but . . .' Her voice faded and Brianna's stomach curled.

Russell always told stories of Josie with love and affection. Angie's could be funny and full of teenage adventures, but they were not always that way. The first anecdote Angie had ever related was about a time she and Josie had gone exploring together.

'Your mother really loved being out in the bush. She knew every tree and plant and bird and always managed to find fox holes. One day we'd been out all day—you could do that back then—and it was nearly dark. Josie was a bit like a Boy Scout, always prepared, so she had a torch with her. This day, she found a really large fox hole—large enough to crawl down into it. Josie wanted to have a look down there—God knows why. All I could imagine was snakes writhing in the darkness.' She shuddered. 'So, your mum tried to wriggle down into it headfirst, torch outstretched. She got in to her waist.

'I can still hear her calling out, "Check this out, Angie, there's no foxes. Just an empty den, but there's feathers and all sorts that he's dragged back here."' Angie took another shuddering breath. 'Then all of a sudden the dirt seemed to close in around her. All I could see was her legs! The top of the hole had caved in on her!'

Brianna could remember the terror and claustrophobia she'd felt when Angie had relayed the story for the first time. She felt them again now, remembering.

No, she didn't want to hear memories like that.

Brianna focused back on Angie's words.

'I've been thinking about Josie a lot lately. I guess when Trent went missing it was hard not to think about her. I have some lovely stories I'd like to share with you. When the time is right.'

~

'Has she done that to you too?'

Brianna was on her way to read the boys a story, but she stopped at the games-room door. It sounded like the boys were talking seriously.

'What, get all angry like that?' Trent said.

'Yeah, you should have seen her today. Her eyes stuck out and she went all red. She looked like a . . . a . . . angry bull. Snorting and stuff. I thought she was so angry she was going to push Granda into the dam!'

'I don't like her.'

'Cos she gets angry with you?'

'I dunno.' Brianna could almost hear Trent shrug. 'Just don't.'

Beau persisted. 'Have you seen her yell?'

'Yeah, but not bad. She gets grumpy and tells me what to do all the time. She can't do that cos she's not family. Only family are allowed to tell me what to do. Mum, Dad and Granda.'

'Good idea. I'm going to do that too. No teachers or nothing.'

'Nah, you gotta do what the teachers say.'

Brianna smiled despite what she was hearing. She pushed open the door and stuck her head into the games room. 'Bedtime,' she said.

'Aw, Mum. Do we have to?' Trent asked. He was sitting with his foot up on the chair reading an Alex Rider book and Beau was sitting in the corner, pushing a train along the ground.

'Well, I guess I could sit here for a little while and talk to you,' she answered, coming into the room. 'How's your foot, Trent?' As she walked by, she gave the boot an affectionate pat.

'Okay. I'm sick of it, though,' he said, putting the book down.

'Good thing you didn't have to have a cast. Those things get so itchy!'

'This doesn't get itchy, but it's a pain in the arse.'

'Trent!' Brianna scolded. 'That's not a nice word. Where did you hear that from?'

'I dunno. Just heard it round.'

'Angie said it,' Beau said, looking up.

'Angie?' Brianna's voice rose in surprise. 'I can't imagine Angie using language like that. She's too proper for that.'

'She said it to me today. "Beau, you sit your arse down on that raft this instant."' He said it in a high and aggressive tone.

'Ah,' Brianna said. 'That's right. She told me she accidentally swore because she was so afraid for your safety.'

'I wasn't going to fall in,' Beau said in a scornful tone. 'Granda said I was fine too.' He looked at her proudly.

'Look, I don't think she'll do it again. It was unfortunate today, but luckily Granda was there to make sure everything was okay.'

'She scared me.'

'Did she, sweetheart?' Brianna motioned for him to come and sit on her lap. 'Sometimes when people get worried, they react in ways they usually wouldn't. I'm sure that's what happened with Angie today.'

'I was only doing what Granda told me he'd done when he was a kid. Sounded cool!'

'Uh-oh! If Granda did it, Angie might have been right to be worried. He was a tearaway, from all the stories I've heard.'

'Yeah,' Trent said. 'Granda did all sorts of fun things when he was a kid. I still don't know why we can't go and camp out on the beach overnight without any grownups.'

'We've been through this before,' Brianna said in a tone that didn't invite argument. 'Camping on the beach by yourselves isn't going to happen. Camping in the cave, closer to home, that's fine. She turned back to Beau, wanting to get to the bottom of what Angie had said. 'And what did Granda tell you he did that you felt you needed to copy?'

'Stand on the raft, out in the middle of the dam, on one leg.'

'Uh, at the risk of telling you what you already know, that's dangerous. What if you fell off?'

'But I didn't, Mum. Anyway, she shouldn't have shouted at me like that and she shouldn't have said nasty things to Granda.' He crossed his little arms and stared at her defiantly.

'I agree with you, Beau. However, Angie came and talked to me before she left today and said how scared she'd been. I think she just overreacted.'

'I've heard her yell at Granda before,' Trent said.

Brianna cocked her head. 'Have you?'

'Yeah. Well, more at the sheep in the yards. This one ewe wouldn't go down the drafting race. She tried and tried but it just wouldn't. Then she called it a bastard.'

Brianna allowed herself a small smile. 'I bet,' she said, giving Beau a hug, then putting him down and dropping a kiss on Trent's head, 'that she was talking to the sheep, not Granda. Sheep can be very, very stupid when they want to be and they can make even mild-mannered, patient people lose their temper. Right now it's bedtime. Which story am I reading tonight?'

Chapter 25

Anna woke to a soft hand on her head, pushing her hair back.

For the first time in days—or was it weeks—she felt safe. The room was cool and dark and her head was healing well. She thought she was almost normal again. Except she couldn't remember who she was.

'The police are here to talk to you, Anna,' Elspeth said. 'I'm going to bring them in now, but I'll be with you the whole time, okay? Did you want a moment to wash your face and sit up in a chair?'

'Do I have to talk to them?' Anna asked. 'I can't tell them anything.'

'I know, but they might have some information on you. Maybe someone has lodged a missing person report or something.'

Anna got out of bed and went to the window to look out. There were white, fluffy clouds drifting along in the blue sky, and the lady who lived across the road was sitting on her verandah, like she always did.

'What's that lady's name?' she asked.

'Oh, that's Mrs Turner,' Elspeth said, coming to stand next to her. 'She's always sitting out there. Sometimes she plays patience, other times she drinks a cup of tea, but mostly she just sits there and watches the world go by. Nothing too exciting happens here. A car might drive past or a dog might cock his leg on someone's rosebush—that's about the extent of it.'

Anna laughed. 'Okay, let's get this over with,' she said.

After she'd showered and changed, two men entered the room. Anna admitted they looked like real policemen, but the familiar feeling of fear started to trickle through her. She couldn't be sure. Maybe they were here to hurt her.

She felt the comforting hand of Elspeth on her shoulder and began to relax. Elspeth wouldn't let anything happen to her, of that she was sure.

After introductions, the younger of the two asked, 'What can you tell us about your injuries?'

'Nothing,' she answered. 'I remember waking up in a shed and everything hurting so badly, then going back to sleep or passing out. When I woke up the next time, I somehow got out of there and then I walked until the good Samaritan found me. He brought me here. I don't know his name. He walked me in, then left before I could ask. I wasn't in a fit state to even thank him . . .' Her voice trailed off.

'Let me get this right. You have no memory of how you came to be in the shed?'

'None. Just waking up there . . . I heard a rat . . . That's right, I heard a rat and it tried to climb on me.' She shivered. 'I was really thirsty. And then there was a dam. Yeah, a dam where I tried to wash all the blood off me. I drank a lot of water but I was still thirsty.' She looked down at her hands.

'Can you think of anything that might give us an idea of who you are?'

'Don't you think that if I could think of anything, I would have?' she snapped. 'I've tried, God knows I've tried . . .' She broke off as a sob escaped from her. 'I might have a family who loves me, children even. Do you think I'd stay in a hospital room all by myself if I had another option?'

The policeman broke eye contact with her and looked at the ground. 'Ah, well, yours is a very unusual case. I'm not quite sure what I should be asking.'

'I suggest then,' Elspeth put in, 'that you take the photos and details and leave, because I'm not going to have you upset my patient. I'm assuming there isn't a missing person report out on someone who looks like Anna?'

'We don't have any MP reports in South Australia right now.'

'Really? None?'

'No, ma'am.'

Anna realised he was very young. He and the doctor could be friends. She'd bet this was his first posting out here . . . wherever here was—she hadn't quite worked that out yet. Clearly he didn't have much of a clue. Perhaps he'd shove all her information into a file and not do anything about her at all. Half of her hoped he would spread her details all over Australia so someone might find her, but the other half of her hoped he'd do nothing. Maybe if she returned to her old life, she'd be right back in the situation that had got her in trouble in the first place.

She breathed a sigh of relief when the policemen left.

'That wasn't as optimistic as I'd hoped it might be,' Elspeth said with a sigh.

Anna sat on the edge of the bed and looked at her new friend steadily. 'Can I tell you something?'

Elspeth's head jerked up, wariness in her eyes. 'Don't tell me you know who you are? Or you've done something illegal?'

'No, no, no,' she answered, shaking her head hard. 'No. I just wonder if it was my old life that got me into trouble. Whether it's worth going back. Do you see?'

Elspeth blinked as she took in what Anna was saying. 'I guess I do. Maybe you were beaten by an abusive husband and left for dead. If that was the case, then you'd never want to go back.'

'Exactly. I had a dream last night. It seemed so real, but I didn't recognise anyone in it. I was up a tree and there was someone else there. We were playing hide and seek. There was lots of laughing and giggling, but the other person there . . . it didn't feel like another girl, but when I woke up I thought it must have been cos of all the laughing.' She paused.

'Anyway, something happened and the other person fell out of the tree. They were lying on the ground and I could see blood. Lots of blood. And the person never moved the whole time I was watching. I felt like I watched until I finally woke up.'

Chapter 26

'G'day, Guy. How are you today?' Dave got out of the car and held his hand out to the old man.

Guy was once again dressed in clean clothes, although Dave could see he'd spilled his breakfast down his shirt.

The old man squinted. 'You're the policeman, right?'

'That's me,' Dave said with a grin.

'You 'ere about me sheep?'

'Yep, but also the wool you're missing.'

Dave brushed away the flies that were buzzing around his eyes while he waited for Guy to connect the dots.

'That's right,' the old man finally said. 'Me twenty bales.' He nodded and his hand strayed down to pat Bob. Dave had worked out that Bob was Gus's security blanket. Whenever he wasn't sure about something, he needed to make sure the old dog was beside him. God only knew what would happen to Guy if Bob passed away before he did.

'That's it. Can we have a chat?'

'Course, come in.'

In the kitchen, Dave once again noticed Isabelle's influence. The kitchen was shiny and the floors clean. The musty smell had gone, replaced with that of disinfectant. On the table, papers were spread out and there was a cup of tea in the middle.

'Got a bit of mess 'ere.'

'Don't worry, you sit down. I'll tidy them up and leave them on the corner for you.' Dave reached down to start collecting them and Guy suddenly leaned forward.

'Don't touch 'em. They're none of your business.' His voice was strong and commanding and Dave backed away immediately.

'No problems, I'll put the kettle on instead.' He glanced down at the papers, wondering what was so secret about them, and saw the word *adoption*.

The old man clumsily gathered all the papers into an untidy pile and took them out of the room, leaving behind a wooden box, which, Dave assumed, they had been stored in. Making sure he wasn't in Guy's sight, he leaned over to look inside.

He saw the birth certificate for Rachael Carol Wood.

More proof.

Grabbing his phone, he snapped a quick photo, before lifting up the birth certificate to see if there was anything under it.

Damn. Empty.

He heard Guy returning to the kitchen, so he swung around and lifted the kettle up to refill it.

'You shouldn't go lookin' at things that don't concern you,' Guy said as he sat heavily at the table.

'Sorry, only trying to help,' Dave said, hoping he hadn't seen him take the photo. Changing the subject, he said, 'I've got a bit of bad news about your wool.'

'And what's that?'

Dave put a cup in front of him and the teapot—now nice and shiny—onto the coaster in the middle of the table, then sat down. He laid an envelope on the table and took some paperwork out of it.

'What's this?' Guy asked suspiciously.

'It's a theft report for your insurance company,' Dave explained. 'Unfortunately, we're at a dead end in investigating the theft of your wool. We've spoken to the local wool buyer and none of his clients have sold any wool out of their normal time frame. My guess is whoever stole it would have opened up all the bales, then re-baled under their brand and sold it that way. Sadly, the best we can do for you is give you a theft report so you can make a claim with your insurance company. I can help you with that, if needs be.'

Guy frowned. 'So you can't 'elp me at all?'

'Not with the wool,' Dave answered. 'I'm sorry. If we find the ewes, then there will be ways to tell they're yours—the earmark and so on. But wool . . . well, it's the perfect item to steal because there aren't any identifying features.'

'Yeah, yeah,' Guy said. 'I understand that. Clever sods. What about me sheep?'

'We've spoken with your neighbours, Goanna Harris and Peter O'Neil. Those two blokes have had a few little items go missing—tools, diesel. But again, unless I can lay my eyes on the items, there's not much I can do.

'Jack took a drive around their farms to see if there was any chance the sheep could've got through the fence, and we've also talked to Toby Jones again. The investigation is still ongoing, but to be honest, Guy, I'm not holding out a lot of hope. Again, unless the saleyards pick up your earmark and realise it's not you who is selling the animals, we're a bit hamstrung.'

'Do I get one of these for the sheep too?' He waved the theft report at Dave.

'Sure, if I can prove they've been stolen. So I'll need your shearing figures, last year's tax return with your opening and closing stock numbers, and all your sales and purchases for the last twelve months. Then I'll need to get the stock agent and we'll do a muster of your farm and count everything on it. If I can cross-reference numbers and find a deficit, I can certainly write you another theft report.'

'Then do it,' Guy said. 'I got nothin' to 'ide. I know I'm right.'

'Okay, no problems, I'll organise a stock agent. Who do you usually use?'

'Rob Walker with Landmark.'

'Can I have all the other papers, and once I've collated all the information, then I'll be able to organise it.'

Guy nodded. 'Right, you pour, I'll get 'em.'

'Tell me a bit about your family,' Dave called as he was pouring the tea. 'You've been here a long time.'

'Yeah. It was just me and Dad for a lot o' years,' Guy said as he sat back down and handed Dave another large file. 'Once me brother died. We worked together—real close, we were. Fenced and bought stock. Put crops in. Hard country to make a living off when there's a drought and we had a few of them in the early years. I can remember seeing the whole land moving with rabbits. Mongrel things. They'd eat any skerrick of grass almost before it was outta the ground. Oh, I seen lotsa things.'

'And your mother?' Dave lifted the cup to his lips, watching Guy carefully.

Guy's face softened. 'Ah, me mum, she was a good sort. Had the softest voice I ever remember. 'Ad a real elegant way o' talking. Not like me and me dad. We're Australian; like, she was more, I dunno, English.

'Never quite understood how she and me dad got together. Different, they were.'

'She sounds lovely.'

'Oh, Ma was. Tragedy the way she died.' He seemed to gather himself and took another sip of tea.

'How did she die?'

'Horseriding accident. When I was fourteen. Don't really know what happened to her but my theory is the horse got its hoof caught in a rabbit hole and went down. She was thrown off and broke 'er neck. I remember the horse coming trotting into the yards, with 'is reins dragging on the ground, but Mum wasn't anywhere around. We had to go looking for her.' He drew in a shaky breath. 'Shouldn't upset me after all this time, but it still does. Guess it's cos it was me who found her.'

'Hard scene to go to at fourteen,' Dave answered in a low voice. 'Hard at any age, but you were very young.'

'It was the way of things back then,' Guy answered. 'Life was tough and we had to be tougher. I looked after me little brother as much as I could, and me dad. You know, with the cooking and things. But then Brett went to Vietnam and never came home. Just me an' dad.'

❧

After Dave left Guy, he called Kim.

'Can you do me a favour?' he asked, when she picked up.

'Oh, honey, I can do you any favour you want,' Kim purred down the phone.

Laughing, he said, 'Can I keep that for tonight? I know what I want to do to you.'

'Oh, tell me. I could do with a little excitement.'

'First, I'd pour you a glass of wine and massage your shoulders,' he deepened his voice, knowing how much she loved it when he did. 'Then I'd kiss you . . .' He heard her let out a wanting sigh.

'You'd better stop unless you can come home right now,' she said in a throaty voice.

'I'd love to, babe, I really would. But I'm about forty minutes out of town.'

'That's what I was afraid of. Okay, what's the favour?'

'Can you google *Joy Anne Wood, horseriding accident, 1962* and see what you come up with?'

'Hmm.'

He heard the keyboard clicking.

'Aren't you cooking?' he asked.

'Looking for new recipes. Hang on, I've got to . . .'

Dave heard her talking to herself.

'Here . . . Nope. I'll just click on this one . . . Nothing there.'

'If you can't find anything on Google, maybe try the Trove website,' he suggested.

'Got it,' she said. 'Okay—hey, this is really cool. I haven't been on here before.'

'It's a great resource. Can you imagine how much time it would have taken to catalogue all those documents for the web?'

'A bloody long time, I'd think. Right, I'll read it to you. It's from the *Goyder's Journal*. *Joy Anne Wood, wife of Warren, from Barker, died in a riding accident last Friday. According to witnesses, she'd been in the township of Barker collecting stores and was on her way home when the accident occurred. It seems unclear why she fell as the horse was uninjured. There has been speculation it wasn't an accident, but Constable Bourke, when interviewed, told* Goyder's Journal, *"There isn't enough evidence to launch an official investigation." Mrs Wood is survived by her husband, Warren, and two sons, Guy and Brett.*'

'There's speculation it wasn't an accident and there's no mention of the daughter again!' Dave ran his fingers through his hair, frustrated. 'There's really something big here,' he said to Kim. 'When I went to Guy's today he had some old papers on his table and I offered to help him shift them, but he wouldn't let me. Told me it was none of my business. I saw the word *adoption* on one of them but I didn't see any names . . . Only Rachael's on the birth certificate.'

'Sometimes, if families couldn't afford their children, they gave them up for adoption,' Kim said. 'Or sent them to children's homes, or to other family members. It happened quite often back in the early days, particularly during the Depression.'

'Do you think the Wood family did that? Gave Rachael up for adoption? In the fifties?'

'Could have done. But if they did . . .' Kim paused. 'If they did, how come she wasn't ever seen by people around here?'

'I suspect people just don't remember. And a lot of the people who were the age of Guy's parents will have died.

'Think about it. They're only in town for supplies once every month or so; sometimes it was only the father who came to town in the buggy to pick things up. There's lots of reasons why she isn't remembered or wasn't seen.'

'Then why get her christened in the church? If they'd planned to give her away, they would have hidden her birth.'

Dave tapped his fingers on the steering wheel. 'What if they never planned to, but something happened—like Joy's death—which made them have to. Rachael would have been only ten when Joy died. It would have been a huge job for Warren to look after two boys and a young girl.'

'Honey,' Kim said. 'They couldn't have kept her hidden for ten years.' Uncertainly entered her voice. 'Could they?'

The excitement fizzed in Dave's stomach. 'You know what? They could have. Perhaps if she had a disability or was disfigured somehow, they may have done just that. Can you google that?'

'Google what?'

'I don't know, something that might find an adoption paper or . . .'

'Hang on . . .'

Fingers clicked over the keys again and he blew out an impatient breath.

'There's something here, I just know it,' he muttered.

'I can't see anything quickly,' she said finally. 'I'll keep looking. When are you going to be home?'

'Won't be until tonight. And then, my precious girl, be prepared to be pampered. Daydream about me kissing you all over.'

Chapter 27

'Good afternoon,' Dave said politely to the woman who answered the phone. 'My name is Detective Dave Burrows and I was wondering if it would be possible to see Pastor Alan McSweeny, please.'

'I'll check if he's having visitors. Hold the line.'

Dave listened to the annoying chimes for a whole minute before she came back on the line.

'His nurse says he is, but she's wondering what it was about.'

Dave explained he would like to ask him about the Wood family from Barker.

'Hold the line again, please.'

'Sure,' Dave said, but was speaking to the chimes again.

It was a different voice the next time.

'Detective Burrows? My name is Gail Kenally. I'm Mr McSweeny's nurse. I'm assuming you want to ask him questions in relation to an investigation?'

'I'm interested in one of his parishioners from his time at Barker. I understand he's, ah, quite, um, "with it" and shouldn't have any problems answering questions.'

'Coherent would be the word, Detective, and, yes, he is. He's the sharpest ninety year old I know. When would you like to see him?'

'I can drive to Adelaide tomorrow.'

'We'll expect you midmorning.'

'Of course. See you then.'

He hung up the phone and let out an excited breath, before getting to his feet and bouncing on his toes.

'What are you excited about?' Jack asked, walking in holding a plastic container. 'I met Kim outside. She was bringing this.' He opened it and let out a little moan. 'Oh my God. Is that her cherry pie?'

Dave sniffed the air. 'Yep, and I've got first dibs on that.'

'Not likely. I'm closer.' Jack grabbed a knife and started to slice it.

'Why didn't she come in?' Dave asked.

'Said she was busy. Something about going to see someone who needed meals.'

'Ah. I'm going to Adelaide tomorrow to interview Pastor Alan McSweeny. Do you want to come?'

Jack shook his head. 'No, I'm going to set up a random breath test tomorrow night just outside of town. There'll be a fair few blokes in for cricket training then, so I think it would be worth seeing which skills they're training—ball or elbow.'

Dave laughed. 'That's a good idea. Don't you have to train too?'

'Not when I'm working. What did you find at the church?'

'Sweet nothing. But I've got a theory.'

'What's that?' Jack spoke through a mouthful.

'I think they adopted the little girl out. Kim tells me it wasn't uncommon, if the family couldn't afford to feed the extra kid or if circumstances changed. Which they did in this case because the mother was killed.'

Jack frowned and swallowed. 'Jeez, that's a bit harsh. Having a kid, then not being able to afford to keep it. The second idea makes more sense. Who would they have given her to?'

'That's what I'm going to find out.'

'How did Guy take the theft report?'

'Right on the chin. Not the ewes so much. I've got all the paperwork here.' He indicated the folders on his desk. 'You can start going through everything while I'm away tomorrow.'

'Right, so cross-referencing opening and closing stock figures?'

'Yeah, and numbers in sales and any replacement stock he's bought in. If everything checks out, then we'll bring Rob Walker in to count the animals. You and I will go out and muster—I don't want Guy involved with that, unless he's sitting in the passenger's seat. Not saying he's too old, especially since he's managed all this time by himself, but it needs to be police so we can stand up in court and say we mustered everything we could find.'

~

The next morning, Dave left before dawn and drove slowly out of town. His headlights followed the road towards the glimmer of the sunrise, promising another hot day. Dave hated the city in summer. All the cement and tar seemed to absorb the heat and make the place twice as hot as it was in the country.

'Shit,' he said as a kangaroo bounced in front of him. He slammed his foot on the brake but kept the steering wheel steady. *Focus*, he told himself as the roo hopped away into the dawn light, unharmed.

Five hours after he'd left home, the driveway of the nursing home came into view and he pulled in and glanced at his watch.

Ten a.m. With any luck he'd be in time for smoko.

Gail Kenally met him in reception and took him through.

'Can I get you a cup of something, Detective?'

Figuring the coffee wasn't going to be all that special, he opted for a cup of tea, then extended his hand to Alan McSweeny.

'It's good to meet you, sir,' he said. 'I've heard a lot about you from Chris Connelly. He was the one who gave me your address here. Thank you for seeing me.'

Alan McSweeny's handshake was weak, but his eyes were bright and alert and he smiled a wide, genuine smile as Dave sat down.

'I admit,' he said in a raspy voice, 'I was surprised to hear you wanted to talk to me. I'm not sure how I can help.'

'I'm not either, and if you can't, it won't matter, but I thought I'd try.'

'Nice man, Chris. Comes to visit me every so often. I always like hearing what's going on in the town all these years later. You live there, Detective?'

'Yes, I married Kim Tucker.'

'Ah, yes, the Tucker family. I remember them. The father had the corner store.'

'Kim owns a roadhouse now. Best in the area,' Dave said proudly.

'Very nice.' He paused, then refocused on Dave. 'What are you interested in hearing about?'

Dave gave a brief summary of everything he knew, finishing with 'I can't find any mention of Rachael's death in the church records and I don't want to ask people and start gossip.'

'Yes, you're right, of course. It seems a shame to have to drag all this back up when he's so old, that's my only concern. That probably sounds strange coming from a ninety year old. Why is it so important you understand what happened to Rachael?'

'It seems like it's a cold case to me,' Dave answered. 'I started looking into this just to find out whether rumours of a third Wood child were true, but now I know there's something not right here and I need to find out what happened.'

'But Guy hasn't asked you to?'

'No.'

'Interesting family.' Alan steepled his fingers and leaned back in his chair.

Gail arrived with the tea and Dave thanked her, waiting for her to withdraw before speaking again. 'I must say, I enjoyed reading the record books you wrote while leading the Barker congregation. I laughed a lot.'

'Humour is very important. Without it, life would be very dull. I enjoyed watching people and seeing things others didn't. Kept me on top of my game as a minister.'

'How so?'

'If I saw a change in someone, then I could investigate it, see if they needed my help. Young women often found motherhood challenging but didn't like anyone to know they were struggling. A kind word here or a brief visit there often made all the difference to them. Likewise, if I noticed a man struggling within himself, sometimes a friendly, confidential ear was all he needed to work things out. Do you see what I mean?'

'You must have had the confidence of the whole town.'

'Certainly of my parishioners I did, but there were others who occasionally sought my help too, which I was always happy to give.'

'Did the Wood family ask you to help them adopt out Rachael?'

Alan rubbed his nose and looked steadily at Dave. 'Why do you think she was adopted?'

'Just a hunch.' He went on to tell Alan what he'd discovered. 'The other interesting thing I observed was the blandness of your entry the day Rachael was christened.

Usually you would ask for a blessing on the child, but there was none of that. Was there a reason?'

'You're observant too, Detective.'

Dave laughed. 'That's my job!'

'I guess it is.' Alan took a sip of water from the glass beside him. 'Unfortunately, I was very busy that day. I remember it well, because it was the only time in my ministerial duties that I had five funerals in one day. If you'd read on, you would have seen them listed, and that meant there were five families to comfort. It wasn't intentional. The thing you need to understand was the Wood family were different.'

Dave nodded. 'Yeah, I'd heard that.'

'They were a tight-knit bunch who relied on each other and no one else. Warren and Joy had tried and failed time and time again to have a child after the youngest boy was born. I think his name was Brett? Or was it Guy? No, no,' he held up his hand. 'Don't tell me. Brett. It was Brett. Guy was the firstborn.'

'Yes,' Dave confirmed.

'Good, my brain still works reasonably well! Unfortunately, it wasn't to be. Joy miscarried several times, and if my memory serves me correctly, there were two stillborn children as well. Of course, that was a time when records weren't kept of these early births, and the bodies were taken away and disposed of by the hospital staff.

'My opinion, if you're interested, is that Mrs Wood worked far too hard. She was a dab hand at roping and breaking horses and mustering and she worked well as a roustabout in the shearing shed. Of course, she was never supposed to be there—it was before women were allowed in sheds—but the Wood family were never ones for conforming.'

'You believe she lost the babies or miscarried because of the hard work she was doing?'

'Of course, I'm not medically trained, but women's bodies are to be adored and revered, not worked into the ground.

'When she became pregnant with Rachael, I suggested she took things a little easier, but that made her withdraw and I didn't see her until she was seven months gone. About that time, Mrs Wood had an accident—a fall from a horse . . .'

'What, different to the one which killed her?'

Alan nodded. 'Yes. It wasn't a bad fall, but it brought on an early labour and Rachael made a speedy entry into the world. Two months too early. Not a good thing back in those times.

'The baby spent some time in the hospital but, surprisingly, she thrived and was sent home when she was about three weeks old.' Alan's face became hard and he looked Dave steadily in the eye. 'The child thrived, that was for certain, but from very early on there was something not right about her. Not right at all.'

Chapter 28

'Dry!' yelled Luke Noble, the vet, and Brianna quickly slashed a red line down the ewe's back and pulled the rope to open the gate so the ewe could run free into the yards.

There was a clatter of gates and steel on steel and another ewe ran into the crate. Brianna watched as Luke shoved his gloved hand, holding the ultrasound wand, up near the ewe's udder and looked at the screen.

'Pregnant,' he called. 'Twins!'

Brianna took the blue marker and sprayed a dot on the ewe's head.

Hearing Jinx's hoarse old bark, she looked around and shook her head. 'Silly old bugger,' she said to Luke. 'He should be at home on the verandah, sunning himself. I call him Woof on Wheels. Wheel him to where you need some woofing and leave him there because he can't walk enough to shift himself.'

'Dry!' Luke laughed. 'Woof on Wheels, I like it! Trouble is with kelpies . . . Pregnant! They don't like to give up working.'

'I had noticed. I did try to get him to retire, but in the past few days he's spent more time with me than in ages. Although he hides when he knows I'm getting sheep in. I think he's worried . . .'

'Pregnant!'

'. . . I'll ask him to go back and he'd have to run. He doesn't want to do that any more!'

'Pregnant. Twins!'

'Oh, goody,' said Brianna as she grabbed the blue rattle again.

'Last four,' Russell said from the back of the race and pushed the next one into the crate.

'Already?' Luke asked. 'Pregnant.'

'You've put three thousand through,' Russell said.

The last sheep was scanned and, with a final call of 'Pregnant!', Luke hung up his wand, and took out a notepad and wrote down some figures before handing it to Brianna.

'There you go, ninety-eight percent pregnant and sixty percent of them are twinners. Pretty good result, I'd say.'

'Reckon,' said Brianna with a smile. 'That's great news. Did you hear that, Dad?'

Russell raised his hand from the back of the yards to indicate he'd heard.

'One of the best percentages around the district, I can tell you, without breaking any confidentiality clauses.'

'That's what happens when you cull for fertility. Get rid of the dries and make sure you've got productive ewes. It's not rocket science. Got time for a cuppa?'

Luke glanced at his watch. 'Not really. I've got to get back to the surgery and then I have an early start tomorrow.'

'I hear you're going to Angie's to bleed her rams?'

'Hmm, yep, that should be a job in itself. How's Trent since the accident?'

'Not too bad,' Brianna answered as she rolled up the rope that had been used to pull the gate open and handed it to Luke. 'Although he's been having nightmares since. Not sure why.'

'Trauma, I guess. When I was a young fella I had a car accident. It took me months and months not to dream about it. I'd shut my eyes and see exactly what was happening inside the car as it rolled. All the drink bottles and crap I had lying on the floor would whiz past me. Not nice to keep remembering through a dream.'

'So you actually dreamed exactly what happened?' And here she'd been telling Trent that what he was dreaming about wasn't real.

'Yeah, I did, and my mate who was in the car with me, he said the same thing. As soon as the dream started, I'd be sitting in the driver's seat, looking out the window. I'd dream about the white line, then see the roo jumping across the road, then the next thing, we'd be rolling. Remember it very clearly. The dreams, as well as the accident.'

'Shit, I wonder if Trent's remembering something too,

then. God knows what, because all that happened was he fell off the bike.'

Luke shrugged. 'Who knows? Have you thought about getting him some counselling?'

'I hadn't, but I might now. Thanks for the tip.'

'Noble Vet Services, offering advice all round,' he quipped and gave a laugh. 'Righto, I'll be off. Let me know if you need anything else.'

'Cheers, Luke. See you soon.'

As Luke drove out, the dust rose in a large cloud and hung in the still air. Brianna couldn't wait until the opening rains. It didn't take long to get sick of the dust and dirt and for her to long for mud again.

She called Jinx to her and he limped over. She lifted him up, then tied him on the back of the ute and sent one of the younger dogs around the mob to herd them towards the gate Russell had opened. They streamed out, longing to escape, and were soon settled under the scrub in the shade.

'Done and dusted for another year,' Russell said as he walked over, stopping to pat Jinx, who was straining on the chain.

'Thank goodness. So, according to Luke, we've only got sixty dry ewes to sell to the abs. That's an awesome result,' Brianna said.

'Top-notch.' Russell smiled, but Brianna noticed it wasn't quite reaching his eyes.

'What's up?' she asked.

'Oh, love, I don't know. I'm a bit worried about Angie.'

'Why? Let's go and sit in the shed and have a cuppa. I've got a thermos in the car. It's too hot to stand out here in the sun when we've just spent the last few hours in it. I'll just wash my face and hands and grab the smoko.' She took Russell's arm and led him up the stairs into the shearing shed before running back down the stairs, splashing cold water on her face and filling up a water container for the dogs. Letting Jinx off the chain, she lifted him down and gave him a quick pat.

In the shed, Brianna poured the tea, handing it to Russell. She sat back with her own mug and observed her father for the first time in what seemed like a long time. He looked pensive.

'What's going on?'

'That's just it, I'm not sure. She's always been so independent and definite about keeping our farming enterprises separate. But since the big hullabaloo with Beau, when I told her off for interfering, she's changed. Suddenly keen for us to merge both of our properties, move in and become partners. I'm not sure why.'

Brianna stiffened.

'You can't run properties together when they're sixty ks apart—or whatever the difference is. And what would we do with her manager? I don't want or need one. I like doing everything myself.' He sighed. 'Everything is suddenly moving too quickly—or she wants it to. She brought up becoming a signatory for the bank accounts and asked if I have a will.'

Brianna looked down at her hands, knowing her father still had more to say.

'Of course I have a will—everything goes to you. But I don't have a power of attorney, so she does have a point.'

'In what way?' Brianna knew her tone was angry. How dare Angie start interfering like this? She'd never once indicated she wanted to be involved in any way other than being her father's girlfriend. The jealousy swirling around in her stomach took Brianna by surprise. She'd never thought she was the jealous type—until she'd seen the photo of Heidi and Caleb.

The thought of Caleb sent another feeling through her—regret. He still hadn't rung her back after the awful phone call three days ago. It was the longest they'd gone without speaking the whole time they'd been together.

Brianna hadn't tried to call him either. But she should. She was the one who needed to apologise.

'In case something happens to me,' Russell interrupted her thoughts, 'we need to make sure you are the one who has access to all the accounts. That you are the only one who can sign, make payments and decisions. So we need to go to a lawyer—Caleb, maybe—and get you enduring power of attorney in the event of my incapacitation.'

Taking a sip of her tea, Brianna tried to work out what her dad was saying. 'You're not sick, are you?'

'Me? Not a chance! Fit as a fiddle.'

'Does she want to move in with you?'

'She does, but as much as I care for her, it's not going to happen. I'm perfectly happy with the way things are.

I'm set in my ways, love. I like my space and quiet. And sometimes when Angie visits, it's not all that quiet!'

Despite herself, Brianna smiled. 'I can imagine that.' She played with her mug, wondering whether to say something or not.

'What's on your mind?' Russell asked.

'How did you know?'

'You're my daughter.'

'Angie suggested that I move to Perth for a while, so Caleb didn't have to travel. She thought it would be better for our family unit.'

Thunder crossed Russell's face. 'Are you serious? What was she thinking?'

'I thought she was thinking about the kids and Caleb's and my relationship. But now you've told me this, I'm not sure what to think.' She took a deep breath and ran her sweaty hands over the cuffs of her shorts. 'Um, I heard the boys talking the other night and they were saying she's mean to them when no one is looking. Tells them off. I wouldn't have ever said anything because I want you to be happy. You've sacrificed so much for me, especially when you were younger.'

'You and the Terrors are the most important people in my life,' Russell said firmly. 'No one will ever change that.'

Brianna toyed with the idea of telling Russell about the photo and Angie's insinuations, but her father looked sad enough already.

Angie would never understand, she thought. Nothing could ever come between Brianna and her dad. They were a partnership on the farm and in life. And they had been through too much together to let anyone tear them apart.

~

'Hello, Bri,' Angie said as she put a paper bag on the counter in Brianna's kitchen. 'Brought you some home-grown apricots off my tree.'

Brianna didn't stop at the sound of Angie's voice—she kept wiping the bench until it was shiny, scrubbing hard at imaginary stains.

'Hi,' she finally answered, throwing the cloth back in the sink and looking up. She was trying to work out how she felt about everything she'd heard today from her dad. Drawing on all her self-control, she pasted a smile on her face and looked at Angie carefully. There was something different about her. Her hair. Again! It looked like she was wearing a wig. What the hell? 'Thanks for the apricots. Trent loves them,' Brianna answered, trying to bed down the anger that had welled up as soon as she'd heard Angie's voice. 'What have you done to your hair this time?'

'Oh, I dragged one of my old wigs out of the cupboard and put it on for old times' sake. I decided I'd go through my cupboards and give everything that doesn't fit me to the op shop.' She patted her stomach with a satisfied smile. 'Lost a few kilos.'

'Why do you have wigs?'

'A phase I went through, before I moved back here from the Riverina. I liked changing my look. Now,' she tapped the bench and looked straight at Brianna. 'I'm a bit worried about your father. He seems very tired.'

'Funny you should say that. So am I,' Brianna said, her voice dangerously low. She held Angie's gaze.

'Well, um, yes . . . What's the matter? Why are you talking to me like that?' Angie seemed to shrink under her stare.

'I heard some interesting things today and I'm trying to work out what it all means.'

Angie straightened before folding her arms across her chest. 'Have you? Do enlighten me. I'd be more than happy to help you understand it.'

To Brianna's ears, it sounded like a challenge.

'This is my farm. Mine and my father's. We are a team—a link that can't be broken. Don't think you can waltz in and change things between us. No matter how much you try, you'll never change Dad's mind when it comes to me and the kids and the farm.'

'Ah, I'm assuming you're talking about my conversation with Russell about merging the partnership. It makes good business sense. More land, more income. I can't imagine why you'd think I'm trying to break a link. That's just ridiculous.

'However, my idea is a good one. A good business decision. That's my forte, Brianna, business. I'm not convinced it's yours.'

'If you think Dad would ever choose you over us, I can promise you, you're wrong. Same with the farm. He'd choose Le-Nue over you too. You know why? Because we're his family.' Brianna smiled coldly.

Angie's posture changed and something flickered in her eyes. Drawing herself up and pushing her shoulders back, she stared at Brianna, not once shifting her gaze. 'We'll just see about that, shall we?' Angie got up and left the room, shutting the door quietly behind her.

Feeling uneasy, Brianna went to the window and watched her drive away, wondering what she had just unleashed.

Chapter 29

'Beau.' Brianna sat next to her son, who was sitting on the dam bank, a line in his hand. He'd been there all afternoon, trying to catch yabbies, and so far he had half a bucket. The nets would have been a much quicker way to catch them but, as he'd informed her earlier, 'not as much fun'.

'Yep?' He jiggled the string and looked up at her.

'I heard you talking about Angie the other night. Did I hear you say she was mean to you when Granda and I weren't around?'

Beau pursed his lips and looked over his shoulder.

'Um.'

Brianna waited, not wanting to put words in his mouth.

'Remember that night you and Granda had to go to the fire brigade meeting and she looked after us?'

'Sure do. You said she cooked chicken parmy, your favourite.'

Beau nodded. 'Yeah. That night I spilled my water on the carpet and she got real angry.'

'Like, how angry?'

'She pinched my arm.'

Clenching her fists at her side, Brianna took a couple of steadying breaths and looked across the dam. There were ripples spreading out across from Beau's line. She licked her lips, trying to work out what to say next.

'Where?'

'Here.' He pointed to his upper arm.

Brianna looked but couldn't see any marks.

'I see. Was that the first time she'd done something like that?'

'Well, she smacked me here once.' He tapped the side of his head. 'But that's all.'

'How come you didn't tell me, sweetheart? You know that you can tell me or Granda anything. We'll always listen.'

'Angie said not to.'

'I don't want you listening to what Angie says any more, okay? You stay with me or Granda and have nothing to do with Angie. Promise me.'

'That's not going to be hard, Mum. I really don't like her.'

Brianna tussled his hair and kissed his head. 'Good man. Now, I'm going to see your brother. Do you know where he is?'

'He took the motorbike down to check his ewes.'

'Don't go hear the water's edge, okay?'

Beau looked at her, vexed. 'I told you, Mum, I won't do anything to worry you.'

'Oh look, you've got one!' She reached around and tugged his line before running up the dam bank, laughing.

~

Trent was sitting on his motorbike, the engine off, watching the sheep. From the gate, Brianna could see a couple of the cheeky ones had started to come closer to him, but she knew they'd never come right up close. Not unless they had been raised as pets, and none of his mob had been.

She drove over and the sheep scattered with the clatter of the tray and sound of the engine. Trent looked over and broke into a smile as he saw her.

'Howdy, Farmer Trent,' she said in a very bad American accent. 'Got some good-lookin' ewes there. Whatchya planning on doing with them?'

'Mum, I'm not five any more,' he said with a frown.

'Sorry, old habit.' Brianna tried to look chastised. 'What are you doing down here?'

'Thinking.'

'Good spot for thinking. Out in the open. There's nothing to cloud your thoughts.'

'I like it. Do you think I'll be able to work here when I finish school?'

Brianna looked across the land, her heart full. 'I'm sure we can work something out,' she said. 'But you might find you want to do a trade first. Like learn to be a mechanic or something, and that's a good thing to do too. You can always use a mechanic on a farm.'

'Hmm, I don't know. I like the animals.'

'There's lots of different options. But you've got a bit of time to figure it out. Granda and I would love to have you home and working on the farm, when the time is right for you.'

'See that ewe out there?' Trent handed her a set of binoculars and pointed to a ewe at the back of the mob.

'The limpy one?' she asked after she'd looked for a couple of moments.

'Yeah. Why's her leg like that? I don't think she was limping when I checked them two days ago.'

'Maybe her hooves are a bit long and need clipping. I don't think it's a problem, though. Not life-threatening.'

'I can't afford to lose any, you know.' His face was serious and Brianna could tell he was thinking hard.

'Unless they get a bout of Barber's pole, or run out of water and feed, which can happen in summer, they should all be fine. Has Granda told you about the signs for Barber's pole worms?'

Trent shook his head.

'They swell up underneath the chin—look like they've been bitten by a bee. It's called having a bottled jaw. They sleep a lot, don't have any energy—like you get when you've had a vomiting bug.

'When the weather is damp, you've got to worry about flies, or different types of worms. Oh, and lambing. Sometimes the lambs get stuck and you have to help bring them out. Huh! Look at me, I'm getting carried away. You know all that anyway. Farm kids learn by osmosis, and you, my handsome young man, are a sponge!'

An expression of delight crossed Trent's face and he seemed to grow in stature as he looked across to his ewes again. 'This is just the start,' he promised. 'I'm gonna be a real big farmer one day, Mum.'

'And Granda and I will be here to help,' she promised.

A crow flew overhead, cawing as it went. 'Bloody mongrels,' Trent said.

Brianna had to hold back a laugh. 'Spoken like a true farmer.'

'Mum?'

'Hmm?'

'I've remembered something about the accident.'

'Oh yeah, what's that?'

Trent shifted on his motorbike and brought one leg up to rest it on the handlebar. 'I'm not really sure about this, but I think there was a rope across the road. That's why I fell off.'

Her heart stood still. 'What do you mean, a rope?'

'It's weird. I've been trying to remember how I fell off. It's been bugging me, you know?' He crossed his arms. 'I'm a pretty good rider.'

At that, Brianna hid a smile. Nothing like the confidence of youth.

'It shouldn't be easy to fall off. Especially off a four-wheeler because it's got all four wheels on the ground.'

She opened her mouth to disagree, but Trent kept talking.

'Anyway, I sorta remember something being stretched out across the road, but I was going a bit quick before I noticed it and then I couldn't stop. I remember the handlebars twisting out of my hands and the bike stopping really fast. I'm sure that's how I fell off.'

'Are you absolutely sure, Trent? That would mean someone had to string it up and I don't know anyone else who goes down to the swamp. That's sort of like our secret yabby place. There's very few who know about it.'

He shrugged. 'It's just what I remember.'

'Have you remembered anything else?' She looked up as the sheep started to walk back towards them, curious as to what was in their paddock.

'No,' he said, far too quickly for her liking.

'I'm not sure I believe you, Trent. You don't ever have to worry about telling me anything.'

'There's nothing else to tell,' he said. 'I'm going to ride over to Granda's, is that okay?'

'Sure, but can you be home before dark?'

'Uh huh.' He nodded.

'Oh, and one other thing. I was talking to Beau about Angie and he told me a couple of nasty things she'd done to him. If she's over at Granda's, I need you to stay with him, okay? Don't hang out with Angie alone.'

'Okay.'

Brianna thought he accepted that too easily, but by the time she went to ask him about it, he'd started the engine of the bike and begun to putter slowly across the paddock.

'Don't go slow just cos I'm watching,' she yelled. 'I know you're only doing that for my benefit!'

~

Back at home, Brianna tried to ring Caleb once more to apologise. Today seemed to be the day for difficult conversations, and she would feel much better if she could just hear his voice. Once again, it went straight through to his voicemail. Should she ring his secretary? Nope, she would wait until he calmed down and called her. Surely he'd received her messages, so he'd know she'd been trying to apologise.

The sun went behind the clouds and Brianna got up to see what was going on with the weather. Thunder. In the distance. She frowned. As far as she knew, there wasn't a storm forecast tonight.

Her mobile phone beeped with a text message. Nina: *Are you home tonight in case there're fires? Severe storm warning just issued by bureau. Not sure if there will be any rain.*

Lizzie was next: *You okay? Heard the thunder. Are you home by yourself?*

Brianna opened the weather website she used and looked at the radar. No rain. She flicked across to the lightning chart. It showed where the lightning was hitting the ground. Looked like there were lots of strikes. It might be a busy night.

Chapter 30

Anna took her first tentative steps out into the sun and tried to get her bearings. Everything looked different up close than it did from her hospital room.

The police hadn't been back and she wasn't surprised. Pleased would be the word. She didn't want to go back to her old life, even though she didn't know what it was.

Her friend Elspeth had suggested the plan and Anna had agreed to it.

Elspeth knew of an old couple who were living on a station by themselves and were getting to the stage of needing a bit of help. Since the police seemed to have finished with her and the young doctor was keen to be rid of her, Elspeth had suggested Anna discharge herself and walk away. After her shift finished that afternoon, she'd come and find her and take her out to her friends.

Anna was impatient to leave hospital. She carved fresh air and space, and she hoped that if she started a new life, the dreams would stop.

There was a new one now. One with a person, a faceless person, holding a kitten in their arms like they were loving it. Patting and stroking, lifting it to their face and nuzzling it. The kitten seemed to like the person too. But the more they stroked and patted, the more playful the kitten became, grabbing at their hands, and clawing at their pants. The kitten got free and turned around to pounce on the person, biting the outstretched hand. Even though Anna couldn't see the face of the person, she could sense their anger in the dream and had watched, horrified, as a hand closed around the kitten's neck and squeezed and squeezed, until the kitten stopped struggling and lay limp. Dropping the body on the ground, the person got up and walked away, not even looking back.

The evil in the dream scared Anna senseless and she would do anything to stop the dreams from happening.

Elspeth had given Anna twenty dollars and told her about a café in the main street.

'Go order a coffee and something to eat. I'll be finished about 4.30 p.m.'

Feeling free, Anna gave a little skip down the steps and turned right, like she'd been told, heading towards the main street.

Today was the start of her new life. A safe and quiet life, away from whatever had caused her to lose her memory.

~

'Hop in,' called Elspeth through the open passenger window. 'We've got about a forty-five-minute drive.'

'Where are we going?'

'A tiny little town called Hawker. Well, we're not going to the town, but to a station just before it. My friends, Liza and Roger Conway, own land there and live by themselves. No family or children. Roger is nearly seventy-five and Liza just a bit younger.'

Anna was watching the mountain ranges fly by, marvelling at the purples and reds of the sun setting that made the hills glow. 'I'd like to know if I know anything about sheep,' she said. 'It's not ringing any bells.'

Elspeth put her hand on Anna's leg and gave it a gentle squeeze. 'You know you might never get your memory back?'

Clenching her teeth, Anna nodded. It really was a horrible predicament.

If she stopped and thought about it.

Which she'd sworn she wouldn't do any more. She had to believe that she was running from something nasty and dangerous, rather than from a loving husband or family. The policemen had said there wasn't anyone missing in South Australia. No one was looking for her. No one loved her. If they did, they would have reported her missing.

'Liza is a lovely old stick,' Elspeth was saying. 'They couldn't have children, but they have had kids in need come and stay with them at times. Very religious people.'

Anna tried to think of something to say. 'They sound nice,' she said cautiously.

'My plan, are you happy with it?'

'No one should find me there, should they?'

'That's the beauty of it. You're well and truly hidden, unless you decide you want to go out in public. Liza and Roger are looking forward to having you in the house.'

'The country is so pretty,' Anna said, wonder in her voice.

'I never get sick of looking at it. There's always something new. See, look over there.' Elspeth pointed to a mob of emus. 'Old man emu with eight or nine chicks.' They were strutting along the edge of the road, but when the father emu saw the car coming, he chased all the chicks away and took them safely into the bush.

They didn't speak for the rest of the journey, but when Elspeth pulled into a dirt driveway and Anna saw the large homestead with rambling gardens and trees, she suddenly felt as if she'd come home.

Chapter 31

Dave cleared his throat, a sense of danger running through him.

'Not quite right,' he repeated, looking at the old minister. 'What does that mean?'

'She was an exceptionally quiet baby. Rarely cried or fussed, the way you would expect. When she was old enough to walk, she took to looking after herself. Independent. Didn't like to rely on anyone. Didn't want anyone. If she hurt herself, she wouldn't look for her mother.'

Alan took a breath and reached for his water again. 'When Rachael was five, Mrs Wood came to me and asked if I would pray for her daughter. "She likes to hurt animals," were her exact words. She'd been playing with newborn puppies and two had "accidentally" died. I don't think Mrs Wood thought it was an accident.

'There were other incidents—chicks found floating in water bowls, dead lizards on the back doorstep. Rachael had turned six when Mrs Wood came to me again. This time she was frightened for her daughter. Mrs Wood had been raising five newborn lambs after a cold snap. The ewes had died, so when she found the lambs snuggled into the bodies of their mothers, she decided to bring them home and put them next to the fire to hand-raise. This was a time, Detective, of waste not, want not.

'Having warmed and fed them, Mrs Wood went to tend to her other chores. When she came back in . . .' He swallowed and put his hand to his eyes. 'Dear Lord, forgive her, all five lambs had had their throats cut and Rachael was standing over them with a knife. Mrs Wood told me that when she looked into the eyes of her child, they were black and she couldn't see her soul.'

'Jesus,' Dave breathed and immediately apologised.

'I think I would have said something similar if I'd been able,' Alan said. 'I arranged for Rachael to spend time in the church with me, and in there she was a little angel, but of course there was nothing to hurt. Nothing young or helpless, which was what she seemed to like.

'Rachael was a beautiful child. Blonde hair and clear blue eyes. Never smiled or laughed. Serious all the time, and seriousness seemed to suit her.

'There was another incident and we decided Rachael needed to go into a home, or to a family where she would be safe from herself and others safe from her. Brett had been climbing trees this particular day, and he never was able to tell me exactly what happened, but he fell and knocked himself out. When he came to, there was a stick pierced through his arm.'

'She sounds like a classic psychopath.'

'Quite possibly that is the term for it these days, but we didn't have fancy labels back then,' Alan stated. 'I made arrangements. After being advised adoption was the best possible outcome, I started the process through church networks. It wasn't a legal adoption, more a handing-over. Both parties signed papers to say there wouldn't be any more contact between them. Then, just as the transfer was about to take place, Mrs Wood was killed in a riding accident.'

'Rachael?'

The old man sighed and rubbed the back of his neck tiredly. 'I couldn't be sure, but I do know she was with Mrs Wood that day. She could have pushed her from the horse or . . . I honestly don't know.

'At first, after Guy found Mrs Wood's body, we couldn't find Rachael. A search party was launched, and three days after the accident we found Rachael asleep in the shed back at the homestead. She wasn't hurt at all and seemed unperturbed by her mother's death.

'Guy, who doted on his mother, seemed to believe it was Rachael who had caused the accident and he was the one who insisted we go ahead with the adoption. Her father . . . well, poor Warren was beside himself with grief and couldn't make a decision. I had a lot of respect for Guy, stepping up and taking charge of his family. That's what the eldest boy did in those days.

'When I picked Rachael up, I took another man with me; I didn't want to take any risks. Happily, Rachael didn't seem to mind leaving. She walked to the car and got in without saying goodbye to any of her family and without showing emotion. It was as if her face was blank.' He shook his head. 'I honestly don't know if we did the right thing. Let me tell you, Detective, I have spent a lot of time praying that we did.'

Dave was silent, trying to take the story in. He was shocked to the core.

'Going okay in here?' Gail popped her head around the door and smiled at them both, took in their serious faces and said, 'Oh, looks like some serious conversation happening. Do either of you need anything?'

Dave shook his head. 'No, thanks, we're almost done.'

'Mr McSweeny?'

'Thank you, my dear. Perhaps I could have a painkiller. I have some discomfort.'

'I'll bring it to you right away.'

'Seems like they look after you well here,' Dave commented.

'I'm happy to see out the rest of my time here. I'm content and at peace. When my time comes, I'm ready.'

Pressing his lips together, Dave tried to formulate the next question. 'Do you know where Rachael was adopted to?'

'Interstate, I believe, but I couldn't be sure.'

'And do you know what happened to her later in life?'

The old man shook his head. 'All I know is that, many years ago now, I had a letter from the person who took her on. She said they had made a difference in Rachael's life and she was now happy and well. There was nothing more. If Rachael was able to change through the support and love of another family, then I'll say we made the best decision for her future.' He folded his hands in his lap and looked steadily at Dave. 'However, I can't say I was surprised when you came to ask questions. Now I have one for you.'

'Of course.'

'Other than needing to know whether Rachael lived or died, what is your interest? I need to know she hasn't come to light in any investigation.'

Dave rolled his head, trying to relieve the tension at the base of his skull. 'Not that I'm aware of, Mr McSweeny.' He tried to think of more questions he should ask. The trouble was, he was still reeling from a story he couldn't possibly have anticipated when he'd first got into his car this morning. 'Do you have any idea what her name would be?'

'I believe they intended to change her name, but considering you aren't here investigating a crime, and I've had word she was happy and content, I don't feel I can tell you.'

Dave wanted to protest, but he held his tongue. 'Can you give me any more information? The whole adoption sounds rather underhanded and strange.'

'I can understand why you might think that. You need to remember that, back then, it was different. There were always people wanting children because they couldn't have their own. I guess in a way it was underhanded, but I assure you she went to a very safe home because it was checked out by the Church.'

'Was her new family made aware of her behaviour?'

'Yes, they were. To be very honest, Detective, I found it difficult to believe that a child, one so young, could have murderous intentions or be as evil as the Wood family had implied. Certainly not without cause. Children aren't born evil. They become that way through traumatic experiences. I was convinced that taking Rachael out of the family situation would help her.'

'As in . . .' Dave stopped trying to find the right words. He'd been led to believe that the Wood family were close-knit. Had there been something underhanded going on at the farm? Was that why they kept to themselves? He tried again. 'So you believe . . .' The old man gave a shake of his head. Further questioning down this particular path wasn't going to be productive.

Again, Dave had to rack his brain for questions. There didn't seem to be any more coming to him, so he held out his hand. 'Thank you, Mr McSweeny,' he said with sincerity. 'This story wasn't at all what I expected.' He gave a sigh and shook his head. 'I'm sure it will take some time to absorb. I'm not sure I want to look into it any further, but I'm grateful for your time.'

'You're very welcome. Please send my best back to Barker.'

~

Dave drove to the beach and sat looking at the waves for a long time. There were young children playing in the waves, laughing and squealing every time the water splashed their legs. He tried to imagine a child who didn't have a soul, who could kill young and helpless animals for fun. He could only guess what, without intervention, she would have grown into. A monster.

His phone beeped with a text message. Kim: *Hey you, ring me when you've got time.*

Fear shot through him. Every time he received a text message like that now, he was worried the news would be from the doctor. That something had changed in Kim's breast cancer status and the test results, which had proven to be false, were true.

He hit speed dial. 'Hey, what's up?'

'Up? You, hopefully!' she answered mischievously. When Dave didn't laugh, she continued: 'Nothing. I miss you! Just wanted to say hi. But I wasn't sure if you'd finished with Alan yet, so I didn't want to call and interrupt.'

Dave let out a relieved breath. 'I finished about half an hour ago. The story he told me was very disturbing. I'm sitting at the beach.'

'Oh, that sounds interesting. Tell me about it?'

He could see her sitting at the desk in the office, her chin resting on her hand, hair tumbling around her shoulders. 'I can't tell you this story over the phone. I'll tell you when I get home. What's your news?'

'Hmm; not much, really. I've been on Trove this morning, just snooping around. There's so many fascinating stories! There's a tiny story in 1982, um . . . March. In the *Goyder's Journal*. Listen to this: *Reports of an injured woman wandering the road between Barker and Hawker have so far been unsubstantiated. Three reports were received by this journal, but so far police and medical practitioners have denied any knowledge. However, the* Journal *has spoken to Mr Shane Hill, who has told us he picked up an injured woman and took her to the Barker hospital. "She was unable to remember who she was or where she came from," he said. More to follow as it comes to hand.*'

'What piqued your interest about that article?' Dave wanted to know.

Kim gave a throaty laugh. 'You know me too well, Detective Dave Burrows. I just wondered if it could link up to Rachael somehow. You know, a woman wandering around in the bush, without a memory. But this is years down the track, so it's probably not connected.'

'Kim, apparently Rachael was an evil child. She killed animals, and her parents were so worried about her, they adopted her out to another family.'

'What?'

'I know, it sounds too strange to be true.'

They sat in silence, trying to take it in.

'I've got an idea,' Kim said. 'When are you going to be home?'

'I'm leaving as soon as I get a coffee.'

'Okay, I mightn't be home when you get here, but I'll leave dinner in the fridge. I won't be too late.'

'Where are you—?' There was no point, the phone had clicked off.

Chapter 32

Brianna and the Terrors sat on the verandah in the dark, watching the lightning show. So far there hadn't been any rain, but she could smell moisture, so she was hoping it wasn't too far away.

'The thunder sounds like growling dogs,' Beau said.

'Yeah, Jinx and Rexy growling at each other because they both want to be the boss,' Trent agreed.

'I love thunderstorms,' Brianna said, 'but I like rain with them, especially in summer. Did you have a good time with Granda this afternoon?'

'Yeah, it was cool. We went out to the weaners and drove around them real slow. They kept coming up to the ute and rubbing on the tray so it moved. Granda told me that when he was little he used to lie out in the paddock and the cows would come over and sniff him.'

Brianna laughed. 'He told me the exact same story. Did you know a cow's tongue is rough, like a cat's?'

'Yeah!' said Beau. 'I've been licked heaps of times.'

'I held my hand out the window today and one of them licked me,' Trent said with a giggle, then he stopped and said sadly, 'Granda said he was going to come over tonight but Angie got there just before I left. I guess he won't now.'

Brianna looked at the disappointment in her son's face. 'Chin up. You had the afternoon with him.'

'I know, but we didn't finish talking about how long it takes a ewe to have a lamb and the stages.'

'Plenty of time for that, Trent,' Brianna said.

'I'm tired,' Beau said.

'How long did you fish at the dam for?'

He shrugged. 'I don't know. I put all the yabbies back in the dam when I finished. When I heard the thunder, I thought you'd be too busy watching for fires to be able to cook them.'

'Oh, Beau! I didn't even think about the yabbies for tea. Would you have had enough?'

'Nah, there weren't very many. Nothin' more than a taste.'

Brianna laughed. 'Did you steal that line from your granda?'

He flashed her a huge grin. 'He stole it from me!'

That made her laugh more. Putting her arms around both her boys, she thought about Caleb. If only . . . *No, not tonight,* she told herself. *Don't think about him tonight.*

Trent twisted his warm body away from hers and walked out onto the lawn. Looking around, Brianna watched as he put his head up and sniffed like a dog.

'What's up, Trent?' she asked, on alert. She checked carefully for the glow of a fire.

'Mum, can you smell smoke?' Trent asked as another flash of lightning lit up the sky. She looked out and saw a black-and-white polaroid snap of land, bush, the hill, the sheep in the paddock. The picture was gone with the lightning.

Jumping off the verandah, she went out into the darkness and looked around, shielding her eyes from the glow of lights from the house. She couldn't see a glow from any direction.

'I can't see anything,' she said, walking further out into the dark.

'I can smell it,' Trent said again, appearing at her side.

'Might be from way out in crown land. Not farming. The weather moved in from that direction. We can't get out there to fight a fire. The department won't let us. Just have to wait until it comes out in farming land, if that's where it's started.'

'Mmm.' Trent sounded unconvinced.

Brianna glanced down at her son, surprised at how grown-up he sounded. For an eight year old, he was so mature. Since the accident, it was as if he had taken on the role of protecting her.

'Okay, you two,' she said, swinging her arms over both her sons. 'I think it might be a noisy night, so you should head off to bed.'

'Aw, Mum,' Beau protested.

'Nope, no arguments tonight. If I need to go out, Lizzie will come over to be with you both, okay?'

Still complaining, the boys went to their bedrooms while Brianna switched off all the lights in the house. It was easier to see a lightning strike or the flow of a fire without any background light.

With her headlight, she checked the back of her ute, making sure all the uniforms and equipment she might need were there, then backed the ute into the firefighting trailer and hitched it up, before parking it right next to the house.

On a night like this, she needed to be ready.

Finally, when she could do no more, she went back to the verandah, grabbed her phone charger and phone, then sat on the bench seat and waited.

❧

The buzzing of her phone woke her and she lifted her head from the kitchen bench, where she'd finally nodded off. Instantly she could smell smoke.

'Shit,' she said, snatching up the phone. She realised the bushfire radio was crackling in the background.

'Nina,' she said.

'Your dad's place,' was all Nina said.

'Okay,' she replied, fighting down the fear that had been sitting in her stomach from the first rumble of thunder that night. She dialled Lizzie as she ran to her ute.

'Don't worry, I'm already on my way,' Lizzie said in greeting.

'Okay, be safe. Talk soon.'

Brianna hung up and started the ute, trying to work out where the fire was. Now she was awake, she could see the glow from the back of the hill. It must be very close to her dad's house. Maybe in the bush that bordered it. That area was full of kerosene bushes and banksia trees. If the fire was in there, it would be very hard to control.

'No, no, no,' she muttered and drove as quickly as the heavy firefighting unit would allow. The pull on the ute every time she went over a bump slowed her down.

'Dammit, come on!' she yelled. The smoke was drifting down the road and she could see only about a hundred metres in front of her. The smoke reflected back off her lights as if it were fog.

The smell was almost overpowering and, every time the lightning slit the sky, she could see thick black clouds towering over her dad's place.

'Merriwell Bay Five, come in?'

Snatching the mic up from the radio, she answered, breathing hard. 'Merriwell Bay Five.'

'ETA, please?'

'Three minutes.'

'Can you come in from the road frontage and make your way to the line of bush to the north of the hill. This area is not, I repeat, not contained. We need places to refill.'

'There's a dam about one kilometre to the east of the house, if you can't use the tanks at the shed.'

'Negative, Merriwell Bay Five, will not be able to use the tanks at the shed. There is fire there as well. Inaccessible.'

'Shit.' She pushed her foot down on the accelerator but found only the floor.

As she came closer, in the light cast by the fire, she could see five other units pouring water onto the burning shed. It seemed everyone had responded as quickly as she had. Thank goodness for neighbours.

At a quick glance the fire was well established, the flames burning the wooden floor of the shearing shed.

Fear and sadness hit her with the force of a waterfall and for a moment she felt as though she couldn't breathe. She gulped in air and followed the road until she saw the other units along the bush.

'Merriwell Bay Five,' she said into the microphone, watching as a large banksia tree was engulfed in flames and threw sparks into the paddock. They would have to watch for spot fires.

The fire drew her out of the ute. As if in slow motion, Brianna stepped out and watched the fire race along—it seemed to lick around a bush or tree, then burn it within seconds. The noise made her want to put her hands over her ears and the heat scorched her face. But she couldn't move. She was mesmerised by the firestorm in front of her. Somehow she took a step towards it, her hand outstretched as if to touch it. She was entranced as the hot wind blew strongly and lifted her hair up in its breeze.

'Brianna!' A hand grabbed her arm and pushed her back into the ute. 'What the fuck are you doing?'

Brianna stared at Darren Wilson and started to shake.

'Pull yourself together. Go back to the shed and help them there. Now! Go! You're no good here and that fire isn't as big. Go now.' He slammed the door shut and pointed to where she'd come from.

'Where's Dad?' she cried over the noise of the fire and wind. Darren just pointed towards the shed, then got back on the fire truck.

Brianna knew she was overwhelmed—her first major fire and she was a basket case. 'Stop it!' she screamed at herself. 'Just get with it! You know what to do.' Giving her face a hard slap, she put the ute into gear and went back to the shed.

The bushfire radio talked to her as she went.

'Need another small unit behind the Merriwell Truck 3-4.'

'Merriwell Bay Five is heading back to help with the shed fire.'

'Need a dozer on the southern side of the bush.'

'This fire is not controlled or contained. I repeat. Not controlled or contained. Another dozer to cut firebreaks is required now.' The panic in Nina's voice was clear.

As Brianna arrived at the shed, she saw small flames starting to creep out into pasture. She pulled up next to it and tumbled out, desperate to grab the hose and start showering water on the blaze. The heat drove her back, but she couldn't let it beat her, finally pulling the cord to start the pump. Water gushed out, but it didn't seem to be making any difference.

'Bri?' She felt the hose taken out of her hand. John, Nina's husband, was beside her. 'Back this way.' He indicated for her to turn around. 'Follow the line of fire. Behind the fire truck. We'll put out the smaller flares while the truck does the larger ones. Okay? He's going to go around the edge of the tree line. Just follow him. I'll get on the back and operate the hose. Leave the shed. It's stuffed. Nothing you can do.'

Without giving her time to argue, he leapt on the trailer and held the hose. 'Come on,' he yelled. 'Move! We don't have time . . .'

'Have you seen Dad?' she screamed.

'Get going!'

Doing as she was instructed, she pulled in behind the fire truck. Slowly and methodically they rounded the edge of the tree line, wetting down the flare-ups. They tried to push it back away from the house and the pasture, but every time Brianna thought they had it beaten, another tongue made its way out and threw flames over their heads.

A tractor with a plough on the back moved slowly, making a large firebreak between the bush and the house.

'Over there,' she heard John yell and looked to her left. One of the rows of trees Russell had planted when she was small was alight. She swung the ute around and drove slowly along the edge while John held the hose steady.

'Out of water,' he yelled before she'd got to the end of the row.

'But—'

'I can't put it out without water!' John screamed.

Without the heaviness of the water in the trailer, she could drive a lot more quickly and was at the dam within a couple of minutes. She grabbed the suction hose and ran down to the water's edge.

'Go!' she yelled as loudly as she could and waited for John to start the engine. The pipe pulsated into life under her hand. For what seemed like an eternity she waited until the pump cut out and John yelled the tank was full.

Rolling up the hose, she ran back, threw it in the ute and took off back towards the fire.

There wasn't time to think about anything other than the flames. The noise of the fire astonished her. She wanted to put her hands over her ears and scream to make the noise stop. And the wind . . . furnace-hot, streaming onto her face. From her training, she knew the fire created its own wind, but no amount of preparation could have made her understand what it would be like.

In the distance she could see the first fire she'd pulled up at; the flames seemed to be touching the sky. She could only imagine what was going on over there.

After what seemed like hours, and five or six—she lost count—water fills, John tapped on the ute roof. 'Reckon this spot is okay. The plough has gone around it three times and contained it to this paddock. I'll check in with Nina.' He jumped down and leaned in through the window to get at the mic. Calling in, he asked for the status of the other fire.

'Contained,' was her answer. 'Just beginning to rain, thank God.'

At that, Brianna saw one drop on the windscreen, then another. Five millimetres would stop any sleeper fires and certainly put a dampener on this one.

'Where's Dad?' Brianna asked.

'I haven't seen him tonight,' John answered. 'But it's been so crazy. He'll be around somewhere. The boundary fence is burnt. Is there any stock in this paddock?'

Brianna shook her head. 'No, there's nothing to shift,' she said, leaning her head against the ute seat.

'What about where the other fire was?'

Brianna turned to look, calculating which paddocks had stock in them. 'No, that should be fine too. Most are down towards my place.'

Another ute pulled up alongside them and Phil, Lizzie's husband, got out, his reflective jacket shining in the ute lights. His face was blackened like John's, and Brianna reached up to touch her own face. Her fingers came away covered in soot.

'All good on this side?' Phil asked.

'Certainly contained,' John answered. 'I'll stay for a couple of hours longer, make sure there isn't a wind shift. If the rain keeps up, we might all be able to go home early. Bri, you want to head home to the kids?'

'No, I want to stay here. Make sure everything is okay.'

'How did it start?' Phil enquired.

'Got to be lightning, doesn't it? Close to the house. I know there's a patch of granite in that bush and lightning is attracted to granite.'

'I heard there were three other fires out the other side of town.'

Bri picked up her two-way radio: 'You on channel, Dad?'

There wasn't any answer.

'You on channel, Dad?' Fear crept into her voice.

Again, no answer.

'Has anyone seen or heard from Dad tonight?' she called to John and Phil. 'Did anyone stop by the house and make sure he and Angie were out?'

'The house was fine,' Phil said, walking towards her. 'But, no, I haven't seen him.'

'Oh, God!' Brianna jumped back into the ute and put it into gear.

'Hold on!' John's voice was steely. 'Let's not go jumping to conclusions. He's not answering the two-way?'

'No.'

He got out his phone and called Nina. 'Did Russell check in tonight?' He listened to the reply with a frown. 'Better have a look, eh?'

Brianna let out a little whimper and Phil put his arm around her shoulders. 'Don't worry, there'll be an explanation.'

Chapter 33

Dave sat in front of his computer and tried to work out how he could search for Rachael Wood without knowing her new name.

Of course he couldn't. There was absolutely nothing he could do to find out who she was. Unless . . .

Snatching up the keys from the desk, he ran out to his ute. It was probably far too late to go calling on Guy, but there wasn't another option.

It was dark, but even with the risk of running into roos, Dave drove quickly. He needed an answer. His gut was telling him there was something very wrong. He suspected that if Rachael were still alive, there was every chance she had a record. A bad one. He wasn't convinced that she had been rehabilitated by her adoptive family. He needed to know where she was. With any luck she'd be in jail.

There was only one light burning in Guy's house when he arrived. The naked globe in the lounge. He hoped he wouldn't frighten the old man too much when he knocked on the door.

Bob barked from within the house as Dave walked up the path and onto the verandah.

'Hello?' he called and rapped three times. 'Guy? It's Detective Dave Burrows.' He listened and heard nothing but crickets and the sound of Bob's nails on the bare lino. The dog was sniffing at the door.

'Hello, Guy!' Dave called a bit louder. Maybe he was asleep. He pushed on the door and it opened. 'Mr Wood?'

Unsure of what he was going to find, Dave reached and turned on the hall light before walking inside. He called out another couple of times, but there was still no answer. In the kitchen the table was covered in papers—the old, yellowing ones he'd seen the last time he'd been here. The ones that Guy had gathered up so quickly. Dave reached out and picked up the first one.

'*An agreement*,' he read.

The next page was entitled *Adoption* and the third one had names. Dave stared. Rachael Carol Wood was adopted by Melanie and Andrew Barry in 1962. The year that Joy Wood was killed. Just as Alan had said. They lived in Western Australia.

Dave took a photo of the document, even though he knew it would never be admissible in court.

He walked quickly through the rest of the house. Empty. Going back into the kitchen and looking around, he saw there was an uneaten meal in the fridge. Guy couldn't have had tea.

He ran to the car and raced down to the shed. Grabbing his torch, he pushed open the door and found Guy lying on the floor.

'Guy.' Dave felt for a pulse and then shone the torch in his eyes. His pulse was weak and his eyes non-responsive.

He called triple zero, then went back out to the car, grabbed a blanket and covered the old man with it. Sitting down beside him, he held his hand and talked to him until the ambulance arrived.

~

'What is that in my laundry?' Kim asked, her tone stern, hands on hips.

'That's Bob,' Dave answered, staring blearily at her through sleepy eyes.

'And who is Bob?'

Dave struggled to sit up, feeling somewhat at a disadvantage. 'Bob is Guy Wood's dog. He needs looking after.'

'Bob looks like a mangy, thin excuse for a dog. He's probably got worms and fleas.'

'He needs some of your good food.'

Kim sank down on the bed. 'What happened last night?' she asked quietly, reaching out to take his hand. 'You were so tired when you came in, you grunted at me and fell asleep before you even took your shirt off.'

He looked down to see what he was wearing. It was the same shirt as yesterday. 'I went to see Guy last night and found him collapsed in the shed. The ambulance took him to hospital but they're not sure if he's going to make it. Must have been a heart attack or something. Just keeled over, I imagine.'

'Oh my God,' Kim's hand flew to her chest. 'Good thing you went out there. When will you know something?'

'I'll have a shower and go to the hospital. Need to talk to Jack too.' He yawned.

'You go and have a shower while I feed the dog and make you a coffee.' Kim leaned forward and kissed him. 'And when you're feeling half human, have I got a story for you.'

Kim put bacon and eggs and a fresh, hot cup of coffee in front of him as he came into the kitchen, doing up the buttons on his shirt.

'Your phone rang,' she said and handed it to him.

It was the hospital. He wasn't sure he wanted to hear what they had to say. Quickly he sent a text to Jack, asking him to run a few names, took a mouthful of bacon and rang the hospital back.

'I'm sorry,' the doctor said. 'Mr Wood had a massive heart attack not long after he was brought in. I suspect he'd had a smaller one when you found him. There was nothing we could do.'

Dave let out a heavy sigh and put the phone down.

'He's gone.'

'Oh, sweetie.' Kim came up from behind and put her arms around his shoulders, hugging him close.

'I'd better get back to the station,' Dave said a moment later, his voice a little gruff. 'Got work to do.'

Kim nodded. 'I'll be here when you get home,' she said.

~

Dave went to the hospital first, where he identified the body and signed all the necessary papers. Gazing at Guy's sunken face, he sighed deeply.

He was so grateful Guy had rung to say he'd had sheep stolen, even though he hadn't. Jack had left him a message on his desk last night to say he couldn't find any discrepancies in the stock figures. It must have been a product of Guy's confused mind, as was the woman in the shed. The wool, well, the insurance money would go into his estate and Dave would continue to keep an ear to the ground as to who may have stolen it. That first phone call had meant Guy's last few weeks had been full of company and good meals. He'd been looked after and enjoyed sparring with Dave and Jack. Dave felt privileged to have played such a role in this man's final days.

'Finished?' the doctor asked.

With one last glance, Dave nodded and walked away.

His next visit was to Chris Connelly.

'Guy Wood passed away last night,' he said without preamble. 'I'd like to organise his funeral. Unless, of course, there's someone else in the family I don't know about?'

'I'm sorry to hear that. No, no other family. I'd be happy to hold the service here.'

Dave nodded his thanks and left.

~

'Did you run the names of the adoptive parents through the system?' Dave demanded as he walked into the station. 'Have you found anything? Charges of some sort?'

Jack nodded, a serious look on his face. 'Yeah. We've got a problem.' He swung the computer screen around and showed it to Dave, who started reading. It was a transcript from an interview with Angela Moore, after her husband, Matthew, had died:

Detective James: Can you tell me about your life with Matthew Moore?

Angela Moore: I didn't like animals. Pets were a nuisance; they required feeding and watering every day. Time consuming. Stock, well, they weren't as bad because they weren't daily. Humans? They could be irritating too. They talk too much, hurt my brain. Matthew changed my thoughts on animals. And humans. In the Riverina, he showed me how to love; animals—the horses, sheep and dogs. Him.

I fell in love with the lifestyle of farming.

That was the buzzword back then—the lifestyle. Not the work side of farming; that was far too intense for my liking. I've always said that when I buy my own farm, I'll employ a manager.

Detective James: How did you meet Matthew?

Angela Moore: After I left home I went to live in Paris for a year and met a gorgeous Frenchman. Unfortunately, that didn't last, so I went to Canada with a new man. Oh, he swept me off my feet. Such a whirlwind romance.

He was a self-made millionaire, but he died unexpectedly. It was terribly sad.

His daughters didn't like me because he'd promised he'd leave me a bequest. I couldn't claim it, though, because his daughters protected his estate like wolves. It was easier to leave and start again.

I met Matthew in Sydney, at a glitzy fundraising do. He was so handsome and kind. But adventurous too. We settled on his farm—it was 25,000 acres! So large. He had a horse stud there as well as sheep and cattle.

Oh, we had a wonderful life together—skiing holidays to Aspen, cruises in Europe. I went with him on business trips, helping him buy new mares or accessing stallions for his racing stud. He appreciated my input.

We had ten wonderful years together, until Matthew's untimely death.

Unfortunately, he had hidden a great deal of debt from me and everything had to be sold to pay what he owed. I had no option other than to return home to Merriwell Bay.

Detective James: Mrs Moore, did you kill your husband?

Angela Moore: I did not kill my husband.

'Holy shit,' Dave breathed. 'She sounds almost deranged. Get this Detective James on the phone. Ask him questions—you know what you've got to do, Jack. I'm going to call the Merriwell Bay Police Station. God, I hope they've got one.'

'Angie,' she said, still holding on to her dad's hand. 'Where are you?'

'At home, *darling*. I didn't stay at Russell's tonight. Too many storms around, and I thought I should be at my own place in case there was a fire here. I haven't been able to get hold of your father, is he all right?'

Brianna let out another sob. 'We're taking him to hospital now.'

'Hospital? What on *earth* for?'

'There was a fire; oh my God, Angie, it was awful. Dad, he . . . We found . . .' She stopped and tried to take a shaky breath. Her last suspicious thought about Angie came back to her. 'What have I unleashed,' she whispered to herself. No! She had to put that aside. All that mattered now was Russell, and Angie had a right to know about him.

'Brianna,' Angie snapped into the phone. 'Tell me what is going on.'

This time she managed to get the words out.

'How far out are you?' Angie asked.

'I'm not sure.'

'Ask the driver.'

'ETA, twenty minutes,' the ambo said, obviously overhearing the conversation.

'I'll meet you there,' said Angie.

By the time they arrived at the hospital, Russell was beginning to come to.

'Don't try and talk, sir, your airways might be damaged.'

'Water,' he gasped.

'Just as soon as we get you inside.'

There was a doctor waiting at the doors to Emergency, stethoscope in hand. 'If you wouldn't mind waiting out here,' he said to Brianna and followed the trolley into Emergency, leaving her staring at the doors.

~

The doors slid open and Angie ran in, looking frantic.

'Brianna?'

'Over here.' Brianna was sitting with her head back against the wall. 'I'm still waiting for news,' she said.

'Oh my God, what happened?'

Brianna could smell Angie's perfume before she sat down. Stretching, she sat up and looked at Angie.

'Shit, what happened to you?'

Angie's hair was wild and unbrushed, while her face had a couple of black streaks down it. Then Brianna saw her hands.

Angie's long red nails were a melted mess.

'We had a small lightning strike at my place. Nothing major. Got it out before it did too much damage. Unfortunately, I got a bit too close and, well, this is the outcome.'

That's what happens when you are a plastics-based person, Brianna thought. *You're flammable.*

Out loud she said, 'Do your fingers need seeing to? They look really painful.'

'There's nothing they can do here,' Angie said, pulling them out of Bri's reach. 'I'll need to go to my beautician when they open in . . . Oh look, it's nine-thirty already.

I'll go when I've seen Russell. They need to be taken off by a professional.'

'Are your fingers burnt underneath?'

'No; honestly, Brianna, you're making a mountain out of a molehill. I'm fine. Tell me about Russell.'

'The doctor is with him. That's really all I know. He was trying to talk when they wheeled him in. I've got no idea how long it'll be before we hear anything from the doctor.'

'I guess we just sit and wait, then.'

Her phone rang. 'Honey, where are you?' Caleb sounded tense.

'At the hospital. We're just—'

'We?'

'Yeah, Angie and me. We're waiting to hear what the doctor says. I'm hoping Dad might get put into a ward soon, but I've got no idea because I haven't seen anyone, not even a nurse since we arrived. The doctor took him into Emergency and I've—'

'Bri, I want you to take yourself away from Angie. Go outside, or to the toilet or something. Don't look at her, just walk away and do exactly as I say, okay?'

'What?'

'No, don't sound surprised. Keep talking normally. Ask about the kids.'

'Are the kids all right?' she asked obediently, getting up from the chair and looking around for a toilet.

Through the windows she saw a police car pull up at the front and two men get out.

'Yeah, they're fine. Staying with Lizzie. Are you away from Angie yet? She cannot hear this conversation.'

'I'm nearly there. Where are you?'

'There has been some information that's come to light about Angie,' he said, ignoring her question. 'You must do as I say and try not to alert her that something's different. Can you do that?'

Brianna didn't know what to say. She looked down at the floor and hunched her shoulders.

'Bri?'

'Yeah. Yes, of course.'

'Can you see any police there yet?'

'Yeah, a couple.'

'Great. Now, tell me, can you see Angie? What's she doing?'

'Nothing, looking at her nails. Caleb, you should see her hands, all her nails have melted onto her fingertips . . . Hang on, what's going on? The police have got her standing. They're . . . Caleb?'

'You're safe if she's with the police. I'll be there soon.'

'Brianna!' Angie's voice was high and frightened. 'Brianna, you must do something. Call Caleb. They're accusing me of all sorts of horrible things.'

Brianna stood back, fighting tears of confusion. 'I don't know what's going on,' she said.

'You must ring Caleb. He'll help me.' Angie tried to twist away, but the younger of the two policemen held her firmly. 'I didn't hurt your father any more than I hurt Matthew!'

'Come on, Mrs Moore, keep walking. We're just going to have a nice friendly chat down at the station.'

A Toyota LandCruiser screeched to a halt next to the police car and Caleb jumped out, not stopping to acknowledge Angie. He ran to Brianna and gathered her to him.

'Thank God,' he muttered into her hair.

'I've got no idea what's going on,' Brianna said in a frightened voice.

'I know, sweetheart. Angie isn't who she says she is. Her real name is Rachael Wood.'

'She killed her previous husband?' Brianna asked incredulously.

'I've been worried for quite some time there's more to Angie. I'd caught her in a few lies over the past two years. None of them made any sense. I'd been sure she'd told me her husband, Michael, had died from cancer, but then she said he had died unexpectedly,' Caleb explained. 'I would have thought she would know how her husband died.'

Brianna nodded.

'Then, a couple of months ago, Geena Adams told me she knew her, and that Angie had been pestering Geena with phone calls recently. She didn't seem to want anything in particular but to chat, however—' Caleb paused, frowning—'Geena couldn't understand this, because they'd never been close. She told me Angie had been asking questions about me.

'At that point, I wasn't too concerned—maybe she was just checking up,' Caleb shrugged, as he rubbed his thumb up and down Brianna's hand. 'But more and more inconsistencies came to light and I started to become suspicious of her. There was something which made me feel she was after more than your dad; call it lawyers' intuition. When she showed you the photo of Heidi and me, and you accused me of having an affair, I knew she was behind it.

'I couldn't work out how she'd got inside your mind to even make you think something like that, but that's how these type of people work. They manipulate and tell lies until they've got you thinking things you never usually would. That's when I was convinced she had more in mind than being Russell's girlfriend.

'And, going back to her husband's death, the police couldn't prove she had killed him at the time,' Caleb continued. 'But I suspect she did *and* she's murdered more people than we know about, so I managed to pull in a few favours and ask for her case to be reinvestigated.

'After you'd left in the ambulance I went and found the jerry can and took it to the police. They're going to fingerprint it, but I'm betting my whole year's wages that her prints are on it.'

'Caleb, slow down. I still don't understand why . . .'

'Perhaps something tipped her over the edge to make her hurt Russell, I don't know. Who could possibly know what goes on inside a psychopath's mind?'

Brianna covered her mouth to hold in a silent scream. 'Yeah,' she whispered. 'I told her Dad would always choose me and the boys over her.'

'That would do it. From my research, I've found two people she'd had relationships with who have died unexpectedly. Three, if you put her great-uncle into the mix.

'When I rang the police station, they said they'd just had a phone call from a Detective Dave Burrows. He'd found evidence of Angie's original identity and how she came to be in Merriwell Bay. It seems she was born in South Australia and was the daughter of Joy and Warren Wood. They knew something was wrong with her, so they adopted Angie out to a family in Merriwell Bay. So she lived and went to school here, exactly as she told us. And she was friends with your mum . . .' He left his sentence hanging.

'Mum? You're going to have to stop because I can't make sense of any of this.'

'Okay, okay,' Caleb smiled and kissed her. 'I'm sorry. There's just so much to tell. Two more things—I think Angie strung the rope across the road and caused Trent's accident.'

Brianna had run out of words to say.

'I'll tell you why. You mentioned you wanted to come to Perth for a while? What's the bet she was trying to convince you the country was too dangerous for the kids. If you moved away, she'd have Russell all to herself. His farm, his money, his everything.'

'And the second thing?'

'I love you and I'm moving back to Merriwell Bay.'

Chapter 35

Dave played with Kim's hair as they sat on the couch, glasses of red wine in hand.

'So you're telling me you've found the lady in the Trove article who lost her memory?' he asked.

'I have,' Kim grinned widely.

'Am I at risk of losing my job to you?'

'Not likely.'

'Tell me then.'

'The day you went to see Alan McSweeny, I went to Hawker and saw Elspeth Williams. I knew she'd been living quietly up there since she'd retired. Dessie, the minister from Blinman, had told me stories about babies they'd delivered, christened and buried together, so I knew where I could find her. Anyway, she was a travelling nurse who helped deliver babies and look after people on remote stations. There was a two-year period where she worked at the Barker hospital. And guess when that was?'

'When the newspaper article was written.'

'Bingo! So I thought I'd go and talk to her about it. See if she remembered anything.'

'And did she?'

'Better than that. She told me the whole story.

'A lady was brought into the hospital after being badly beaten and left for dead. In fact, Elspeth thought she should have been dead when she first saw her. As time went on, the two became friends, but Anna—that was what Elspeth decided to call her—never regained her memory. Between the two of them they hatched a plan.

'Anna was taken to Liza and Roger Conway's station, where she worked for them until they both passed away. It was for about twenty years. Apparently, Liza lived well into her nineties and wouldn't leave her home. All this time, Anna worked there not knowing who she was.'

'Didn't she ever try to find out?'

'No. See, because she was badly beaten, she was frightened of what her life had been like beforehand and didn't want to go back. Elspeth told me she thought her husband must have been violent, or that someone wanted her dead. Anna was quite insistent she never find out who she was.'

Dave nodded and took a sip of wine. 'I almost understand that thinking.'

'And get this—in 2013, when Liza finally died, Anna inherited the station.'

Dave stiffened as he joined the dots.

'She's still living there?'

'Yep.'

'Did you see her.'

'And talked to her too,' Kim said softly.

Chapter 36

Angie sneered at Brianna through the glass.

'You've got no idea what I've done. You think you do, you *all* do, but you don't really know.' Her voice had become a screech and she looked wildly dishevelled after two days in a cell. Her melted fingernails still hadn't been removed.

'You said you knew my mum?'

'I didn't just know her, we were friends.'

'I don't believe you. My mother wouldn't be friends with someone like you, you're despicable.'

'Is that right? Well, when you find her, ask her about the time we climbed the tree together. She wasn't a very good climber, Josie wasn't. She fell. Just like my brother. Oops.' Angie put her fingers to her mouth and widened her eyes in innocence.

'Keep her talking,' Caleb whispered out of the corner of his mouth.

'She fell or you pushed her?'

'She was such a clumsy girl. I could never understand how she managed to snare your father. He was such a handsome man. I tried to get him to notice me, but he only had eyes for her. She had to go. Away!' She waved her hands towards the sky.

Brianna could hardly believe what she was hearing. Angie seemed to have transformed into someone she barely recognised. 'Did you kill her?'

'I think she was cooking tea—you were in the cot, screaming as always. She thought she was going mad with the noise you made. It was easy for me to get her outside. Not so easy to get her into the car. She didn't want to leave you. Kept shrieking at me. Tried to hit me a couple of times. In the end, drugs were her best friend. They kept her sleeping on the back seat of the car, all the way across the Nullarbor.' Her voice was singsong now. 'But then I couldn't keep her with me, so I dumped her. In a shed. Don't know what happened after that. Probably died.

'And now, here I am. Ready to be the best wife I can be to Russell.' She smiled, her eyes glassy.

Brianna turned to Caleb. 'Get me out of here.'

~

Later that night, as Brianna, Russell, Caleb and the Terrors were sitting around the table, still in shock, she brought up the idea of trying to find her mother.

'Maybe she isn't dead. We have to try!'

'Of course we have to try,' Russell said shakily. 'The police have a missing person report now; they'll circulate it and hopefully we'll find something.' He took her hand. 'Bri, I think you need to prepare yourself for the fact that she might be dead. If Angie is as evil as it seems, then . . .' He stared off into the distance, his jaw working frantically. 'God, I can't believe I was taken in by her.' He stood up. 'I'm embarrassed . . . A fool. Looking back, it's so easy to see, isn't it? The little pieces of manipulation; the conversations that didn't add up. The way she dropped hints about you leaving, Bri.' His voice cracked. 'I can't think about this any more.'

He shoved his hands in his pockets and walked out onto the verandah. Brianna got up to follow him, but Caleb caught her hand.

'Leave him,' he said softly and tipped his head towards the boys, who were picking up their plates and following their granda. 'They'll be better for him than either you or I could be at the moment. Kids don't judge.'

Bri found a small smile in acknowledgement. He was right.

She leaned into his body and breathed in her husband. She was a fool too. Angie had only planted one small seed, one small photo, and her overactive brain had grown it into something that could have destroyed her precious marriage.

'I'm sorry,' she said softly. 'Sorry for everything I said to you. For everything I implied.'

She felt Caleb's arm tighten around her, but he didn't say anything.

'We do have some problems, though, Bri,' Caleb finally said.

She nodded against his shoulder. 'I know. But I want to work them out. The one thing I'm certain of is that I love you.' Brianna pulled away and looked up at him. 'Do you love me?'

'I do,' Caleb said quietly. 'You're the most precious thing in the world to me.'

'So we'll work on us, then?' She crinkled her eyes at him.

'Yeah,' Caleb answered, leaning in to kiss her.

Before his lips reached hers, Brianna pulled back. 'But you're coming home?' she asked. 'You're going to start your own business here? Really?' She needed confirmation.

'I handed in my resignation before I came home. I'm going to start a practice in Merriwell Bay so I can be home at night. Because you and the boys mean more to me than any career. You're my everything.' And then he kissed her.

Epilogue

Guy Wood's coffin sat at the front of the church, covered in a wreath of gum leaves and native blossoms from his farm. Kim had chosen them and, knowing how much Guy had loved his place, Dave was sure he would've approved.

Dave sat in the front pew, a dog leash in his hand. Bob was lying on the floor, his head on his paws, watching the casket. With some fast talking, Dave had managed to convince Kim that Bob would be better off with them than at the pound.

Glancing down, he saw Bob heave a deep, deep sigh. He leaned forward and gave him a rough pat. 'Don't worry, old fella,' he whispered. 'You're going to be our station mascot. If you're lucky, Jack's crumbs will fall right where you're lying and you won't even need to move to lick them up.'

'Do you think he knows?' Kim asked, her lips close to his ear.

Dave shrugged. 'I think so. Look at his eyes, they're full of tears.'

He glanced around and saw the church had filled since they'd arrived. Jack was sitting behind him, and he caught Toby Jones's eye. He wondered whether the 'young upstart' had made an offer on Guy's land yet. Meg gave him a small, tight smile and he noticed her hands were clenched around a wad of tissues. A funny feeling of regret passed through him. He wished Guy had known he'd been cared about.

Chris Connelly came to the pulpit as music began to swirl around the church. He held his arms out in welcome and began to speak.

Dave listened without hearing, thinking instead of the drive he and Kim had taken two days ago. It had been a long drive to a station near Hawker, but a worthwhile one.

He'd tried to break the news to Anna as gently as he could. They'd found her family. There was no danger in them at all. Would she like to meet them?

Elspeth had gasped and grabbed her friend's arm, while Anna had stared straight ahead.

'Family?' she asked.

'Yes,' Kim answered gently. 'A daughter, Brianna, and a husband, Russell.'

Anna tested the names: 'Russell. Brianna.'

Elspeth said, 'I wonder whether that's why you chose the name Anna, because it somehow linked you to your daughter.'

Dave had seen no recognition in Anna's face, but had been heartened when she'd said she would meet them.

'Please rise.' Chris gestured that the congregation should stand.

Dave reached for Kim's hand as the coffin was wheeled to the waiting hearse.

As they milled around outside, Meg came up to Dave, her eyes red.

'Thank you for everything you did for him at the end. He would have appreciated it, even if he said he didn't.'

'I'm glad I could help. He did need a bit of extra care, didn't he?'

'I would have given him more if I could've,' Meg said.

'We all would've,' Dave said gently. 'But sometimes it's not possible. He was happy out there by himself. Isabelle made his last days much more comfortable for him.'

Meg swallowed and nodded, before digging in her pocket. 'I brought you this.' She held out a piece of paper.

Dave took it and unfolded it.

'*Dark purple V8 Holden ute. Rego number S807-145*,' he read. 'Ha! You've seen the phantom ute carving up the roads? Well done!' He gave her a big smile.

'Just by luck,' she said, then she glanced over to where Toby was talking to Kim. 'Better go. But thanks again.'

'What have you there?' Jack asked, appearing at his shoulder.

'Details of the phantom ute,' Dave said with a glint in his eye. 'Only one person I know in town with a purple ute. That new young bloke from Landmark. Guess he's been having a bit of fun at the road's expense. We'll have to have a little chat with him.'

Bob whined, and Dave squatted down and patted the old dog. 'It'll be okay, old mate. It'll be okay.'

❧

Brianna held the photo that Detective Burrows had emailed to her and tried to imagine finally meeting this woman who was her mother.

Anna. Not Josie. Brianna wondered at the name. Perhaps her mother hadn't forgotten her entirely. She could see her own eyes reflected in her mum's: hazel with gold flecks around the iris. Anna's smile had a hint of mischief, the same as the Terrors' when they'd been pushing the boundaries. In some slightly discomforting way, it was like looking at an older version of herself.

Russell glanced across from the driver's seat. 'She's exactly as I imagined she would be,' he said, his voice catching in his throat. 'You're very similar.'

'Look! There's the turn-off,' Brianna pointed.

The ramp was covered in the purple dust of the mid north and the two-wheeled track looked like it led to the house visible at the bottom of the hill. Brianna could make out the shiny tin roof.

'Detective Burrows said the house is two-and-a-half kilometres from the road. Can you see it?' she asked, her voice low and shaky.

Russell nodded, his eyes fixed on the track.

They drove in silence, as they had for most of the journey, both lost in their own thoughts. Brianna's heart was thudding now, and despite the airconditioner blowing hard, her brow was beaded with sweat. There were too many questions running through her head.

What if Josie didn't recognise her?

What if she didn't recognise Russell?

What if . . . What if there ended up being nothing between them?

Russell cleared his throat. 'Looks like they're expecting us,' he said, nodding towards the house. Two older women were sitting on the verandah in worn-out chairs.

Brianna couldn't say anything; she just reached over and took Russell's hand.

'I know,' he whispered. 'Me too.'

Parking under a tree, he turned the engine off, opened his door and got out. He faced the verandah and lifted his hand in greeting.

Brianna looked up and saw Anna getting up from the chair, a polite smile on her face.

'Oh God, Josie! Sweetheart . . .' Russell's voice seemed to boom out across the silence.

Anna froze halfway down the verandah steps and seemed to look again. She didn't say a word, just stared.

With a sharp intake of breath, Brianna said, 'Mum.'

Anna's eyes shifted to Brianna's. For a moment her legs seemed to buckle beneath her, but the other women put her arm out and steadied her. Anna looked at her friend and gave a faint nod.

'Russell . . . Bri . . .'

Acknowledgements

Suddenly One Summer is the last book I've written for my publisher, Louise Thurtell, who left Allen & Unwin earlier this year. After so many years with the company it is not an understatement to say it is the end of an era.

Louise barrelled into my life in 2007 after I submitted *Red Dust* to her initiative, Friday Pitch Day. Her response was: 'Your writing is strong and commercial.' It wasn't what Allen & Unwin were looking for at the time and she strongly suggested I try another publisher.

I didn't. Instead, I waited a few weeks, rejigged the first three chapters, then sent it back in to Friday Pitch again. This time she bought it on those first few chapters. Thankfully she never asked to read the full manuscript, because it wasn't finished! I didn't tell her that piece of information until after the book had been published. From there, I guess you could say the rest is history. We've published ten books together.

Louise, I can't thank you enough for the opportunity you gave me when you rang to say you were offering me a contract. Thank you for your belief that *Red Dust* had a market and for convincing your colleagues that it did too. There is no way either of us could have foreseen what was to come. I'll miss working with you.

About a month after I heard of Louise's departure, I had a phone call from my rock and editor, Sarah Baker, to let me know that she was leaving. At that point, I was reeling after losing two of the three most important people in my publishing world. (The third—not in any order—being my agent, Gaby Naher.)

Sarah is the most incredible editor I've ever worked with. We've worked on six of my ten books together. As well as my editor, Sarah is my friend and I am devastated to see her leave. (Although I can't help but wonder if it was my lack of making deadlines that caused her so much stress, and she didn't have a choice but to go!)

So, to my 'editor extraordinaire', thank you for your gentleness, insightfulness and kindness. I'm looking forward to the time you hang out your editor's shingle again but, until then, sending you much love, respect and gratitude.

Now I have a new team. Christa—I'm looking forward to working with you as my new editor. Thank you for pulling this book together with ease and professionalism, despite the time frame. Tom—your steadfast belief in my work and the support and time you've given me is appreciated more than you could know.

Gaby, as always, agent extraordinaire, keeping me calm, on track and well looked after. Many, many thanks, my friend.

And to Carolyn—we create good books together. Thank you for being my first reader, critic, biggest supporter and friend. We seem to have modified how we produce together now, but it still works! Love you long time.

This might sound strange, but it still surprises me how many people love me! Especially when so often I feel unlovable. Cal and Aaron, Heather, Em and Pete, Jan and Pete, Robyn, Scottish, Tam, all precious friends with large hearts and so much love to give. And especially to Heather, who has proven herself again and again, at being the best drinking partner a girl could have! (And everything else. Love you.)

To Garry, again, my calm amid the chaos!

My daughter and friend, Rochelle. You are so impressive. So much fun and I love hanging out with you!

Hayden, gorgeous Hayden. Thank you for being you.

As I write this, I'm sitting in my camp, just south of Kalgoorlie, on a beautiful, cold winter's day. The campfire is blazing, the birds singing and trees are rustling in a gentle breeze. For me, it's a time of reflection, to look back on the past eight years since first being published. There have been so many changes! To the people who have helped me reach this point and where I am today, there aren't enough thanks in the world.

However, in the end, it all comes down to you, the reader. If you hadn't bought these books, then I wouldn't be writing them. Thank you for allowing me to live my dream of creating characters; for making them come alive through your imaginations.

Writing has always been an escape for me. I hope I can continue to create your escape through reading these books.

With love,

Fleur x

COMING IN NOVEMBER 2018

Where the River Runs

FLEUR McDONALD

Nine years ago, thirty-year-old Chelsea Taylor left the small country town of Barker and her family's property to rise to the top as a concert pianist. With talent, ambition, and a determination to show them all at home, Chelsea thought she had it made.

Yet here she was, in Barker, with her four-year-old daughter, Aria, readying herself to face her father, Tom. The father who'd shouted down the phone nine years ago never to come home again.

With an uneasy truce developing, Chelsea and Aria settle into the rhythm of life on the land with Tom and Cal, the farmhand, who seems already to have judged Chelsea badly. Until a shocking discovery is made on the riverbed and Detective Dave Burrows, the local copper, has to tear back generations of family stories to reveal the secrets of the past.

Chelsea just wants a relationship with her dad but will he ever want that too? Or will his memory lapses mean they'll never get that opportunity?

Chapter 1

2018

Chelsea drove slowly through the small country town of Barker. Her home town was nestled at the base of the Flinders Ranges and had a population of only a few hundred people. Her eyes searched the streets to see what had changed in the past nine years. The trees that had been planted in the middle of the main street were green and lush, but the lawn beneath them was dry. So dry she'd probably cut the soles of her feet if she ran on it like she and Lily had in the middle of the night, the last summer she lived here.

The town was quiet. The streets were empty and there was a total of three cars parked in front of the supermarket. The supermarket was the first change she noted. It used to be owned by Mrs Chapman, now it boasted the logo of the IGA chain.

The newsagency seemed the same, as did the post office across the road. There was a war memorial near the trees in the medium strip, and her mouth pulled up in a half-smile as she remembered the night she'd stayed at Lily's place and they'd snuck out after midnight to roam the streets. They'd thought they were so adventurous and daring. Nothing, *nothing* could have happened to them during that night! Barker was as quiet and safe as a church. Ah, the naivety of youth. What the kids had forgotten was Barker was on the main road from Perth to Sydney so there were strangers passing through all the time, but they hadn't ever imagined anything untoward could happen in Barker. It was a sleepy town where nothing exciting took place.

Chelsea pulled into a parking spot next to one of the three cars already there in front of the supermarket. As she looked around, she realised that the chemist, where she'd always been given black jelly beans by old Mr Ford, had been replaced with a small café. Good, she might be able to get a decent coffee when she came into town. Chelsea would bet her last pay cheque that the cars parked in the street still wouldn't be locked and the keys would be in the ignitions. Even with the few changes on the main street. No one ever locked their cars in Barker.

'Mummy?'

The sleepy voice of her four-year-old daughter, Aria, startled her and she turned around to the back seat. Her daughter's black curls were stuck to her head and her cheeks were flushed.

'Hello there,' she smiled. 'I thought we'd stop for an ice cream.'

'Are we at Papa's place yet?'

'No, this is the town where I went to school. Do you remember how I told you I had to catch the bus from the farm to school? Papa's place is a bit more of a drive yet.' She unclipped her seatbelt and opened the door. Unprepared for the blast of furnace-like heat, she gasped and slammed the door shut, before walking around to get Aria out of her car seat.

'It's hot, Mummy,' Aria said, pushing her hair back from her face. She was hot and sweaty, but still gave a couple of hops and a jump up onto the footpath.

'Summer in the Flinders Ranges is always hot, honey. I'd forgotten how hot.' She wiped her long, slim fingers across her brow and pushed her hair from her eyes. 'Come on, I think the airconditioner will be on inside the shop.' She pushed open the door and waited for Aria to go in first.

'Hello,' said the man behind the counter.

Chelsea tried to keep the look of shock from her face. Even though she'd realised Mrs Chapman probably wasn't running the supermarket any longer, she hadn't expected her to have been replaced by a man who looked like he came from the Middle East. This was Barker, after all, hardly a multicultural hub.

'Hello,' she said, gathering herself.

Walking around the store, she saw that along with all the other food there was a section dedicated to Middle Eastern and Asian cuisine that never would've been here if Mrs Chapman still owned it. And very different to the chops and three veg that her mother used to dish up to her dad every night. She grabbed a few essentials and then lifted Aria up so she could look into the freezer and choose an ice cream.

With the most important items selected, she put them on the counter and the man rang up the items, before putting them in a box. No plastic bags here. 'Where's Mrs Chapman?' she asked as she handed over a fifty-dollar note.

'Who?' the man gave her a confused glance.

'Mrs Chapman. The owner. Or doesn't she own the shop anymore?' She wondered how well he spoke English.

'Ah, Gloria,' he answered fluently and Chelsea wanted to kick herself for making assumptions. 'She is no longer here. I bought the shop from her two years ago.'

'Right. Of course. I guess she'd be pretty old by now. Been a while since I was home.'

'You used to live here?'

Chelsea nodded and reached down to stop Aria pulling on her T-shirt, wanting her ice cream. 'Wait, honey.' Turning back to the man she answered, 'Yeah, I'm Tom Taylor's daughter, Chelsea. Haven't been home in nine years. I guess a lot has changed.' Opening the wrapper, she handed Aria the icy pole and picked up the box.

'It is nice to meet you, Chelsea. And you too, little one. I am Amal. Enjoy your time being in your homeland.'

Giving him a curious smile, she guided Aria out the door. What did he mean 'homeland'? How did he know she'd been away overseas?

'Let me just put this in the car and we'll go for a quick look around,' she said, placing the box on the back seat, then taking her daughter's hand.

They walked down the main street together, the heat rising from the pavement, Chelsea looking in each window in the hope of catching glimpses of people she knew—kids from school, or their parents. There was no one. How could there be a few hundred people living in Barker but the footpaths were empty?

At the end of the street they came to the butcher's shop and Chelsea wondered if she should get some steak for dinner tonight. Her dad always liked steak as a change from chops. Still, he might see it as a suck-up job.

The door opened and an old lady carrying a string bag stepped out onto the footpath. Something about the woman was familiar.

She glanced at Chelsea, then down at the little girl, and she stopped. 'Chelsea Taylor? Is that you?'

Chelsea couldn't place her, so she just nodded. 'Yes,' she added for good measure.

A look of disgust crossed the woman's face. 'Got a bit too big for your home town, did you? Well, it's about time you came back. Fancy, never turning up for your—' She broke off and shook her head 'Well . . . I can't say that your father will be pleased to see you.' With that, she turned and stalked towards one of the three cars parked in the street.

Chelsea blinked, a sliver of anxiety running through her.

'Was that lady angry with you, Mummy?' The icy pole was now finished, and Chelsea could see Aria's hands were covered in a sticky mess.

'Let's go and clean up those hands and get going out to Papa's. What do you say?'

'But . . .'

'Aria, let's go.' Chelsea wanted to get off the street, and away from prying eyes before anyone else could see her and pass judgement. Was that what they thought of her now? Chelsea, the town darling had become too big-headed for her home. She knew how a small town could have a person charged and guilty without any proper evidence, but the thought made her sad. If only they all knew . . .

A few minutes later they were back in her little red Ford Focus and heading out towards the petrol station, which boasted three petrol pumps and the best takeaway in the area.

Chelsea's mouth dropped open as they drove by. It was gone.

Actually, that wasn't strictly true. The shell of the building was still there, but the windows had been smashed in and graffiti covered the walls. There were empty spaces where the pumps had been. Where did people get their fuel from?

'Mummy, what are those bushes? They look really prickly.'

Chelsea ignored Aria's chatter from the back and concentrated on the road. Now she had left the town boundary, she still remembered to slow down as she went through the creek that had an unexpectedly deep dip and to keep an eye out for kangaroos near the grove of saltbush on the side of the road. Her dad had always said it was the best place for a roo to jump out and surprise them—especially since the roos were the same colour as the vegetation.

One kilometre out of town she saw the turn-off to the cemetery and lifted her foot off the accelerator.

Was her mother buried there? She didn't even know. Just as she hadn't known about the funeral. Or about her death. Until it was too late.

The lump which had threatened all day finally made its way to the middle of her throat and sat like a stone. She swallowed. It didn't move.

Tears were there too, but she couldn't cry in front of Aria. She had to be strong. Like she always had been. No tears, no emotion, no thinking about things which would make her feel overwhelmed by sadness. That was why Aria's father was never mentioned either.

'Mummy?' the high-pitched voice was now pleading. 'Mummy! You're not listening . . .'

'What?' The word came from Chelsea which such anger that Aria stopped talking and looked down at her hands, her lips trembling.

The cemetery was behind them now and Chelsea pushed her foot down and blew out a breath. 'I'm sorry, I'm sorry,' she told her. 'Look, let's sing something. To take our mind off the trip. It's been such a long drive and you've been so good. I know it's hard being cooped up for hours. What would you like to sing? Your choice, honey.'

'One hundred green bottles!' Aria said, her voice triumphant as though she'd been waiting all journey for this moment.

Chelsea closed her eyes briefly and sent a silent plea for patience, then started to sing.

Chapter 2

Scenes from Chelsea's childhood kept her company as she drove the dirt roads towards her parents' farm, Shandona.

Aria had drifted off to sleep at about the fifteenth green bottle and, by the twentieth, Chelsea knew she could stop singing without waking her.

As she passed through the deep creek lined with river red gums, she flicked on the radio to the local station she used to listen to when growing up. More memories. She recognised some of the ads from years ago. Had no one thought to update them?

Ed Sheeran's 'Castle On The Hill' began playing, and goosebumps rippled over her skin as she listened to the words. He was singing about driving the roads home and how he couldn't wait to get there. Maybe he was singing about England, but the words still resonated with her in South Australia. The verse about Ed's friends started and she wondered if Lily still lived in Barker. And what about Jason, or Kelly, or Shane?

She thought about the time a boy she'd known from primary school had smuggled a bottle of wine out of his parents' bar fridge and they'd sat on the edge of the reservoir while they drank under a star-studded sky. The moon had been nearly full and, if she closed her eyes, Chelsea could see its reflection on the water. Chelsea had been home from the conservatorium on summer holidays. The wine had been cold while the air in her body was warm. That was the first time a boy had ever tried to kiss her. With her cheeks burning from the alcohol, she'd kissed him back. Kelly had told her later he had only done it as a dare. The hot flush of humiliation swept over her, even after all this time.

Chelsea narrowed her eyes and focused on the road to banish the memory. She'd been in two minds about coming home. Part of her was pulled by some invisible force, a need to be where she grew up. To show Aria where she'd spent her childhood and to sit on the bank of the creek where she'd once played in the puddles. It was a place she could breathe in the peace. The other part of her was saying there was nothing here for her anymore. Hadn't been for years. Why would she put herself through all the emotion of a homecoming when she didn't need to?

Rounding a corner, she saw the boundary fence of Shandona snaking its way down the rough hill onto the flood plain. Taking her foot off the accelerator, she slowed to take a better look. There had been an outcrop of trees up on that hill when she'd been in primary school. The only stand of trees within a few miles. She'd wondered why they grew in that spot when there were no others around. Her Papa had followed the winding track slowly down that hill one Sunday afternoon. He and Gran had taken Chelsea for a drive after church to check the lambing ewes. It had been bitterly cold, but she'd still ridden on the back of the ute, enjoying the freezing wind against her face. One of those trees had caught her beanie and pulled it from her head and she'd called out to her Papa to stop. She'd watched as her bright red beanie snared on a bare branch, waving in the wind, until he'd turned around and they'd gone back to pluck it from the tree. Her favourite beanie had been ruined. Gran had comforted her when they'd finally got back to the house and promised to knit her a new one. 'You'll need something to keep your ears warm when you're riding your horse,' she'd said.

But Gran had died before she'd been able to finish knitting the new one. She'd gone to bed one night and not woken the next day.

Chelsea hoped the half-knitted red beanie was still in the bottom drawer of her bedside table, where she'd put it after her gran's funeral so she'd always have part of her close by.

Driving slowly, Chelsea noticed changes to the road—it was smooth and well cared for now, not the potholed, two-wheel track it had been before the council had taken over managing it. It was the opposite when it came to the boundary fences of Shandona: they were sagging and the wires were a combination of rusty and new. It looked as if someone had tried to patch them the best they could without a lot of money.

The land they contained was bare, save for scrubby bushes scattered here and there. On one side of the road, the paddock had hundreds of emus in it—it looked like they were being farmed, but she knew better. The country was in the grip of a drought and the emus would be looking for any skerrick of grass they could find.

But the rivers, her favourite places, although dry and devoid of grass, looked just the same as they had when she used to ride Pinto through them. The beds were still filled with stones and river sand; the trees, hundreds of years old, towered overhead as though they were the river's guardians.

The road turned sharply, and there was a turn-off to the homestead just in front of her. She saw the white forty-four gallon drum posing as a mailbox, then the cattle grid. Bumping across the grid, there was a short drive until she passed the dam on her left and then turned through the gates of Shandona for the first time in nine years.

When she saw the house, her breath caught in her throat. The raised voices of the past screamed at her.

'You won't amount to anything by following that path,' her mum yelled.

'After everything we've done for you, this is how you repay us?'

And the pleading—'Why?'—from a different time, after Dale had died.

With a deep breath, she pulled her small car—her jelly-bean car, Tori had called it—underneath the large gumtree on the corner of the disused tennis court and shut off the engine.

'Mummy?'

Chelsea turned in her seat. 'We're here, honey. Ready to get out and meet Papa?'

Aria's deep brown eyes were serious. 'Yes.'

'Okay, then let's go.' She unclipped her seat belt and got out, this time ready for the heat. The galahs, which had been perched in the tree above her, rose with screeching protest as the noise of the slamming door echoed around the empty area. Chelsea hadn't even got to Aria's door before they settled straight back down into the tree again.

As she helped Aria out of the car she couldn't keep her eyes still. The old meat house which stood in the middle of the yards looked like it was disused and derelict, while the overseer's house seemed well tended. The gardens were neat and tidy and the walls, although covered in a thin film of ever-present red dust, she could tell were newly painted. This house was where she had lived with her parents until her grandfather had retired and moved to Adelaide and the family had moved over to the main house. She wondered if the kitchen walls were still painted the same pale blue.

Looking at her old home, she assumed there must be someone living there. A grey ute was parked out the front, chooks in the hen house and a pile of logs on the verandah. Not that whoever was living there now would be needing them in the middle of summer, she thought. Her dad must have employed a workman.

'Come on.' She took Aria's hand more for her own comfort than her daughter's and started up the gravel pathway. She kept her eyes peeled for snakes, out of an old habit she thought she'd long since forgotten.

Her family had moved into the main house when she was eight, the year Gran had died. Leo had decided he didn't want to farm without his wife and that decision had stopped the arguments between Leo and Tom about succession. Tom, at forty-one, had more than enough experience to run Shandona as his own.

The pathway leading to the main entrance was slate and wound its way through a large free-flowing plumbago bush, which seemed to be planted in the ground but let grow wild. They had to push it out of their way as they walked. Opposite the garden was a stone building that had been her dad's schoolroom when he was a kid. Shandona was too far from Barker for him to attend a school so, along with School of the Air, Leo and Evelyn had employed a governess to help educate Tom, before sending him to boarding school in year eight. The last time she'd peeked into the disused room, the old desks and faded times-table charts had still been on the wall, long since forgotten.

The laundry was next to the schoolroom and Chelsea wondered whether the twin tub washing machine her mum had used was still there. Chelsea knew she'd kept it because it didn't use very much water, but it had always seemed like a lot of extra work to her.

Pip had always loved maintaining a tidy and strict house. And a nice garden.

As well as forcing you to play netball and not understanding you, a tiny voice in her head told her.

Shush!

The house was built from stone and had an enclosed verandah on one side, which had always been called the sunroom. The louvred windows, which bordered the area, were open and dusty—something which never would have happened when Pip was alive. Chelsea's stomach constricted. The temperature gauge which had always hung just outside the door was still there.

Everything was the same, but it wasn't. The house didn't have the same loved feel as it had the last time she'd been here, and what she was seeing made her realise it was really true, her mum was gone. Swallowing hard, she blinked, hoping to see her mum raking the leaves from the lawn or walking down from the shearing shed.

There was nothing, except an old-looking border collie sleeping on the end of a chain near the laundry door. He sat up as they pushed past him and gave a sharp bark. Aria squealed and made sure Chelsea was between them.

'It's okay,' Chelsea told her. 'He'll be for chasing the sheep, and warning of visitors. He won't hurt you.' She realised Aria had never seen a border collie before. And yet they'd always been there when Chelsea had been living here. Hers and her daughter's childhoods had been very different.

'Hello? Dad?' She knocked on the screen door and pushed it open. The dusty door squeaked and she called out again.

'Papa?' Aria copied her mother and pushed in front of her.

'No, Aria.' Chelsea grabbed her shoulder and pulled her back. 'You can't go into other people's houses if they're not home.'

'But he must be. He lives here,' Aria said frowning. 'I want to see him!'

'Maybe he doesn't expect us yet. Perhaps he's still out in the paddock. I didn't see his ute here when we pulled up.' Truth was, after all this time there could have been ten utes parked out the front and she wouldn't have known which one was her father's. She tried again. 'Dad?'

There was a crash from deep inside the house, then, 'Hold on!'

Chelsea recognised her father's deep, gravelly voice and instinctively held Aria's hand tighter. She hadn't realised she was so nervous about seeing him after all this time. Of course, the lady whose face she'd recognised but name she couldn't remember, and who'd warned her father wouldn't be pleased to see her, had made her even more anxious.

'Who is it?'

The noise of boots on wooden floorboards echoed through the large house, but they weren't his normal footsteps. It sounded like he was limping.

'It's me, Dad. Chelsea.' She paused. 'And Aria.'

'Chelsea?' His tone went up in surprise and the footsteps stopped.

Then started again.

'What are you doing here?' he asked, appearing in the doorway.

Chelsea sucked in a breath as she saw him. This wasn't her dad. Stubble covered his chin and cheeks, and his eyes were sunken into his head. His shirt hung loosely from his thin frame. He was nothing like the jovial, heavy-set man he'd been nine years ago. Chelsea wasn't sure that he could have shrunk in the years she'd been gone, but it certainly looked like he had. His hair, which had been the same mousy brown as her own, was now grey, and he had a look of bewilderment on his face.

Clearly he'd taken her mother's death hard. *Of course he has,* that little voice told her. *On top of Dale's death as well. Don't forget you haven't been here to support him either. He's been alone.*

'Dad.' The words felt like they were stuck in her throat.

'Who are you?' He looked down at Aria, who was standing next to Chelsea, her eyes wide.

Shaking off her mother's hand, she took a step forward and smiled up her grandfather. 'I'm Aria and you're my Papa.' She opened her arms and ran to give him a hug.

Startled, Tom's eyes flew to Chelsea. 'You've got a daughter?' he managed to ask before Aria connected with his legs and threw her arms around them. His hands came down on her head and he touched her lightly on the crown, before looking back up at Chelsea.

Cold fear dripped through her. 'I've told you about Aria, Dad,' she said softly. 'I wrote to you and Mum when she was born overseas. I sent photos too.' She paused. 'And I told you about her on the phone, when I rang to say we were coming for Christmas.'

'Christmas?' Then recognition flashed across his face and something seemed to shift inside him. 'Of course you did. Although I don't know why you bothered after all this time!' He focused on Aria, 'Hello Aria, aren't you a sight for sore eyes. Now you come into the kitchen and tell your Papa all about your drive up to Shandona. Was it a long drive?' He took her hand and led her through into the kitchen and opened the fridge, offering her a cold drink of cordial.

Chelsea followed, a lump of anxiety in the pit of her stomach. She was grateful Aria hadn't noticed and was chatting happily away.

'I'd forgotten you were coming,' her father admitted, his initial anger seemed to be gone, his normal tone had returned. He took the empty glass from Aria and lifted her down from the bench where she'd been sitting. 'You can see it's pretty dry. We've been busy. Feeding the sheep and keeping everything alive. I haven't made up your beds or got enough food.' He looked distressed. 'Maybe . . .'

'It's fine, Dad. We brought some supplies with us and I can easily make up the beds.'

Tom looked around vaguely. 'I guess there are spare sheets somewhere. Your mother . . .' As his voice trailed off, then without warning, the anger was back flashing across his face. Chelsea braced for the onslaught.

'Hello? Tom, it's me, Cal.' The screen door slammed, and a silhouette of a man wearing an Akubra appeared in the doorway, stopping any verbal attack that might have followed.

'Cal, how are you, mate? Meet my daughter Chelsea and this little one is, um . . .' Tom paused.

'I'm Aria.'

'Well, hello there, Aria,' Cal said, squatting down and holding out his hand. 'I'm Cal, which is short for Callum. How do you do?'

Aria giggled and held out her own small hand and said shyly, 'Hello. Are you a real cowboy?'

Cal snorted. 'Nope. No cows out here, and I ride a motorbike. My hat is to keep the sun off my face so I don't get burnt.' He stood up and looked at Chelsea. 'Nice to meet you.'

He didn't smile or hold out his hand and Chelsea got the distinct impression he was not happy to see her. Apparently the nameless lady in town wasn't the only one.

'Nice to meet you too,' she answered, twisting her fingers behind her back. 'You work here?'

'Yep. I do.'

Chelsea nodded. That explained the tidy overseer's cottage.

'Be lost without him,' Tom said.

'That's great,' she said, then wanted to kick herself. What was great about it? Her dad needed help?

Cal turned and focused on Tom. 'The tank at the back of the shearing shed is leaking,' he said. 'Reckon it's just about buggered. We can get the bloke to come back and poly-weld it, but because it's the main tank, I think we should order a new one. You right for me to give RuralCorp a call to order a newbie?'

'Damn, I was hoping it would hold. I noticed a split in it a couple of days ago.' Tom sighed. 'No point in ginning around with poly-welding it. Get a new one, but get a different brand. That's the second one we've had that's split down the join.'

'Sure thing. Right, I'll be on my way. Do you need anything in town?'

'Can you pick me up another script? I phoned the order in this morning.'

Chelsea wondered what the medication was for. Depression maybe? That could explain the way her father was looking. She imagined living here, just one person rattling around in a house which could've held six people. It would have to be lonely.

Cal nodded. 'I'll be back out tonight after tennis. I'll drop it in then.'

'Thanks, mate. Have a good game.'

The room was silent after Cal had left and Tom looked around as if unsure what to do.

'Which rooms can we sleep in?' Chelsea finally asked. 'I'll go and set them up.'

'The top two. Think the bathroom up there works okay. Well, it did when your mother was alive. I haven't had any need to go up there since then.'

'Thanks. I'll get our bags.' She felt like she was talking to a stranger. But what more could she expect? She hadn't visited since she was twenty-one and her parents hadn't tried to see her either. Chelsea had hoped her mother would come when Aria was born, but she'd been born overseas, and by the time she returned to Australia, Chelsea's circumstances had changed . . . and life had continued on without her parents in it.

She'd been left to cope by herself.

Anger swelled up in her as she remembered the endless nights rocking Aria to sleep, the pain of the birth which lingered for months afterwards, the silence from her mother. All in a foreign country. Well, her dad might have reason to be pissed off with her, but she had a good reason to return the feeling. Maybe coming back here wasn't going to be the therapy she needed. Perhaps all it would do was unsettle her and make her angry again.